QUIET HEARTS

A Promise McNeal Mystery

Morgan James

Also by Morgan James

Quiet the Dead, A Promise McNeal Mystery
Quiet Killing, A Promise McNeal Mystery
And
Sing Me An Old Song

Quiet Hearts is a work of fiction. Names, characters, places, and incidents are either the product of the author's imagination, or are used fictionally. Any resemblance to actual persons, living or dead, events, or locations is entirely coincidental.

This book is dedicated to my cousins Susan, Patti, Lydia, and Kay. Especially Kay, who makes it possible for us to gather at St. Simons every year and remember that no matter where we go or what we do, we are still The Creek Women. Love y'all.

"He hath set me in dark places, as they that be dead of old."

Lamentations 3:6

THE BEGINNING:
JEKYLL ISLAND, GEORGIA
...AUGUST 1948...

She stood on the rusty pedals slowing her bike to a near stop, then put her left foot on the ground for balance and squinted into the shimmering distance. By the bamboo whistle's two-note song drifting to shore ---the whistle Jon whittled for him---she was sure he was out there with Caretaker. She reckoned he was sitting with his back to her, up on the flat bow of the skiff, facing out to sea.

She listened, didn't hear the bass voiced rumble-sputter-rumble-sputter of Caretaker's outboard engine as the boat rocked and dipped over lazy waves. It was the silent motor, she decided, that allowed the whistle's sad notes to ride a breath of August wind and find her on the beach. So yes, when she settled it in her mind later, he was there playing his whistle on the bow, sitting in the chair---that evil chair pocked by twisted wood faces, gnashing teeth, and long, licking tongues.

She wondered why they would be out there facing ocean-side in the hot afternoon when the flounder and sea trout were better caught around the tip of the island, nearer Jekyll Creek. She got off the bike, rolled it into a cover of slash pines, and put the kickstand down. Now she had both hands free to raise the army-issue, field glasses hanging around her neck.

While she was adjusting the glasses and waiting for an exploded shard of sunlight to pass behind a cloud, Caretaker stood up, the limp brim of his canvas hat barely stirring with the listless breeze. He closed the distance between where he sat at the stern and the boat's bow, braced his left hand on the gunnel, raised his right foot, and shoved the chair and boy off their perch.

From the beach, she thought she heard the dollop-splash of something breaking the water's surface. The whistling stopped. When she finally found the boat in her sights, Caretaker was alone, the skiff rocking like a toy boat given a jerk. He stood for a few seconds looking overboard, then wobble-stepped stern-end, balancing with outstretched arms, and sat down. Unhurriedly, he wound out the starter cord again and again until the engine turned over. Then he revved the outboard to full life, made several wide passes, churning up a foaming wake as he circled, and aimed south, chugging in the direction of the island's dock.

After the boat moved away, she wiped sweat from her eyes with her shirttail and scanned the empty plain of ocean. She saw a bile green rope of seaweed snaking lazily atop the water, bobbing and nodding in the sunlight, but nothing surfaced. Nothing.

It was a good two hundred yards from where she stood on the hot August sand swatting mosquitoes to where Caretaker's fishing skiff had been. As much as she loathed, feared, the man, she hoped, then prayed to Mena's Jesus that she was wrong---that she'd not heard a splash or the bamboo whistle.

She kicked up the stand on her bike and straddled it without pushing off, sitting, both feet on the ground, thinking. If she rode back to the cottage and told Jon or Mena what she'd seen, there would be trouble, one way or another.

If Caretaker had done this terrible thing, not one of the other six left on the island could pilot the island steamer over to Brunswick for help. Only Caretaker could manage the passenger boat. That was part of his job---ferrying people and supplies on and off island, and taking care of Sparrow Cottage, the island generator, and the water plant.

Without Garr Lemley as Caretaker, where would they be? He knew how dependent they were on him. Did what he wanted. Took what he wanted. She gritted her teeth, remembering his rough hands on her arms, his dead-rat smell breath. She hated him. Wished she had the courage to kill him.

And if she was wrong, if nothing had happened out on the skiff, he'd make her pay for accusing him. Punish her. There'd be no one to stop him---certainly not Jon. Jon had told her again and again to be clever, to avoid Caretaker. And the sad, ancient, black man who lived with his gray haired daughter beyond the cemetery would be no help either. The daughter said that some days her daddy's mind walked in another time, a back time of white, Sea Island cotton stacked in burlap bales on the dock, and an island owned by the du Bignon family.

That left Mena with her fluttering heart and eyes that saw only what she wanted to see. Unless you counted the other older boy, the boy whose brother was probably lying on the sandy reef bottom, waiting to be bloated enough to surface. She shivered. No, there would be no help if she told.

Maybe if it had happened in the spring when the loggers and construction bosses were on the island harvesting pines for pulpwood and planning a bridge to the mainland---but not now. The workers stirred up the mosquitoes, raised the yellow fever from the marsh when they cut the trees, and then left. All gone. Bad luck for her.

Only the six of them now, alone, in an empty village of boarded up fancy houses where ghosts walked in the shadows of the palm trees.

Mena told her the State of Georgia bought the entire island from the rich men who owned it---even the old hotel---everything except Sparrow Cottage. Mena wouldn't sell. Swore she would spend her last dollar on lawyers to keep Sparrow and stay on Jekyll Island. Easy for Mena to say---Caretaker left her alone. And Mena had Jon. Even the pitiful old black man had his daughter.

She'd heard the construction workers say they would return when the summer heat was gone, when cooler weather killed off some of the mosquitoes. They would build a bridge. A bridge meant a way off the island that didn't depend on Caretaker's steamer boat. *Maybe* she could leave the island then. But who knew? Maybe the workers were never coming back. *Maybe* was a deep pit waiting to swallow you if you dared to hope. Men talk big, but don't always do what they say.

She pushed her bike out of the trees and walked it back to the beach road. She was thinking about the fever raised by the mosquitoes. Wasn't the killing fever why those two boys were left motherless in Caretaker's house? And him not even their daddy. Yes, it was the fever that killed the mother, and the curse brought by that chair---the curse that Jon said to be quiet about because such talk upset Mena. Made Mena's heart race like a hummingbird's wings.

She nodded her head, knowing she was right about the fever, and remembering the morning when a cool night had spilled fog across the island and left it to billow here and there between the oak trees.

She had been working in the vegetable garden when the black man's daughter walked out of the mist and down the dirt road, bareheaded, droplets of dew marking her forehead, and carrying a bundle of kindling in the crook of her arm. The black man's daughter stopped beside the garden. She had rested on her upturned hoe and waited. They seldom spoke, but that day their eyes met, both understanding they were two women bound to do other people's bidding.

The black woman had stepped over a bushy row of green beans, her bare feet sinking into the moist soil, and whispered to her from behind the secrecy of her large black hand. "He fetched me to the little house to wash and wrap that poor dead lady's body for burying. Her skin was yellow as a mustard plaster, and her two lips was all split open, crusted with dried blood. It was the most awful thing I ever did see. And him?" She spat on the ground. "He paid me one stinking dollar and don't even say thank you."

That was almost two months ago. Yet, Caretaker had not told Mena about his wife's death. If word reached the mainland that the fever was on the island they would be quarantined. But what difference would that make? They were alone anyway. She wondered where Caretaker had buried his wife. Maybe he buried her in the du Bignon cemetery. Who would know, or care?

She pushed off from the grassy verge onto the crushed shell and sand road, riding the old Schwinn up island, grateful for the cooling breeze her pedaling coaxed from the afternoon stillness. She would finish her ride. Go back to the cottage as though nothing had happened. Wait, listen out for trouble, and plan what to do when it came. Turning her head one last time out to sea, she looked into an afternoon sky of impossible blue and saw only white gulls trolling for dinner.

She was thinking this was how it was the day before that terrible time back in Taiwan---quiet blue skies. She'd stood on the beach and watched fishermen leaning over the edge of a little boat, hauling up nets heavy with catch. Then she'd heard the excited chatter of the men, seen their waving arms, and watched them hoist and then empty full nets overboard and make for land. An old woman with a tobacco juice brown, leathery face and squinting eyes had stood near her also watching. She'd asked the old woman what had upset the fishermen, and the old woman's voice crackled, "Monsters in nets. Bad thing coming."

And a bad thing did come. First came the rains, then the next day, Easter Sunday, earthquake. She'd felt the ground heave, seen it crack open and swallow a man and woman. She remembered their faces, screaming, terrified, their arms around each other as they disappeared into the mouth of the earth. Her parent's house, the village, cedar trees with long feathery needles, everything sliding down the mountain, burying her sisters and mother in gray mud.

Betty pumped faster on the pedals, outrunning memories. *Wait and see* droned the spokes of the bike. *Wait and see.* Perhaps nothing had happened, nothing at all.

CHAPTER ONE

I t seemed like a good idea at the time. Leave Western North Carolina early in the morning. Drive down to St. Simons Island, get married over on Jekyll Island, and enjoy a few days of Georgia sunshine. St. Simons was my idea. Daniel is a North Carolina boy, thus he heads for Wrightsville Beach when the ocean calls. Not me. It's the Georgia barrier islands that sing to me. I feel as though St. Simons and Jekyll Island are in my blood as surely as the Irish Sea defined the hearts of my mother's ancestors even after they kissed Ireland goodbye and boarded ship for America.

When I was seven, it was my mother, the beautiful and always elegantly dressed, Rose Marie Fitzgerald

McNeal who suggested our little family vacation on St. Simons. After that first year, the Georgia coast became an almost yearly pilgrimage. I say almost because when I was a child, there were summers when my father's sporadic income or my mother's career as a buyer for Rich's Department Store's Fine Ready-to-Wear department kept us bound to the heat of our apartment in Atlanta's Virginia Highlands neighborhood. But the few years we missed the beach were eclipsed by the good times we had on St. Simons Island as guests at the Georgian Sands Motel where the Spanish tile floors were always cool underfoot, and the window air conditioning unit blew across our sunburned bodies with the ferocity of the Ice Queen's breath.

I loved the draw and push of the ocean waves, the feel of the swirling sand under my toes as the tide sucked it out to sea, and the possibilities of other worlds beyond the flat blue horizon. My mother loved walking on the beach, her lovely, unlined face shaded by a straw hat, the orange scarf she'd tied about the crown whipping in the wind like fire dancing around her head, and the wide brim dancing a tango as she moved.

Mother was also fond of praying in Christ Church at old Frederica on St. Simons, or in Faith Chapel on Jekyll Island---especially Faith Chapel with its dependable Gothic design punctuated by rainbow fused stained glass windows. One window, I have read, was wrought by Tiffany and the other by Maitland Armstrong and his daughter

Helen. Both are breathtakingly beautiful. Faith Chapel, Mother always said, was a place undeniably loved by God.

Now, forty-five years later, when I think about those vacations, it occurs to me that one reason my mother probably relished being at the beach and away from Atlanta was that those six short days assured her of my father's undivided attention. Before the days of cell phones and laptops, my dad couldn't get a call at the beach from a card-playing buddy and disappear for parts unknown to chase the poker win of all poker wins. The operative word here is *chase* because I don't recall him ever catching the elusive jackpot.

Ah yes, my father, the charming, irresistible, James McNeal--- the *flipside* of an Irish coin stamped with religious fervor and a strong work ethic. Jimmy Mac, as his friends called him, never met a bad bottle of Irish whiskey, seldom folded with a three of a kind hand, and never failed to entertain. But that is another story, one played out long ago in my childhood.

Today I remind myself, I am a semi-retired psychologist, one who closed her Atlanta counseling practice several years ago in a crazy moment of mid-life disorientation. I can use the word *crazy* because I'm talking about myself. The details of my decision amounted to giving up my steady income, selling my almost mortgage free condo in Atlanta, buying a general store in Western North Carolina that didn't earn its keep, and moving myself to the mountains. I now have two sweet, Alpine milk goats, the proverbial hound dog, two cats, and a hefty mortgage on a house and five acres with a creek and mountain views. Beautiful---but what was I thinking?

Don't get me wrong. I'm not complaining. Along the way, I have been lucky enough to gain the love of a good man, Daniel Allen, who recently retired from the post office and from raising beef cows---both occupations chosen so that he could be fully present to raise his daughter after her mother died in an accident on an icy mountain road.

On weekends, Daniel plays a mournful fiddle with a bluegrass band called The Lickers. Susan plays banjo and sings with the same band. Recently, the two of them purchased my non-earning general store and converted it to a restaurant. Thus, I am down to just the one mortgage on the house and land. Thank goodness.

There are times I miss owning Granny's Store, but I'm truly delighted with Susan's idea to repurpose the once tobacco barn on the Little Tennessee River into a restaurant. Truth be told, after the barn was outfitted as a grocery store in the 1980's, I suspect the only time it ever turned a profit was when the Goddard twins were selling homegrown pot from behind the counter. Of course, I didn't know that when I bought the store from the twins. Can you spell naïve?

Since he retired, Daniel handles the business side of the new restaurant venture, and approves all barbecue recipes. Besides being a gourmet pork taster, and handsome, Daniel is good at managing money, is easygoing, organized, well read, and tolerant. Of those admirable attributes, I am somewhat organized, and well read. Enough said about that.

Our plan to travel south to the coast to be married was especially enticing considering cold weather was hanging on in Western North Carolina like the last drunk at a party. Early May and this morning I was on the back porch in a jacket folding sheets of damp newspaper I'd draped across my tomato plants as protection against the morning frost.

My adopted hound Alfie lowered his head until his long, red ears nearly touched the porch, and eyed me with a look mixed of equal parts puzzlement and concern. Puzzlement because he probably knew newspapers usually belonged in the house, and concern because he'd gotten one or two sharp words from me lately for peeing on the five-gallon plastic buckets repurposed into pots to grow the tomatoes.

Or, it's possible the dog knew that trying to grow tomatoes on the porch was not the best of ideas. But what could I do? Last year the deer ate my tomato plants down to the roots before one, single juicy specimen appeared. This year I'm banking on the deer not having the nerve to prance up on the back porch to dine. Another naïve thought, no doubt.

Alfie woofed a half-hearted alert, and I looked up to see my neighbor Fletcher Enloe emerge from the pine thicket that separates his property from mine. His limp, a visible reminder of last year's car *accident* when the infamous Goddard twins tried to hurry him into the great beyond, didn't seem to slow Fletcher down. Even with the slight hitch in his gait, he certainly didn't move like a man in his early eighties. I said a silent prayer that in twenty-five years I'd have Fletcher's endurance. In fact, I wished I had it now.

"Morning Fletcher," I called to him. "You're up early."

"Not early, girl. Daylight's wasting. I come to milk Pearl and recollect with you everything I need to do whilst you and Daniel are down in Georgia."

Fletcher, even though making a career from a daily recounting of all the ways I am an ignorant flatlander and an outsider to the mountains, is also the best neighbor a single lady like me could have.

Single lady. I supposed that was about to change. An ugly, niggling doubt worked its way to the front of my mind and stood on ragged haunches, wiggling boney fingers at my face. At fifty-eight, wasn't I too old and set in my ways to accommodate a husband in my life? An occasional over-night tryst with Daniel was exciting and totally satisfying, but marriage was unchartered land where the possibility of disappointment and failure lurked. Could I survive a second failed marriage?

Visualizing a stiff broom and dustpan, I swept the doubt back behind the door and told myself that Daniel was nothing like my ex-husband---may he choke on a peach pit. After a three-year relationship, I'd agreed to marry Daniel. And truly, that's what I wanted. The dress was bought, and the reservations made at the King and Prince Hotel on the beach at St. Simons Island. I had to hope that, once I jumped in the water---pardon the bad pun--- married life with Daniel would be a happy life. It's just that...

What exactly was it? If I were one of my clients back before I retired from being Dr. Promise McNeal, I might work with me for several sessions, uncovering the roots of my doubts about marriage. But all that hard work really wasn't necessary, not for my situation anyway. All I had to do was be honest--- as if that is ever easy for any of us---and admit my doubts were more about me than about Daniel.

And maybe more about fearing my irascible, good neighbor, Fletcher Enloe, is right. Daniel was born and is deeply rooted in Perry County, North Carolina. Except for the eight years he served in the Marines, part of it in Vietnam, he's lived and worked within fifteen miles of where he was born. Daniel is a man at home with the mountains, with his people. He is as comfortable in his own skin as any man I've ever known. And me? Even though my great-grandparents are buried up on Fire Mountain, not two miles from my house, their son, my grandfather, deserted Perry County for Atlanta long before my father was born.

In some ways I'm Atlanta through and through, and fear I will always be a flatlander, an outsider to the mountains. I straddle the two worlds, ever so precariously, and some days I need a nametag to remember who I am. I left my friends and familiar haunts behind in Atlanta and said goodbye to the secure income and spiffy office with my name printed in gold letters on the door. I'm no longer Dr. Promise McNeal but will never be mountain made. Shoot, I can't even grow tomatoes that look better than crushed Ping-Pong balls.

Staring back from the mirror, on my worst days, I see a visitor to Perry County, a summer resident up from the city who has outstayed the leaf season. I see someone who doesn't really belong to the North Carolina Mountains; hasn't been able to say *home* and feel the peace of the word in her heart.

Yet, I love my house with its massive stone chimneys. I love that Fells Creek is so close that from my front yard I can feel a spray of cold, mountain water galloping over laurel roots, and settling on my eyelashes like a veil. And I love the times when Fire Mountain, leaning against a lonesome sky of bruised peach and amber, steals my breath away. But I've asked myself: are these mountains home? I'm not sure.

As I stood on the porch, drifting on worry and anxiety, marriage approaching, I had a sense that if I weren't sure, then I wasn't home, and saying *I do* with Daniel wouldn't quiet my restless soul.

Fletcher's heavy booted footfall on the lower step of the porch brought me back to the cool morning, back to Fire Mountain hiding in fog off in the distance and back to my beautiful goats, Minnie and Pearl, who'd peeked out from the barn at the sound of Fletcher's voice. I don't need an alarm clock. Fletcher appears every morning at seven to milk Pearl, even though I tell him I can manage on my own.

Fletcher makes the same harrumph noise every time I say I'm ready to do my own milking and usually points out to me that I might have been a good psychologist down in "Hot-Lanta", but I don't know jack about taking care of my land or animals. Fletcher's criticism used to cut me to the bone. I like to think I'm fairly self-sufficient and certainly wouldn't take on the responsibility of two nanny goats if I couldn't take care of them. And besides, the local vet tells me my girls are as healthy as any goats in North Carolina.

So now, after four years, my neighbor doesn't get to me the way he once did. When Fletcher starts with his grousing, I smile like a blackjack dealer who knows the card about to be played. That's because I finally realized the real issue is that the old man needs to be in control of everything---even if control is about milking a goat he so skillfully blackmailed me into buying, so he could have fresh goat's milk.

I offered Fletcher a seat in one of the porch rockers and headed for the kitchen to pour two cups of coffee---his heavy with sugar, mine heavy with cream.

Back inside the house, where the furnace had kicked on, and last night's embers lay cold in the fireplace, I felt a tingle of anticipation for warm sunshine and six peaceful days at the beach. I was packed and ready to go, thinking our trip to St. Simons was as well organized as any papal visit, sans the popemobile with the bulletproof windows. Ben Owens, Susan's restaurant manager, would even cover for her so she could come with Daniel and me.

Good plan. But what's the old saying about the best laid plans? I'll always wonder if things would have been different if we'd made no plans and just stayed at home.

CHAPTER TWO

In Atlanta, in the lobby of the quick oil change and service store, Betty Wu stands straight and tall, as tall as her four-feet ten inches in high heels can stand. At eighty-seven, Betty prides herself on excellent posture, insisting the ivory, dog-head cane under her right hand is only for dramatic effect. She will also tell you that her obsidian black hair, today wound in a tight French twist on the back of her head, does not require monthly color from a bottle to hide the gray.

A black, Yves Saint Laurent leather tote with wide silver clasp occupies her left hand. It compliments her cardinal red, light wool, Chanel suit, the jacket of which is tastefully piped in black braiding. The slim skirt of her suit fits exactly as it did when she purchased the outfit from her favorite Phipps Plaza shop in Atlanta during the first year Jackie Kennedy was First Lady. Betty Wu believes fine things do not go out of style, and that some things do not change. Not ever.

Her nose is assaulted by the mixed odor of motor oil and gasoline when the young Latino man opens the door from the garage where her white Cadillac waits, hood up, the driver's side door ajar. She is taken back to another time when the smell of crude oil wafted ashore, house wide slicks of fuel undulating atop calm seas, and tins of Spam, chicken, and peaches washed up on the beach.

The young man, now wiping his hands with an oil stained rag and stuffing the snuff-colored piece of cloth into a back pocket of his blue workpants, is saying something to her, but she takes a long, slow moment to return to this day, this time.

The oil smell seems like yet another warning to Betty, another affirmation that evil has stirred. As if she needed a third warning today. Hadn't she heard the hungry bleating of the devil in the wind of last night's storm? And hadn't the neighbor's cat killed a mouse and left the head and entrails at her front door this morning? No, Betty didn't need any more signs. She knew what had awakened.

"Did you hear me, Mrs. Wu?" The young man asks.

She snaps back, "Yes, I hear you. You think I deaf old lady? Think you can say anything to me and I won't know you insult me, showing me no respect?"

He pulls back from her, frowning at her sudden outburst, and then holds his hands up as a sign of peace. "No, no, Senora. No insult. Just say your Cadillac ready. Clean, new oil. New windshield wipers. No problemo. You good to go now."

When he says *you*, the word sounds like *chew* to Betty. She shakes her cane in his face and makes tsk-tsk sounds at him. Then she tells him several times that he needs to practice his English if he wants to be American. He smiles and says nothing. Finally, she writes a check for her bill, and he drives the Cadillac around to the front door of the shop and opens the driver's side door for her.

On the way back to her condo, located in the affluent Sandy Springs suburb of Atlanta, she fills the gas tank with high-test and stops by the ATM to withdraw two hundred dollars in cash. After she slips the money into her purse, Betty checks her cell phone again, still no return call from Aileen.

She talks to the empty car as she drives. *What that foolish girl doing down there? You wait. I give her big piece of my mind. And I find out why she didn't call me herself. Instead I find out where she is from some switchboard girl down at her TV station. Ha! She thinks she can leave town and I not find out? You bet that girl doing something she don't want her Nai Nai to know about. And now that big-time evil, that akuryou, is free again. And you watch. My girl is stirring up the pot. I know her. Going to get burned for sure. Foolish, foolish, she doesn't know what she stirs.*

To further irritate Betty Wu, there is no return call from Aileen's husband either. *That Garland Wang, Mister-self-important lawyer who can't stop his work to talk to wife's mother, even when she tells his floozy-blond British secretary that her call is very important. Life and death important. That boy worthless. An umbrella in a Tsunami.*

Fifteen minutes later Betty Wu is dragging her suitcase from the hall closet and making mental notes of what clothes she will need for Jekyll Island. She sheds her Chanel suit for a flax colored linen sheath, ties a red and black patterned scarf loosely around her neck, exchanges her high-heeled pumps for comfortable espadrilles, and sweeps what cosmetics and toiletries she needs from the bathroom vanity into her makeup bag. As an afterthought, Betty swallows two aspirin for the headache she's had since early morning, and adds the aspirin bottle to her bag.

By now it is after four o'clock; she doesn't relish the idea of battling the Atlanta traffic at rush hour or driving east to the coast in the dark. Her night vision isn't what it used to be, and there are times when she admits to herself---but to no one else---that at her age, she probably shouldn't drive long distances alone.

But then, she asks aloud in her native Chinese, "Do I have choice? No."

Betty knows evil doesn't care if an old lady has difficulty seeing the highway centerline at night. *All the better for that*, she thinks. *This akuryou, this hungry spirit, she will laugh if I die on the highway and be happy to carry me off to hell with her.*

Before she drags her suitcase downstairs and out to her Cadillac, Betty opens the safe hidden in her closet behind a stack of shoeboxes. She removes a small, purple velvet bag. From the bag she takes a necklace--- a gold disc about the size of a half-dollar bound to a worn, braided leather chain. She strokes the Chinese characters embossed on the face of the disc, whispers the protective charms written there, and hangs the necklace around her neck.

Another thought comes to her before she closes the safe. Fishing under a packet of deeds and stock certificates, she finds what she's looking for and pulls it out by the chain. She hasn't looked at the crucifix in years and is surprised the gold still glows with a deep luster, the Jesus figure still capable of filling her heart with such sadness. She adds Mena's Jesus to her Chinese good luck charm around her neck.

The last item Betty removes from the safe, its cold metal waiting at the very back, is her late husband's Snub Nose .38 revolver and the box of shells nesting beside it. Her hand shakes as she checks the gun to make sure it isn't loaded and then stuffs it, and the shells, into her already bulging suitcase.

CHAPTER THREE

After we'd taken a short walk through the village of St. Simons Island, we strolled over to Barbara Jean's restaurant. There was a line of hungry people snaking out onto Mallery Street, so we left our name with the hostess and milled about on the sidewalk enjoying the warm Georgia evening and the murmur of waves washing ashore under the pier at the end of the street.

We'd left North Carolina at dawn. Daniel and I took my Subaru because I refused to travel to the beach in his oversized, macho truck, and Susan drove with Sam Quinn in Susan's jeep. Susan's friend Sam, the Reverend Samantha Quinn, a young Episcopal priest from Asheville, would marry Daniel and me on Thursday in the garden of Crane Cottage, located on Jekyll Island in the historical district.

Though Sam was Susan's suggestion, Daniel and I were comfortable with her officiating at our wedding. She was the perfect compromise to unite a lifetime, but not zealous Methodist, and a lapsed Anglican with, shall we say, varied spiritual beliefs. Besides, Sam had become almost part of the family since she and Susan became close friends during a pottery class at the community college. And she took a place in my heart when she'd journeyed up Fire Mountain with us last March to pray belated funeral rites for my great grand-father January McNeal, who died on Fire Mountain over a hundred years ago.

The plan was for Susan to stand up with us. That was fine by me. The only complaint I have with Susan is that she insists on calling me Ms. P instead of my given name, Promise. Other than that minor irritation, we get along well, and I love her for the quirky, openhearted person she is.

Susan, in turn, has more than welcomed me into the Allen family fold. In fact, it's Susan who has promoted our marriage at every opportunity. I usually tease her and say if she wants a wedding in the family, why doesn't she let one of those mountain guys chasing her catch up? My remark usually elicits a look from Susan like she's tasted sour, un-ripe blackberries. With her twenty-seven years lived in the same area of North Carolina, I suppose Susan is well ac-quainted with all of Perry County's finest bachelors.

The rest of our wedding party would be Daniel's cousin Mac Allen, Perry County Sheriff, who is like a brother to Daniel. Mac would drive down Wednesday night and be Daniel's best man. My son, Luke Barnes, who worked for Acadian Oil---or said he did, though probably really worked for a classified, government agency---didn't think he could get stateside for the wedding. I was disappointed not to have Luke, but understood, especially since he'd come up to North Carolina for a visit in March. So long as my son was safe, I could certainly get married without him being present.

And, oh yes, we'd asked Daniel and Susan's MaMa Allen, as well as Fletcher Enloe to come along, but MaMa begged off, saying she'd as soon have us to dinner when we got home than make the long drive to the coast. Fletcher announced he hated weddings, had no use for beach sand or South Georgia gnats. Besides, he pointed out, without him holding down the fort, my dog, cats, and goats would likely be neglected by some lazy-good-for-nothing, hired-out pet sitter. You got to love Fletcher.

We were left with only one full day to complete our remaining wedding plans. But that was okay. Our ceremony would be simple---more of a commitment to each other really. Since we wouldn't be in Georgia long enough to satisfy the state's waiting period for marriage, Daniel and I applied for a North Carolina marriage license the Friday before. When we returned from the beach, we'd go down to the courthouse, "seal the deal" for the state, and make it legal. A little complicated. But being joined as man and wife in sight of the ocean, where I felt life was forever renewed, was what I wanted. I don't think Daniel cared one way or another, so long as the marriage finally happened.

As we watched the line into Barbara Jean's Restaurant dwindle at a slow trickle, I doubt any of us were thinking about weddings. After a long drive and hurrying to settle in---Daniel and I over at the King and Prince Hotel, Susan and Sam into adjoining rooms at a charming 1930s restored inn in the village of St. Simons, The Village Inn and Pub---we were hungry and irritable. At least I know I was. I'd been up since five that morning and all I could think about was Barbara Jean's juicy crab cakes, squash casserole, and a key lime tart for dessert.

When Susan and Sam meandered back in line after window-shopping down the block and back, she announced she would definitely order *Chocolate Stuff* for dessert. Just the mention of this yummy concoction made my mouth water. I can't describe Barbara Jean's signature dessert except to say it is gooey, not really a brownie, not really a pudding, but hyper-chocolate, warm, and the best thing you ever put in your mouth. Maybe I'd change my mind and have that instead of the key lime tart. Daniel listened to Susan and me debate which dessert would be better and rolled his eyes in our direction. He smiled knowingly at Sam. She smiled back, and I was glad to be with these people in this place, where marsh grass waltzes in the wind, and the sea brings a new world with every high tide.

The door to the restaurant swung open. A tanned, trim, pony-tailed, young woman in white shorts and a black, Barbara Jean tee shirt came out carrying a tray of sweating glasses. "Hey y'all. Welcome to St. Simons. Barbara Jean is real sorry y'all have to wait. I promise it won't be long now. Anybody want a glass of iced tea? It's on the house."

Hands went up all over the sidewalk. Daniel, being the closest to the waitress and arguably the most handsome man in line, got the first glass. Knowing the tea would be Southern sweet, I turned down a free drink. Believe it or not, as much as I love sweets, I don't like sweet tea. When the restaurant door opened a second time and the hostess ushered a group of six inside, the line actually looked shorter. I felt like cheering. We would not go hungry after all.

Susan tapped me on the shoulder. "Ms. P, isn't that Barkley with Paul Tournay over there across the street? I think they're coming this way."

Daniel turned around. "Well, I'll be a monkey's uncle. It really is Paul, and with Barkley."

"Yes, it is. Paul looks well, doesn't he? I'm sure I told you that Paul and Barkley have been together for a couple of years now. Remember, we got a Christmas card from them?"

Daniel did another eye roll. "Yeah, I remember. Cute card. Golden Retriever puppies under a Christmas tree.

I guess I'm just surprised they're still together, considering what you've said about Barkley's reputation for going through lovers like Kleenex."

Sam Quinn broke into the conversation. "Which one is Barkley? The dark-haired, shorter guy is drop-dead gorgeous. He looks like a movie star. Look at those upper arms peeking out of his Polo shirt. How many hours of gym sweat would it take to earn those arms?"

Susan grimaced. "The dark-haired guy is Paul Tournay. He's way too perfect for me. Yuck, yuck. I think he co-starred on a soap opera for a couple of seasons. It was cancelled for some reason. He's still an actor, I think." Susan looked at me for clarification. "Isn't he the director for one of the theaters off 14th Street in Atlanta?"

I agreed that he was and watched the pair approach. Sam was right about Paul being movie star material, right down to his perfectly chiseled chin line and tanned cheeks. And Barkley, at over six feet, lithe and elegant in his lavender silk shirt, was no ugly child either. They made a handsome couple. Hmm. I noticed Barkley had lightened his usual duo hair colors of deep brown paired with platinum spikes to an overall softer, pale brown. The color looked good on him. I wondered if this change was fashion or some subtler banner of maturity.

Susan continued to fill Sam in on the gossip about the two men. "Ms. P and Daddy saved Paul from a murder charge a couple of years back. I can't believe I've not told you that story---stolen art from the Nazis and Paul's ex-lover killed in the basement of his house in Atlanta. Daddy and Ms. P trapped the real killer and recovered some of the stolen treasures hidden in Paul's basement by his grandfather. Then Paul came out smelling like a rose and got signed as a regular guest---an art expert, no less--- on Aileen Wang's Atlanta TV show. He's on the show a couple of times a month. That's how he met Barkley. He's the taller guy in the fancy shirt."

Susan took a breath and continued, "Barkley has the most elegant hands I've ever seen on a man---or on a woman for that matter. I've gone down to the TV station with Ms. P a couple of times. Barkley told me he danced with a professional troupe in New York before moving to Atlanta. Now he's Ms. Wang's assistant. From what I've seen, Barkley keeps the Aileen Wang show together. She'd be in deep doo-doo if he ever walked out."

"Hmm," Sam pursed her mouth. "How interesting. I don't watch the Atlanta stations. Who is Aileen Wang? Does she do a talk show kind of thing?"

Susan's eyebrows arched. "Oh yeah. Aileen talks to her guests. But mostly she skewers them. I tell you, that woman is fearless in digging up the dirt on her guests. Grown men cry after she trots out their dirty laundry. I don't know why anyone would ever go on her show."

CHAPTER FOUR

I waved to Barkley and Paul. Barkley wiggled one of his gracile hands back at me, and they fast walked over to hug each of us, even Sam, who didn't know either of the men from her yellow house cat.

Barkley was the first to speak. "Well, as I live and breathe, Dr. Promise McNeal, the bodacious Susan, and you must be the groom, Daniel Allen." He and Daniel shook hands, and then Paul took Daniel's hand and told him it was good to see him again.

I stepped forward to introduce Sam Quinn as Susan's friend from Asheville. As he took her small hand in his, Barkley arched an eyebrow and tasseled a curly lock of her pale red hair around a finger. "My, my, Miss Susan. Just where have you been hiding this gorgeous, sexy creature?"

Morgan James

Susan slapped Barkley's hand away. When she glared at him square in the eyes--- a feat not difficult for Susan since she's every bit as tall as Barkley--- her nostrils flared, lifting her gold stud nose ring. "Watch it, Mister. Sam is a priest."

Sam closed her eyes for a second, maybe trying to will away the uncomfortable moment or maybe to say a prayer that Susan wouldn't deck Barkley on the sidewalk.

Barkley however was not to be deflated. He laughed and gave Susan a big brother look. "She can't be a priest, Susan. Priests are only *guys*. And don't be so tetchy. You know I'm harmless."

"And ignorant," Susan shot back. "Sam *is* a priest, so you can shut up your smart mouth."

Barkley gave Sam's hand over to Paul and then announced with exaggerated respect, "Reverend Sam Quinn, may I present Mr. Paul Tournay." Paul looked embarrassed and shook her hand briefly. So much for thinking Barkley was waving a banner of maturity by his new hair color--- same old Barkley.

Daniel wisely changed the subject. "So, what are you guys doing down here? And how did you know I'm finally going to be a groom?"

Barkley smiled and shrugged his shoulders. "You tell them, Paul. I don't want to put my foot in my mouth again."

Paul patted his partner good-naturedly on the back. "It's okay, Bark. We all know you are well acquainted with the taste of shoe leather." Barkley smirked and remained silent. "We know about the wedding because Promise told her old friend, the illustrious attorney Garland Wang. And you know Garland, being the good husband, had to tell Aileen. Aileen passed along the good news to us. We weren't sure when or where, though. Are you getting married down here?"

"Yes," I answered, "at Crane Cottage on Thursday morning. Y'all come on over. It's at 11:00, very informal, on the side lawn near the fountain. We'll have lunch in the dining room afterwards. Sam will conduct the ceremony."

Barkley couldn't help himself. "Oh, a garden party. I do love a garden party. Susan, will you wear your usual attire of Goth basic--- black leggings and black shirt?"

"No," I interjected before Susan could volley back some smart comment. "Susan is wearing a long white skirt and white islet blouse--- very becoming with her dark hair and olive skin tones. The fair and much older bride will be in a light blue, silk skirt with matching mandarin collared tunic. Daniel insists on getting married in clean Levi jeans and a western shirt. *Whatever.* He will remove his Stetson for the ceremony though. Right, Daniel?" Daniel kissed me on the cheek but offered no reassurances about the hat. "Sam will wear her...what are you wearing, Sam?"

Sam piped up cheerfully, a grin spreading across her freckled face, "Oh, not to worry. One of the *real* priests---a short guy I know--- loaned me a snappy outfit. You know: long white robe thing we call an alb and one of those lovely, embroidered stoles to drape around my neck. And then

I'll probably finish off the outfit with a pectoral cross---just to remind us of why we are gathered together."

"Touché," replied Barkley.

Paul cut in. "Sounds wonderful, Promise. We are so happy for you. The plan is for us to drive home tomorrow morning. But if we're still in town, we'd love to come to the wedding. Wouldn't we, Bark?"

Barkley nodded and bent down to give me a hug. For all his foolishness, he is a good soul.

"So, are you guys down here on holiday?" Susan asked.

"Lord no, child. Aileen has commanded me, Paul, the show crew, and as many of the press as she could cajole down here for one of her attention grabbing extravaganzas. As we speak, she is holding court at a cocktail soirée over on Jekyll Island, no doubt trying to look like the white princess instead of the black witch of the north. We grew tired of her peacocking around and the little bitty canapés, and cut out for some real food."

Daniel shot Barkley a confused look. "Jekyll Island is a long way from Atlanta. What's Ms. Wang up to?"

I could only imagine what high drama Aileen had invented to boost her TV ratings.

Barkley stepped in a little closer and lowered his voice. "Well, you know that Aileen's mother, Betty Wu, lived over on Jekyll Island during the 1940s and early 1950s. All the millionaires had pretty much abandoned the Jekyll Island Club and the island at the end of the 1930s, and it was closed to the public during the war. But a few families stayed on fulltime. Betty lived with one of those families, the Simpsons. Did you know there wasn't a bridge to drive over there until the State of Georgia bought the island after WWII? You had to take a ferry from Brunswick. Can you imagine? Also, there were a few soldiers stationed as lookouts on Jekyll during the war in case Germany tried to invade us from the Atlantic. And I read that German U-boats were, in fact, actually seen off the coast during the war. They sank two, maybe three, tankers in the area. Can you believe that?"

Sounded like Barkley had been researching Jekyll Island's history. I had heard about German submarines off the coast of Georgia during the war, but was surprised Aileen's mother had lived on Jekyll Island during that time. I'd met Mrs. Wu on a couple of occasions and thought she was an Atlanta native. Well, I mean I thought she'd lived in Atlanta since she emigrated from Taiwan. As I remembered, Betty Wu was the wealthy widow of a Chinese-American diamond merchant.

Paul jumped into Barkley's history lesson. "Why Aileen has us all down here is a long, long story, and if Bark doesn't get to the point with it, we will all be ordering breakfast, not supper, before he's done."

Barkley made a face at Paul. "All right, dear. You made your point. Let me see if I can cut to the crux of Aileen's grand plan to play the benevolent patroness." He took a deep breath and continued. "So here is the thing: when Aileen was growing up, her mother told her wild stories about this fabulous, intricately carved Chinese chair---or maybe it's Japanese. I'm not sure. Betty even had an old photograph of the chair. Anyway, according to Betty Wu, the chair was possessed by evil spirits and brought a curse on anyone who owned it."

I noticed Daniel doing the eye roll thing again and almost smiled. Then an eerie picture of Stephen King's book with the evil, possessed car Christine wavered across my mind and I shivered. Chairs, cars, whatever---evil is evil.

Susan interjected, "Sam could do an exorcism on it. Couldn't you, Sam?"

Paul arched an eyebrow at Sam, as though he was about to ask a question. But before he could, Sam told Susan to hush and Barkley continued. "As I was saying, the chair sat in the Simpson's Millionaire's Row cottage where Betty Wu lived until the house caught fire and the gardener died of some strange fever. I think that was in the late 1940s. Then something happened and the chair went missing. Anyway, now the Simpson cottage is in ruins, but all the other fancy houses that once belonged rich folks like J.P. Morgan and John D. Rockefeller have been restored."

Paul groaned. "Enough history. Please get on with the point of this long, boring story."

"I am, I am. So a few months ago, Aileen sees what she is sure is the cursed chair at an auction in Atlanta. She knows this from the old photograph, you see. She buys the chair for some ridiculous price and sets up a foundation to restore Sparrow Cottage, all around this chair. She also plans to make a big production of her somehow breaking the curse. You know--- all that drama Aileen is so good at creating. The curse breaking ceremony should be good for at least two Aileen Wang specials for the afternoon audience. She's also trying to get a bunch of her Atlanta society friends on board for restoration money. Of course, she's making a big deal of her gift of the chair back to the cottage. We hauled the heavy old mother down here in the back of our van, and I can tell you one thing, it's ugly enough to be possessed by evil spirits, that's for sure."

Susan's eyes sparkled with curiosity. "How cool is that? What does it look like?"

Paul gave a dismissive wave. "Oh, it's your typical oriental, dark wood thing. Grotesque, covered in heavy carvings, oversized, probably cost a fortune in its day. You'd expect to see Theda Bara draped across it holding an ivory cigarette holder. Has what looks like dragons, and truly hideous, puckered up faces all over the back, and down the arms--- I mean the chair, not Theda Bara. Gives me the creeps. The whole thing looks alive. No wonder Betty Wu thought she could hear ghost spirits whistling through it."

"Whistling through it? What do you mean?"

Paul shook his head back and forth at Susan's question. "More of old Betty Wu's bogyman story from Aileen's childhood. If you sit in the chair and the wind blows through it, you can hear the screams of damned souls trying to escape from hell, or something like that. Aileen doesn't believe that, of course. She's just in it to plug the TV show and to make Aileen look good. Lord knows the woman is running out of heads to roll on the air for publicity. Honestly, she is a truly bitchy female. Treats Barkley like pig sty dirt. If anyone is possessed by evil spirits, it's Aileen Wang."

Barkley shushed Paul. "Shut up, Paul. Someone might hear you. The woman pays our salary, which enables you to keep up your vintage Jaguar and pay the exorbitant taxes on that bleak old house you own in Atlanta. Don't forget that."

Ah yes, Paul's Atlanta house. I remembered the Tournay house very well and Barkley was right. It was bleak. I wondered for one fleeting second if the ghost of Paul's grandmother was still in residence. Paul's voice brought me back.

"I know. But truly, Bark, you should have your own show. Screw Aileen. You do all the work anyway."

Did I denote a little palace revolt going on with Paul? I wondered what Aileen had done to upset him. "Sounds like Aileen hasn't changed, still doesn't mind stepping on a few toes to get her way."

Barkley waved Paul's complaint away like a gnat. "Oh, you know how it is, Promise. Aileen is a master at what she does. Half of Atlanta wants to be Aileen Wang; the other half wants to kill her."

I did remember Barkley telling me that a couple of years ago. I wondered which half Paul Tournay could be counted in.

About that time, the hostess called our name. We invited Paul and Barkley to join us, but they declined saying they were going down the street to a pub overlooking the pier for a quick bite and then back over to Jekyll where Aileen was hosting the cocktail party. Their assignment, they told us, was to collect Aileen and the ugly chair and then ferry both to the beach house she'd rented for the week.

The food at Barbara Jean's was as delicious as it was the last time I visited St. Simons Island back in the late 1990s. And I did have a couple of bites of Susan's *Chocolate Stuff*, as well as a key lime tart. Most of the dinner conversation was for Sam's benefit, with Susan recounting how we knew Paul, Barkley, and Aileen Wang. Daniel and I were content to listen to Susan's rendition, which was mostly correct, and eavesdrop on the table next to us chatter about a cougar sighted on Jekyll Island and about the deer overpopulation over there because the State of Georgia had banned deer hunting on the island.

Daniel leaned in to me and asked, "You hear that? Cougars. Bet that's bad for the tourist trade. I wonder if there really could be big cats here. They live in Florida, you know? An old guy from north Perry County was telling me recently that he'd seen one crossing his pasture this past winter, called it a catamount. He knew it wasn't a bobcat cause of the long tail." I shook my head and wondered if a cougar might attack my goats.

What Susan was telling Sam was true; Daniel and I did rescue Paul from a possible murder charge, though I didn't like to dwell on the incident. Probably because it involved Paul Tournay's grandmother and her unsolved murder haunting my dreams. Not to mention my being attacked by a very tall person of undetermined sex who turned out to be the person who killed Paul's ex-lover. Way too complicated for a happy occasion like this.

Still, seeing Paul and Barkley did stir old emotions. True, Paul Tournay had been grateful when we'd helped prove he wasn't a murderer, but I'd been disappointed with his blasé manner about the stolen artifacts found in his basement. He seemed too quick to parlay the art crimes committed by his grandfather into celebrity status for himself, and that disappointed me.

Against the backdrop of a noisy Tuesday night crowd in the restaurant and Susan's across the table chatter with Sam, I stirred my after dinner coffee and resolved, not for the first time, to give up being judgmental of other peoples actions. Who was I to throw rocks from atop my own glass house?

There was another more personal reason I didn't want to think about the Paul Tournay affair. Back in Atlanta, I'd been forced to deal with my ex-husband, the obnoxious, Atlanta homicide cop RB Barnes. My failed first marriage to Randall Barnes was the last thing I wanted to be reminded of on almost the eve of my marriage to Daniel.

I stole a sideways glance at Daniel sitting next to me, his thigh brushing mine. This was a good man, a caring man who loved me. Daniel was not RB Barnes. Sure, Daniel was probably too handsome to be as sweet as he was---with all that wavy black hair and slim body---but in the more than four years that I'd known him, he hadn't waivered in his quiet, steady, devotion, hadn't given me any reason to think he'd disappoint me.

The committee that sometimes meets in my head convened. "Hey girl," they whispered. "Don't mean to be too, too cynical, but really, nobody can be that sweet. Not on a day-to-day basis. Are you sure about this marriage thing?"

I closed my eyes and told the committee to shut up. I was marrying Daniel and that was it. The *Shoulda-woulda-coulda* girls sounded a Bronx cheer above the restaurant's tinkling glasses and laughing diners as they dissipated into the seafood- fragrant air. I realized Sam Quinn was asking me a question.

"What kind of work do you do for Garland Wang?"

Well, that was a loaded question. I noticed that Daniel had paused, fork in midair, waiting for my answer. I thought for a long moment trying to simplify my somewhat complicated relationship with the Atlanta attorney Garland Wang, my sort-of friend and sometimes employer, whom I met through, of all people, my ex-husband. How RB Barnes and Garland Wang had gotten to know each other, I wasn't sure, since each told a slightly different story. Maybe that's why the two men get on so well. They both have selective memories.

Garland calls me for all sorts of reasons, sometimes as a consultant because of my expert witness credentials as a psychologist and sometimes just to whine and complain about his life with Aileen. Maybe every successful man who thinks of himself as running with the big dogs feels his equally successful wife doesn't appreciate him. I don't know, and I really don't want to take a poll to find out. The bottom line is that my conversations with Garland are usually about Garland, and that's the way he wants it.

A couple of years ago, he'd called me about the Tournay case because he was representing Paul's mother, Becca Tournay, in an issue with the Tournay estate. Boy, that phone call unleashed the harpies from Pandora's box for sure. Oh, and I guess I should mention, Garland labors under the delusion that I possess some sort of psychic abilities, even though I've told him repeatedly that my education in the workings of the human mind and pure blind luck have more to do with my success rate than my having what Daniel's MaMa calls *the sight*.

I could also tell Garland that I try to pay attention to those around me, to their body language, and sometimes to the things they don't say. For me, those observations offer big clues about a person. But I won't go there with Garland because if I did, I'd have to point out to him that he, on the other hand, pays only one third attention to those around him and reserves the other two-thirds for himself. Oops. There goes that judgmental side of me again.

I parroted Sam, "What kind of work do I do for Garland? Well, for one thing, he may call me to testify in court if my opinion will help his side of the case. And sometimes I interview clients for him or do a little research. No much really. But the consulting fees come in handy, especially now that I've closed my counseling practice in Atlanta."

Daniel's eyes widened. "Research? Is that what you call chasing a killer around in the woods and getting yourself thumped black and blue with a piece of rebar? Or having your Subaru riddled with bullets by cigarette hijackers?"

Somehow I knew Sam's question would set Daniel off. He has no use for Garland Wang, though, as I remember, Paul Tournay and Daniel struck up a kinship almost immediately. Daniel has reminded me more than once that Paul is young, has a great deal to overcome from his sad upbringing as Becca Tournay's son, and the whole business of the stolen art was not so black and white. After all, Paul didn't steal the art and had no idea it was hidden in his basement. True enough.

"Daniel, really, you know neither of those things were actually Garland's fault. Well, at least the rebar thing wasn't."

Fortunately, our waitress came over to the table with the check. Our discussion about Garland Wang then segued to a discussion of who would pay the bill. Daniel won. I'd settle up with him later for part of the tab.

It was after eight-thirty when we left Barbara Jean's. A strong breeze blew off the ocean, whipping and popping the canvas awing outside the gift shop next to the restaurant. We walked Susan and Sam back to the Village Inn and Pub and then backtracked to the public parking lot by the pier where we'd left the Subaru.

Before we left the village, Daniel and I strolled along the public park path following the water's edge from the pier to the St. Simons lighthouse, enjoying the quiet and letting our eyes wander out to sea. Pillows of darkening clouds crowded the horizon. I hoped we wouldn't have storms for the wedding and said as much to Daniel. He replied that it could rain torrents for all he cared, that he was so happy I'd finally agreed to get married, a little rain couldn't spoil the day for him. Yes, he is a sweet guy.

I took his arm and snuggled in closer against the wind, satisfied from the delicious food, happy to be at St. Simons Island with Daniel, and humming with blissful peace. Daniel was right. Who cared if it rained? I think we fell quiet again, streaming our own thoughts of the days and years ahead as we drove back to our hotel. An hour later, exhausted from our long day to reach paradise, we drifted off to sleep, lulled by the voice of low tide lapping against the beach beyond our room.

Sometime during the night, I woke with a jerk from a disjointed dream peopled with leathery skinned, pucker faced, spirit creatures with hair made of dripping seaweed and mouths studded with tiny sharp teeth. Daniel slept soundly beside me, his breathing relaxed and peaceful. The sleep of a clear conscious, my mother would have said. Rain gusted in short puffs against the French doors to the balcony, and beyond our open drapes the sea had turned restless. Stars hung cloaked in dark sky.

I tossed and turned for a few moments trying to make sense of my dream. When I recalled Paul's animated conversation about Aileen Wang's infamous Chinese chair, I decided I'd eaten too much rich food. Careful not to wake Daniel, I eased out of bed to find the Tums tucked away in my suitcase.

CHAPTER FIVE

He is unnoticed, in shadow, apart from the dwindled crowd. His summer tuxedo jacket is damp against his white dress shirt, and beads of sweat line up along his trim, gray mustache. Even for May, the island evening is unusually warm and humid, ripe for a storm to roll up from Florida.

He glances off to his right. Without electricity and away from the gaiety of the paper lanterns draped between live oaks for the party, the pitted tabby walls of Sparrow Cottage seem a grimy smudge on the landscape, not the grand dame she once was. He sighs and questions if those years were truly as he remembers them, or if they are un-reliable specters.

Reporters and social climbers trying to impress the TV woman have left. Catering staff from the mainland have swept away leftover shrimp canapés, half emptied bottles of wine, white table cloths, and bud vases festooned with white roses, in a flurry of wanting to clean up and get home to air conditioning and family. The chattering, witty repartee and posturing have all but stopped.

He sees the director of the Georgia Sea Turtle Project, a serious young man he'd recently met at a fundraiser, and then notices the new hotel's public relations guru, a man they all call Bud. Both men take leave of the small, dark haired woman who assembled this self-serving carnival. Finally, she is alone, her white evening suit illuminated by the lantern glow cast on the ragged grass lawn.

As he parts bushy branches of the camphor tree screening him from the woman, moisture from his hands releases a rosemary-like scent into the air. He watches the woman; debates whether approaching her would be of any use, maybe spin some argument that the ugly chair she is making such a big deal about is better anchored with cement at the bottom of the Atlantic Ocean. What could he say that might change her mind? Where was her weak spot? Out of a habit learned long ago, he slows his hunter's breath and wills himself to be one with the trees, with the grass, and with the lone armadillo moving from the exposure of the lawn into the safety of a nearby sago palm thicket.

No, he decides, as he watches the woman drag the chair away from the lantern light and out into the dark, open grass. She doesn't have a weak spot. She always thinks she holds the winning card. She'd made a grand speech at the cocktail party, detailing how she would personally lead a foundation to restore Sparrow Cottage, to tell the story of its past. She would not change her mind.

The house will be rebuilt, the neglectful years gutted, every square inch restored to its former beauty. Sparrow will return as the jewel of The Jekyll Island Club cottages.

What a bunch of bunk, he thinks. Sparrow Cottage was never quite a jewel. It was a rich woman's playhouse, to be sure, but there were larger, more opulent homes on Millionaire's Row. She's a fool and a glory hog.

He already knew who she was from flipping through late afternoon TV channels looking for news and weather, and had introduced himself to her at the party. He had closed his large calloused hand around her delicate, red-polished fingers in an empty gesture of cooperation for her Sparrow project, and even managed to say how lovely she looked. She returned his compliment with a smile as empty as his offer of cooperation. What he noticed most about her was her cold, searching eyes and tightly clenched jaw. Both told him this was not a woman to be derailed by talk or by verbal threats--- not even from him, a seasoned expert in talking smooth and minimizing the competition.

And then, to make matters worse, he has the Peterkin sisters to worry about. Who would have thought old Pris and Paula were still above ground? What were they now, ninety-something? Didn't look much different than they did the last time he'd seen them. Dried up old women even back then. Tonight, they told the TV woman they had their chauffeur drive them over from Brunswick to the party because of their "fond, fond memories of dear Cousin Mena and lovely Sparrow cottage."

Oh yeah, he thinks ruefully. That's probably true. Nobody spent more time sucking up to Mena Simpson or fondly enjoying the free sweets and drinks she served at the cottage than they did. Even during the war when sugar and just about everything else was rationed, old Pris and Paula could always cajole a Brunswick fisherman to ferry them over to Sparrow for free eats.

The way the Peterkin sisters fondled the TV woman's hands when they were introduced you'd think she was Moses come to free the children of Israel, not some ego-inflated celebrity looking for publicity. He wonders what the old sisters were really after. What do they really want from the TV woman?

He seethes--- a palpable burning inside his chest--- at the thought of the two old spinsters and their remark about their chauffeur driving them over. With gas at over three-fifty a gallon, who even has a chauffeur these days? Waste of good money driving around in that old, gas guzzling, Lincoln limo. Burning American oil independence mile by mile. Making us lackeys of the Muslim terrorists. He wants to drown both of them, along with their Lincoln, in Jekyll Creek. No one that useless should live so long.

To calm himself, he slowly counts to five. Then he measures the issue of the old women and their memories. They are certainly old and perhaps forgetful. Maybe for all their annoyance he has nothing to worry about from the Peterkin sisters. At their age, how much could they remember? After all, they were living in their fancy house in Brunswick when it all happened. Probably didn't care what happened to the hired help or their kids. Yet, he wasn't sure, so he had not risked being introduced to them at the party. Instead, he'd drifted away after he heard their conversation with the television woman and kept to the fringe on the far side of the crowd---just to be safe.

His mind snaps back to the dark haired, TV woman when she sits down in the chair. His stomach lurches at the memory of someone else sitting in the chair. How that one loved the stupid chair, even wanted to eat and sleep surrounded by the carved demon faces, thought their ugly puckered mouths sang a song just for him.

As the woman closes a hand around the dragon's head carved on each arm of the chair, she closes her eyes. He swallows and waits, anticipating a low, wailing cry carried on the wind. When there is only the sound of frogs calling from the trees, he reminds himself that the screaming sound was heard only in his nightmares, never in the waking hours. The waking hours held a different kind of terror.

He's thinking now about his plan, not sure if the TV woman arrived in her own car or if one of her staff drove her. He decides she is waiting for one of her staff to return and collect her and the chair. She rests her head against the carved wood back, combs her hair away from her face with her hands, and tucks it behind her ears. Pity, he thinks, she is beautiful.

He checks the lighted dial of his Rolex watch, shading the glow with his right hand. How much time does he have? Can he walk back to his car, assemble the rifle, and get a clear shot before she moves? He feels a mosquito bite his neck but doesn't try to swat it away. An itch pulsates on the tender skin near his collar line. He waits for several seconds, weighing his chances, before he scratches, and then fast-walks to the black Range Rover parked on the other side of the deserted cottage.

Ten minutes later he is driving up-island, careful to stay within the speed limit, his heart still racing from the rush when the shot broke the air with a gloved, whack sound. Three miles along, he cuts his lights and, guided only by a thin memory of day reflected in the early night sky, he leaves the road to drive across the sandy verge of du Bignon Cemetery, past the historical marker naming those buried there, and around to the backside of the low, tabby wall surrounding the graves.

He kills the car engine under a curtain of Spanish moss and sits for a moment, listening. Over the riverbank to his left, he hears something slap the water's surface, perhaps an alligator, but nothing more. Assured that he is alone, he breaks down the rifle lying on the floor of the passenger's side of the Rover.

Once the rifle is fitted into its compact, padded nylon bag, he surveys the cemetery again through the Rover's tinted windows. Confident that no curious tourists are wandering among the graves in the dark, he flips the overhead light switch to the off position, preventing it from coming alive when the door opens, and quickly exits the vehicle.

He decides against climbing over the cemetery wall. Instead, following the oyster shell encrusted barrier to the street side, he enters through a modest, wrought iron gate, tonight left askew on rust-cankered hinges. His steps are quiet on the sand and sparse grass between the graves. When he finds the crypt he's searching for, he moves the stone enough to drop the rifle bag inside, and then forces the gritty slab back into place. He would come back in the daylight, mill around like a tourist, and make sure the grave looked undisturbed.

By the time he drives to the other side of the island, to the house he leases at the end of Thorne Lane, the wind is picking up, shaking out the palm fronds like dry, paper bags. After he showers and sits on the screened porch, a double Scotch in one hand, a Cohiba cigar in the other, the rain is moving ashore, skipping across the metal roof. He smiles. Any footprints left behind would be gone by midnight.

CHAPTER SIX

Warm croissants with apricot jam and strong Jamaican coffee helped cheer an otherwise dreary morning. Daniel and I were having a late breakfast at one of the three tables cozied in the big bay window of the hotel restaurant. Susan and Sam, sitting across from us, their backs to the window, insisted they'd eaten earlier before walking on the beach in the rain, and nursed only coffee.

Susan was saying something to me, and I looked up from my cheese eggs. Her head was silhouetted by rain blowing outside against the window. Swollen drops clung and then separated into rivulets as they slid down the expanse of glass behind her, creating the illusion that she was crowned with long, wet dreadlocks. The dream from last night had dimmed, and I fought to connect what I was seeing with the fear that had interrupted my good night's sleep. Didn't the nightmare have something to do with twisted seaweed that looked like hair?

"Ms. P? I don't think you heard one word I was saying."

I tried for an apologetic look. "I'm sorry. Tell me again."

Daniel joined the conservation. "Susan and Sam were just suggesting that, since the beach is a rainout this morning, we could go over to Jekyll Island and do the historical thing. There's a museum, as wells as a trolley with a guided tour. We can even tour a couple of the millionaire's cottages."

"Right... a ninety-minute trolley tour." Susan waved an unfolded color brochure in my direction. "Listen to this: 'by 1900, the Jekyll Island Club's roster of members represented one-sixth of the world's wealth.' *The world's wealth*, not just little ole America. Can you believe that? Millionaires like Astor, Vanderbilt, J.P. Morgan, Pulitzer, Gould, Rockefeller---all the big guns had houses over on Jekyll. They'd come down here during the worst of the Yankee winters and stay in what they called cottages, and we'd call mansions. But, since you've been down here a bunch over the years, you probably know all about that, huh?"

Sam interrupted before I could answer. "Is that the same Vanderbilt who built the Biltmore house in Asheville? I think that mega-mansion is bigger than this hotel."

Susan gave Sam the infamous Allen eye roll. "Well, duh. Was there another Vanderbilt with that kind of money?"

I fortified myself with another swallow of coffee and answered Susan. "True, I've been to Jekyll and St. Simons before, but I really don't know all about the Jekyll Island Club. And I've probably forgotten half of what I did know. So I'm game for a tour of Jekyll. It'll be fun. And we can check in with Crane Cottage about the wedding while we're over there. Anyone heard the weather report for the rest of today and tomorrow?"

Daniel looked at his watch and rose from the table. "You ladies relax and finish your coffee. I'm going out front to see if my phone will get better reception. I'll bring up the weather on the web, and I want to call Mac. Make sure he leaves the department in plenty of time to get here at a decent hour tonight. You know him, if I don't bug him, he'll hang around the office being sheriff until the last second, and then get in here at midnight all revved up on coffee and wanting to talk about what the bad guys are doing in Perry County. Y'all know I love my cousin, but I don't want to hear any of that shit, at least not for the next few days."

I watched Daniel cross the restaurant, snugging his Stetson on his dark curls as he walked, and wondered just what that was all about. It wasn't like him to use the s-word in front of Susan and certainly not in front of Reverend Sam Quinn. I wondered if Daniel hadn't slept as well last night as I'd thought. True, Daniel had joked that Mac probably wouldn't leave Perry County long enough to keep his promise to join us at the beach for the wedding, but I'd taken it as humor, and not thought Daniel was truly worried about Mac showing. Yet, just now he sounded genuinely concerned. And when did Mac start sharing updates on the bad guys with Daniel? I'd never heard the two men talk about Mac's cases. But then, they probably wouldn't talk in front of me, now would they?

My thoughts came back to the restaurant in time to hear Susan saying to Sam, "You see what I mean, Ms. P gets that faraway look in her eyes when she's drifting off into a parallel universe."

What could I do but smile?

Daniel drove my Subaru, Susan beside him. Sam and I took the backseat because we are both short and require less legroom than the two six-foot Allens. After we crossed the bridge onto Jekyll Island, we stopped at the tollbooth to buy a Georgia State Parks parking pass, and followed the signs to board the trolley tour. By then the rain was more of a heavy mist seeping down through the Spanish moss and live oak leaves. Maybe because of the weather, the tour was packed with gawkers just like us. I found it restful to take a seat in the open-air bus, cleverly donned as an old timey trolley, and catch snippets of conversations spoken by travelers from Michigan, Arkansas, or Germany.

By the time we'd made the rounds of the historical district and toured a couple of restored Victorian mansions, the sun was pushing its way from behind scattering clouds and our well informed tour guide had educated us on the beginnings of the Jekyll Island Club. In 1886, the great-grandson of the island patriarch du Bignon---the family who'd owned the island for almost a hundred years--- joint ventured with his savvy brother-in-law Newton Finney, a Northerner, to incorporate the roughly seven-mile-long, remote barrier island into a hunting and fishing paradise for wealthy businessmen.

The rest is history. Business alliances were made and strengthened on Jekyll Island, where the rich gathered to close ranks, hunt quail, and forge marriage proposals for their young. American presidents were entertained at The Club, and powerful bankers and advisors met there to hammer out plans for the Federal Reserve System when the country was on the brink of financial ruin. However, beginning during the Great Depression and continuing into the start of the Second World War, Jekyll Island's star dimmed. Even the rich and famous don't live forever. Fortunes shifted, younger descendants stopped coming south for the winter, and the island fell into disrepair. During the war it was closed after the State of Georgia bought it for a state park from the remaining shareholders of the Jekyll Island Club, giving all of Georgia, they declared, public access to the great Atlanta Ocean.

When our trolley ride ended back at the Jekyll Island Club Hotel, Susan and Sam continued to chat about Jekyll's millionaire residents and suggested we collect the Subaru and take our own driving tour around the island. That seemed a good idea to me, but first I wanted to stop at Crane Cottage to confirm our wedding arrangements. With that in mind, we walked across the damp lawn to Crane Cottage,

Susan recounting what the tour guide had said about Crane Cottage being built about 1917 by the Chicago plumbing fitting and fixture millionaire Richard Teller Crane, Jr.

Inspired by 16th century, Italian Renaissance villa designs, Crane Cottage was the largest private residence built by a Club member. The cottage boasted 20 bedrooms and 17 bathrooms. Its design represented a shift from the existing, more rustic cottages to lavish ostentation. I didn't know about all that; I just knew that I'd loved Crane's pale stucco façade, Spanish tile roof, and front arches since I'd first seen the house as a child. To me, Crane Cottage suggested all that was beautiful, safe, and secure. Who could walk the promenade of manicured shrubs and flowers to the fountain at the far end of the green and not feel that all is right with the world? I'm sure it was not by chance that Crane's garden came to mind when Daniel asked where I wanted to have our wedding.

We entered Crane Cottage through the enclosed courtyard at the restaurant side and passed under one of the arched balconies of the loggia into what was the library but now served as a reception area for guests. I noticed the temperature was much cooler and less muggy than the 76 degrees outside. Smart man that Richard Crane. Those thick stucco walls were for more than just good looks. As we waited for someone to meet with us about the wedding, Susan and Sam drifted into the cottage to look around, giving me an opportunity to talk to Daniel alone.

"So, what's up? You haven't said twenty words since we left the hotel. Do you think Mac isn't answering his cell phone because he's out of range, or do you think he's avoiding you because he isn't coming?"

As if on cue, Daniel's phone beeped telling him he had a voice mail, and he walked back outside to try for better reception. When he returned he was smiling. "That was Mac. I guess my phone didn't pick up the signal while we were on the bus. He left a message saying he had one stop to make and then he was leaving town, headed down here. He said not to wait on him to eat supper, that he would catch up with us at the hotel."

Before I could say how glad I was that he could now stop worrying about Mac changing his mind and standing us up for the wedding, the Crane Cottage representative appeared, and we joined Susan and Sam to reaffirm plans for the next morning.

Our sampling of Crane Cottage smoked salmon paté with fresh dill was the subject of conversation when we left. Susan hooked her arm through her dad's. "You know what? These guys down here use salmon, but we're slap in the middle of the greatest trout fishing there is. We could use fresh mountain trout, smoke it, and make our own signature paté for the restaurant. I mean we'd have to call it something other than paté, cause who expects a French dish in a barbecue place. But hey, why not marry up a bit? What do you think, Dad?"

Daniel eased his arm up to give his daughter a quick hug. "What I think is I'll be buying a smoker when we get back home. The worst that can happen is the fish doesn't catch with the beef and pork restaurant customers, and I get to eat all the leftovers. What do you think, Promise? You like the idea of marrying up?"

I winked at Sam behind Daniel's back. "I think smoking trout might just be your true calling, Sweetheart." Sam covered her mouth to stifle a grin.

We walked across the Crane Cottage lawn to Faith Chapel, the small, shake-sided building originally constructed as an interdenominational church for island residents. Before entering, we stood in front and looked up at the pointed top-hat configuration of the steeple. I was taken aback when I noticed the terra cotta gargoyles perching under the roof overhang of the steeple. How could I not have seen those gothic creatures in all the times I'd visited the Chapel before?

Once inside, we moved reverently through the interior, stopping to savor the famous Tiffany stained glass window to our left, stroking the backs of the hundred year old wood pews, and finally finding our way to the front where the magnificent stained glass window, *Adoration of the Christ Child*, created by Maitland Armstrong and his daughter Helen, looks down at visitors from behind the altar. My mother was right: surely God lives in this place.

The four of us sat for a few moments in silence. I said a prayer for Rose Marie Fitzgerald McNeal, bless her optimistic Southern heart. She loved my father, unconditionally, in the face of his many faults. Through all the little betrayals and large disappointments, she remained convinced that her husband gave her all that he had to give. I'd always found that concept infuriating. My mother's willingness to settle for less angered me as a child and as an adult. All he had to give simply wasn't enough, and often times his all left my mother sorely shortchanged. She deserved so much more. Yet, Jimmy Mac's love, however flawed, sustained my mother.

I'd always felt there was a big takeaway from their relationship, yet with all my education and experience counseling other people, the truth of it still eluded me.

My eyes strayed over to Daniel--- generous, loving, not a selfish man. Why is it that daughters are forever cursed with comparing all men to the one father of their childhood?

CHAPTER SEVEN

We walked back to the Jekyll Island Hotel parking lot under a bright midday sun riding high in a cloudless sky. I decided to do the driving for the remainder of the tour. Of course, that would be once I managed to crack the code of how the devil to follow the one-way-no way-can't-get-there-from-here signs blocking off several connecting streets in the historical district. After a couple of false turns, I traced my way back and wound up out on the main road. So who cared if we drove by the Goodyear cottage more than once or twice?

Beneath an umbrella of live oaks hung with tendrils of Spanish moss, I drove past the last restored cottage along the historical district's avenue searching for a street allowing a left hand turn to connect us with the rest of the island. Susan reached from the back seat and grabbed my shoulder. "Stop," she ordered. I, being a person who usually follows directions, applied the brakes. Then Daniel spoke up and told me not to stop in the middle of the road. There were two too many drivers in the car. I pulled off onto the narrow shoulder.

"Which is it? Stop? Or don't stop? I can't do both."

"I'm sorry Ms. P, I didn't mean to startle you, but look over there. Isn't that Paul Tournay?"

We all turned to look, Daniel leaning over me to get a better view from the driver's side window. Sure enough, just outside a wide ring of yellow tape encircling a dilapidated structure's side yard, stood Paul, hands in his pockets, his head lowered. A Georgia State Trooper's car was parked off to Paul's left. An officer stood by the car talking to Barkley, who was shaking his head and animating his conversation with wildly gesturing hands and arms.

"What's he saying, Ms. P?"

Daniel sat back in his seat. "We have no idea, Susan. And it doesn't matter. Whatever trouble those two have walked into isn't our business. Just drive on, Promise. We don't want to get sucked into whatever's going on."

Sam spoke up. "Didn't Paul say that Aileen Wang was having a party last night over here at a cottage she wants to restore? Do you think that old, run down house is the one he was talking about? Maybe something happened at the party."

Susan rolled down her window, probably hoping to hear the conversation, but we were too far away to make out what Barkley was saying. "Hmm. You may be right.

That trooper looks pretty serious about something. Daddy, you know we can't simply drive on. What if the guys are in some kind of trouble?"

Daniel groaned as I pulled across the road and down the short drive to stop behind the trooper's car.

Paul, his face twisted into a worried gnarl, was beside the car opening my door before I'd even unbuckled my seat belt. We tumbled out of the Subaru and Susan fired several questions at Paul, but he seemed too upset to answer. All he managed was a sad-dog face and a gesture towards the yellow taped enclosure. Sam stepped forward. I couldn't hear what she was saying as she guided him away from our group, but in a few seconds Paul was nodding as though he agreed with something Sam was telling him, and his face began to relax. She reached up and rested her hand on his shoulder. He covered it with his own and looked away in the direction of the rundown house.

From the corner of my eye, I caught a glance of Susan's face. Was I seeing concern, or was it jealousy? I knew she and Sam were close friends, but how could she feel threatened by Paul? *Interesting.* Momentarily, Susan looked down and kicked at the sandy dirt with her hiking boot.

When I looked around again, Barkley and a bull-dog-framed, female, Georgia State Trooper were approaching. Even in motion, with her hat sitting drill sergeant square on top of her head and one arm close to the right hip, poised just above her gun belt, the trooper looked firmly attached to solid ground. I reckoned she was a half-foot or more shorter than Barkley, though I'd back her in *any* street fight.

"Good morning, Dr. McNeal," she said without offering a handshake. "I'm Trooper Olean Hopper. Mr. Barkley here tells me you are acquainted with the victim."

Mr. Barkley? What was this? Then I remembered Barkley insists on using just one name, Barkley, as though the singular moniker were sufficient for the world to remember him. I guess the trooper didn't know what to do with that piece of information, and for that matter, neither did I---thus the Mr. Barkley. The trooper's other words struck home: *acquainted with the victim.* What victim?

Barkley spoke in a calm, factual voice. "I suppose we shouldn't be surprised y'all came over. Is it on the news already?"

Daniel stepped forward, introduced himself, Susan, and Sam to Hopper, and then spoke to Barkley. "We don't know what you're talking about, son. What's happened here?"

Hopper studied Daniel for a couple of seconds as though she were measuring him for a prison uniform, then put both hands on her hips and answered, "There was a shooting last night…"

Paul whined, "Ai-le-en." Drawing out her name into three syllables.

I sucked in a breath. Susan was quick to ask, "Is she…?"

Barkley shook his head. "No, she's hanging on. She's in the hospital over on St. Simons Island. But she's unconscious, in a coma because of the head injury. Paul and I found her last night slumped over in that crazy Chinese chair of hers. Remember, we told y'all we had to come back over here to collect her."

"But who would do such…"

Olean Hopper held up her hands to stop me. "Let's not go there for now, ma'am. We're operating under the likelihood that Ms. Wang was shot accidentally by a deer poacher. You've probably heard there's no deer hunting on the island, but some fools think they are above that law. In any event, our Georgia State Patrol office is in charge of keeping the peace on Jekyll, but when we have a suspicious incident, we call in the Georgia Bureau of Investigation. I've done that this morning and we're waiting for the agent to arrive. When he gets here, Mr. Barkley and Mr. Tournay and I will talk to him and the GBI will sort it out. Now, unless you folks have something you can tell me about what happened last night, I want you to stay out of our way. Let us do our job. You understand?"

Before we could answer, Hopper held up her hand for silence and responded to the cell phone sized radio squawking on her shirt lapel. Ignoring us, she then pivoted around, walked back to her car, and leaned against the open door frame, talking to the person on the other end of the call. I strained to hear the conversation but couldn't make out a word. In a few moments she'd completed her call and slid into the driver's seat of her vehicle. Her words to us seemed like an afterthought. "I need to go," she called out. "You people stay out of the area marked by the yellow tape. You hear?"

I'm sure I frowned. I'd been given that order once before--- by my former husband---at Paul Tournay's house in Atlanta when Paul's ex-lover was murdered. Trooper Hopper turned her car around in the sandy yard and drove slowly along side us, shaking an index finger in our direction as she passed. A reminder about the yellow tape, I guess, as though we hadn't heard her the first time.

It was a relief to know Aileen had survived. I admire much about her. She's tough and pursues what she wants with tenacity I could only hope to have. And Aileen usually wins. Winning is good. But then, fair play is also good. Aileen could use a little work in that department. Regardless, I wished her a full recovery. Knowing her, I figured she would fight for her life with every ounce of her strength, if for no other reason than she wouldn't tolerate anyone else in her prime spot on TV.

Did Barkley say she had been shot in the head?

Barkley answered my unasked question. "Oh, Promise, I can't believe this has happened. Someone shot her in the head. I mean not between the eyes or anything; the bullet hit the left side of her skull. What did the doctors say, Paul? Something about swelling of the brain from the trauma so they've induced a light coma until the swelling goes down. Am I explaining that correctly?"

Paul nodded, and Barkley continued through tears. "I feel so horrible---all the complaining and bitching we've done about her over the years…"

Sam immediately reached up and gathered Barkley into a hug. Paul and Daniel must have felt uncomfortable by the emotional display because they drew closer together, apart from Barkley, and exchanged a couple of *man remarks* to deflect Barkley's outburst. You know what I mean by *man remarks*: those impersonal statements that describe the weather, the price of gasoline, the possibility of the Braves going to the World Series this year, or who makes the best burgers and onion rings in town.

Susan spoke up. "For cripes sake, Bark, get a grip. Nobody blames you for what happened to Aileen. It's not like your complaining put a curse on her or anything. It was an accident. It would have happened even if you had been kissing her fucking feet in adoration."

Susan's angry remarks left me speechless. I didn't dare look at Daniel. Sam stepped away from Barkley, took Susan's arm, and steered her a few feet off to the side. I could hear Sam say something like: *what's with you?* Susan replied, but I couldn't hear her response, and then Sam said a little louder, "It's what I do, you know. A minister is supposed to minister."

I felt a need to say something distractive and looked around for a clue. Off in the distance at the far end of the yellow crime scene ring, I noticed a second Georgia trooper. This officer, a male, was pacing up and down at the edge of the grass just outside the tape enclosure. I realized he was doing his sentry routine about twenty feet from what looked to be Aileen's auction find---the Chinese carved chair, her anchor for the Sparrow Cottage renovation project.

"Paul, I just noticed there is another officer out there at the far end of the yard. Is he guarding Aileen's infamous chair?"

After a deep sign, he replied, "Yes, Hopper left her cohort here to make sure the crazy chair doesn't get moved. It's part of the crime scene, you know, because that's where we found Aileen. That is, if it is a crime scene. I guess an accident isn't really a crime scene."

"Hmm. Do you think she was shot while she was sitting in the chair?"

We looked off at the dark hunk of carved wood sitting in the open yard. Paul took a long time to answer. "Well, I don't really know, but I guess so. She was slumped over in it, unconscious, when Bark and I found her."

The chair continued to hold my attention. I was having trouble imagining how a poacher could mistake Aileen sitting in the chair for a deer. And besides, Sparrow Cottage sat near all the other cottages, the museum, and the hotel, in the historical district. Seemed like a poacher would seek out a less populated area to shoot a deer, if he didn't want to be seen.

We turned around at the sound of a car driving up behind us. Not just any car, but a silver-gray BMW sedan. I knew before I got a look at the vanity license plate on the rear that it would say: GALAW2. When I'd first seen the plate, I'd asked Garland Wang, in jest, why he didn't get Georgia Law 1 instead of 2. He replied casually that he would have, except "1" was already taken by

Georgia's Attorney General. That, my dears, is why they call it a *vanity* license plate.

After all the pleasantries were exchanged, and I introduced Sam Quinn to Garland, I asked about Aileen. Garland seemed truly concerned. "She's tough. Vital signs are stable. Doctors are telling us they are encouraged. Whatever that means. Now we wait. Give the swelling in her brain a chance to go down. Then we see…"

His voice trailed off, not completing his sentence. I couldn't find a reply that didn't sound canned and insincere so I just nodded my understanding. Besides, Garland knows me well enough to know my heart is with him.

Barkley cleared his throat, then said, "Paul and I feel terrible about what happened. We should have stayed at the party with her, not gone over to get supper. Maybe if we'd stayed…" He shook his head sadly, leaving his own uncompleted sentence hanging in the air.

Garland gave Barkley a light pat on the upper arm. "It's okay, Bark. Wasn't your fault. I know the party was still in full swing when you left. Aileen was probably holding court like Cleopatra. Hell, I would have probably left for her to wind down, too."

I don't usually think of Garland as being a compassionate person. Made me wonder why he was tiptoeing around Barkley's feelings. Having seen Garland on more than one occasion sizing up a witness in court, I waited to see what piece of information he was probing for with his soothing remarks. I didn't have long to wait.

"Speaking of the party, who was still here when you guys took off for a bite to eat?"

Barkley looked a bit puzzled, then glanced over at Paul. I waited for his response, knowing Garland was headed somewhere specific with his casual question. After several seconds, looking at Paul the whole time, Barkley answered, "Well, most of the partygoers we don't even know. I mean Aileen drew up the list of guests and I sent out the invitations, but there weren't nametags or anything. Let me think."

Garland waited, as we all did, for Barkley's answer.

Finally Paul spoke up. "Let me say who I remember first. I have a better memory for a crowd than Bark." Paul held up his left hand and began to tick off fingers, "Besides the catering crew, there were maybe four men milling around Aileen. Then there were two guys without sport coats, probably media types, with a medium height woman in a tacky, gypsy looking long skirt. Maybe she was with the media also? Yeah, I think she probably was. They were all standing off to the side talking to each other."

Barkley broke in, "Yes, the two very casual dressed guys and the tacky woman were with the media. I talked to them."

"Anybody else?"

"No, Garland, the real crowd had drifted away. We spoke to Aileen and she waved us off, saying she didn't want to leave yet, for us to go ahead and come back in about an hour or so for her. She said there were a couple of people she wanted to buttonhole for restoration dona-tions, one in particular, and she wanted to have time to… to…I'm not sure what she said."

Paul finished Barkley's sentence, "*to snare him.* That's what she said. I thought it a strange word to use, *snare.*"

Garland raised an eyebrow as though to say that, Aileen being Aileen, snare would be exactly the word she would use.

Barkley added one more comment, "And oh yes, those two old ladies, the Peterkin sisters, were leaving as we were. Paul and I escorted them to their chauffeured limo. Can you believe that? A chauffeur. Now, those two I know for sure were not on the guest list. Aileen thought it was a hoot that they crashed the party."

"Right. I know about the Peterkin sisters, Paula and Pris. Aileen checked in with me during the party. She was laughing about the sisters; told me they got her cor-nered with stories about Sparrow Cottage back before WWII, how the house looked, that sort of thing. They even pitched the idea of her hiring them as consultants for the restoration. Aileen told me they proposed a fee of twenty thousand dollars--- up front---for their servic-es. She thought it was funny."

Somehow, the scenario didn't sound funny to me. I wondered how the sisters had arrived at a twenty thousand dollar fee. "What did Aileen tell them?"

Garland shook his head. "I don't know. She laughed and made some kind of comment like: not in their dreams. Aileen was in a hurry to get me off the phone and we moved on to something else pretty quick. Knowing Aileen…well, it doesn't matter now."

I think Daniel had been quiet as long as he could stand it. "What difference does it make who was still at the party when Paul and Barkley left? Are you thinking someone at the party may have seen the poacher?"

Garland winced. "I'm not so sure about the poacher angle. I got a call from Trooper Topper as I was driving over here…"

I interrupted, "Hopper, Garland. Her name is Olean Hopper. Topper was a 1950s TV show, starring Leo G. Carroll and a husband and wife who were ghosts." Daniel nudged me to hush. I nudged back. "Sorry, I thought you'd want to know."

Garland forced a smile. "Thank you, Promise. I can always count on you to educate, and correct, me."

I guess I had that one coming. I studied my feet.

"Anyway, Hopper's office called her. A jogger had called in, said he was running by here last night at dusk and heard a muffled gunshot. He also saw a dark SUV pull from around the cottage over there and drive away." Garland pointed to Sparrow.

"What do you mean by muffled gunshot?" Daniel asked.

"I asked the same thing. Hopper said the jogger did two tours in Afghanistan; knows the sound of a sniper rifle. Unfortunately, last night the guy chalked the shot up to his imagination, or maybe recurring memories, and didn't stop to look around. Finally, late this morning, he decided to call in the incident. Said he couldn't sleep last night. Kept hearing the gunshot in his mind."

"Oh, my God," Barkley blurted out, "the trooper told us they are assuming a deer poacher shot Aileen by accident. Are you saying someone deliberately shot her?"

"It's possible. In fact, I think it's likely. The GBI is sending an agent down. I decided to swing back by and wait for him." Garland paused and then held out his hand to Daniel. "By the way, I understand congratulations are in order. I wish you both much happiness."

Daniel and I murmured a thank you. Garland forged ahead with his agenda. 'That being said, Promise, I'm glad you happen to be here. I need your clairvoyant skills, or your intuition, whatever you want to call it. You're on my clock, starting right now, at your regular consulting fee rate. If someone meant to kill my wife, I want to know who and why. I want you to work with the GBI agent and get to the bottom of this mess."

For a second or two, I couldn't quite comprehend what was coming out of Garland's mouth. *He wants what? I'm a bride this week, not a PI.*

Daniel was quick to respond. "Uh, no offense, Mr. Wang. I know you're upset and all, but we're down here to get married, have a short vacation with family. I don't want my wife trailing around all over Jekyll Island after some would-be sniper."

My mouth probably dropped wide open. These two men sure did seem eager to get in line to give me orders. Especially Daniel. We hadn't even gotten married yet and he was singing the *my wife* song---saying he didn't want me trailing around Jekyll. Where did he get off telling someone, right in front of me, what *he* wanted me to do and not do? Besides, I knew Garland. He was only posturing, trying to get some control over a bad situation. He really didn't want to hire me. When the GBI agent arrived like the cavalry to the rescue, Garland would be fine, and I would be dismissed like an extra escort at a debutante party.

Susan checked her watch, giving me a cue for an exit. "Garland, let's see what the GBI learns today, and then we'll talk. It's almost two o'clock now, and we need to get back over to St. Simons Island. You have my cell number. I guess Aileen will be in ICU with no visitors for a while?"

"Yes, until she's conscious. After I meet with the GBI, I'll go back over there, make sure her mother hasn't been arrested for making another high drama scene."

"Betty Wu is already here?"

"Oh yeah, she got here last night before the hospital even reached me. She showed up at the emergency room having a Chinese-checkered-full-blown fit. Told them she knew her daughter was there because she'd had some crazy premonition about that damn chair and the curse."

Susan opened her mouth to say something, probably to ask about the curse, but Daniel herded us out of there before she could get the words out of her mouth. Once we were back in the car and driving across the bridge leaving Jekyll Island, Daniel asked me why we had to be back over on St. Simons. I didn't answer. I was still struggling to be reasonable and not jump him about his *my wife* remarks. Fact is, I was trying too hard to can my temper and had given myself a raging case of acid indigestion. I should always carry Tums in my purse.

Susan reached over from the backseat and patted Daniel's shoulder. "Well, duh, Daddy. That was just an excuse. Ms. P probably just wanted to leave without telling Mr. Wang she has no intentions of getting involved in what happened to Aileen. Right?'

When I didn't answer right away, Susan continued, "You aren't, are you?"

Now I answered, "No, of course not."

"Anyway, the chances are someone she burned to char and ashes on her TV show took the opportunity to even the score with her. I mean the woman has probably made a lot of enemies over the years. Don't you think so, Ms. P?"

"Hmm. Yeah, a lot. No doubt."

"Promise, may I ask you something?"

"Sure Sam, what is it?"

"Does Mr. Wang really believe you are clairvoyant?"

Susan snickered and, though I couldn't see him because I was driving, Daniel probably did the Allen eye roll.

"Who knows what Garland Wang really thinks? I tell him I'm not, but then Garland tends to believe what he wants to believe. When he gets a letter from the Republican Party to attend a fund raising dinner, he also believes it's because the governor believes he's a fascinating conversationalist."

Daniel laughed. I guess he thought I was kidding. I wasn't.

CHAPTER EIGHT

B etty Wu leans over her daughter's still body and listens. Is she breathing? There is an oxygen tube at her nose and wires patched from her arms leading to a computer monitor on the wall. The oxygen machine makes a low, sad hum while Aileen sleeps. But is *she* breathing? Betty worries the only life her daughter has is the one animated by the machine and the wires. She brushes back a dark strand of hair from Aileen's cheek and tucks it behind one ear.

This deep sleep the doctor calls a coma--- where has it taken my tiger daughter, the child with dancing fire in her eyes and great hunger in her belly? Is she dreaming? Does she dream the man who shot her?

Betty resists the urge to shake her daughter's shoulder, to tell her to wake up. Time for school, time for ballet class, busy day today. She knows her daughter is strong, will fight for her life, and wants to believe she will win. Then the bottomless, gaping mouth of guilt opens up inside her, wanting to swallow her, wanting to burst her ears with its accusing cries, and Betty Wu knows this coma is her fault. She was a coward, and now her daughter pays. What would Mena's Jesus say about a mean and spiteful god who punishes a child for the sins of the mother?

Betty takes one of Aileen's pale hands in her own. It is surprisingly warm. She studies her daughter's closed eyes, watches her walk a place of deep sleep holding her soul a prisoner, and remembers how this strong daughter came to be in her life. How storms can blow a person into dark places. How one terrible thing happens after another, and then sometimes, when a person believes her world is broken, one perfect, undamaged smile is there, and two innocent eyes are looking back.

Betty allows the beep-beeping sounds of the machines keeping her daughter alive to carry her back to that hot August afternoon. Hours after she'd ridden her bike back to Sparrow Cottage and stored it in the shed and hours after she'd helped Jon tend Mena's rose bushes, she stood at the kitchen sink with the tap water on, washing and peeling carrots from the garden for the night's supper.

A dirty hand reached around her and shut off the spigot. She smelled his rancid sweat, knew it was Caretaker before she saw him. She sucked in a ragged breath and tried to back away. He pushed his body against her backside, scraping his belt buckle along her spine, blocking her escape.

"You're wasting fresh water, girl," he breathed in her hair. "You run the pump dry and there'll be hell to pay."

Betty scrunched to the side, freeing herself and daring to turn and look him in the eyes, searching for a sign of what she'd seen from the beach. Nothing. His cold blue eyes were like the sea. They gave up nothing easily. "What you want?" she asked.

"I need Jon. Go get him."

"Jon is sleeping. He has fever. Anyway, he always rests before supper. I tell him you asking for him when he comes down from rest."

Caretaker stepped back and smirked down at her. "Resting, eh? I'll just bet he is. Now aren't you the good little wife to look the other way while he *rests*." He turned to put a dirty hand on the kitchen doorknob. "Go get him. Tell him the boy fell overboard off the skiff and I need him to help me hunt. Tell him to meet me down on the beach by the old hotel path. The simple-minded little shit has probably dog paddled ashore and is looking around for shells."

Betty knew the boy couldn't swim, knew she'd seen the skiff out too far for him to dog-paddle to shore, knew that she'd waited on the beach, watched with her field glasses long enough to know he wouldn't be found looking for shells. She wanted to run---run from the kitchen, run from Caretaker---but she couldn't allow herself to panic. She had to be calm, not let him see what she knew, not let him see her fear. She dropped the carrot and the peeling knife in the sink. "I get Jon," she said and hurried out of the room.

Jon and Caretaker took out in the skiff while there was still a low sun on the horizon. But now, in the deep twilight, the boat and the men were dark silhouettes marked only by a single flashlight sweeping the water. She and the old, black man's daughter walked up-island until a jagged city of half-submerged cypress trees blocked their way. They turned around and retraced their steps down the beach until they reached the island marina where Caretaker kept the Jekyll Island steamer. The women crossed the wide wooden gangplank and boarded the steamer. The black woman called out several times, her voice scattering a heron from a night perch on a dock pylon, but the boy wasn't there. Betty knew he wouldn't be there.

The black woman said, "Now what do you suppose done happen to that boy?"

Betty said nothing.

"You know he don't hardly walk good. I don't see he could get very far on his own. I used to stay with him sometimes when his mother wanted to go over to Brunswick. He didn't ever wander off. All he ever wants to do is help me roll out da biscuits, or tag along after his brother. Where is that brother? How come he ain't hunting with us?"

"Caretaker told Jon he took the older boy over to Brunswick yesterday, to visit with his dead mother's aunt, or maybe he said cousin. I don't remember who he said. But he tells Jon the boy is gone for some days."

The black woman walked silently beside Betty for a while and then said, "Uh-huh, well this be the first time I hear of Mr. Garr doing that boy a good turn by taking him to see his mama's folks. All I seen him do is work that boy like a full growed man. I don't know why his mama's family didn't come get those boys after she died. That younger boy, you know he ain't right. They say he got water on his brain. Nearly nine year old and can't hardly talk enough to tell you what he wants. But he be a sweet child. Yes ma'am, a real sweet child."

It was after midnight when they gave up the search and returned to Sparrow. Mena's bedroom light was out. Betty decided, by the state of the kitchen, that Mena had made an attempt at cooking supper and eaten boiled vegetables and left over cornbread. Jon said he was too tired to eat and went to bed. Betty ate cold cornbread with milk, cleaned the kitchen, and fell exhausted into her own bed.

The next morning Jon's fever was higher. Betty sponged him with cool water and encouraged him to drink the tea she'd made for him, though each sip came back. Finally, she gave up trying to get Jon to drink and squeezed cool water, drop by drop, into his mouth with a washcloth. By that night, when his body was racked with chills and the fever raged, Betty knew he was dangerously ill. Several times he vomited blood; his nose bled.

Late into the long night, Mena called her doctor in Brunswick and sent Betty to Caretaker's house to tell him to take the steamer to the mainland and bring the doctor back over to Jekyll. Betty knocked and knocked on Caretaker's door, but there was no answer, and no lights came on. She backtracked to Sparrow and rode her bike along the shell road to the marina. The steamer was gone.

Mena called the doctor again, and he promised to hire a boat to bring him over from the mainland. Daylight was rising over the marsh when Betty met the doctor at the marina. When they reached Sparrow, Mena was standing outside Jon's closed bedroom door. Her eyes were red and swollen, her chin quivering. She whispered, "He's gone. Jesus has taken our Jon home."

The doctor pronounced Betty's husband dead at six forty-three a.m. on that Wednesday morning in August 1948. She didn't cry. Mena had cried enough tears for the both of them. What Betty felt was a growing panic, a swelling fear for what would happen now. Jon was dead. No more Jon, no more *paper husband*, no more reason for Betty to be at Sparrow Cottage. Could she leave now? Would Mena want her to leave? Where would she go if Mena did want her to leave?

Betty remembered well how she'd been given this new life in America. Mena, the missionary who came to Taiwan after the earthquake, was married to the rich Mr.

Simpson who lived in a faraway place called Grand Rapids and didn't visit Jekyll Island. Mena had told her they had a *catholic* marriage, though Betty didn't understand what Mena meant by that, except Mr. Simpson was happy in Grand Rapids with his friends, his parties, and his mistresses. There would be no divorce, Mena said. His family would not approve.

Later Betty understood Mena didn't care what Mr. Simpson did, so long as she had her secret happiness, her Jon. But a secret must remain a secret, so Betty married Jon, on paper, and came to America as his wife. And that arrangement was fine with Betty. She was fourteen and didn't want a real life husband. Jon was a gentle, honorable man, her teacher at the Methodist missionary school, and much older. Betty had no interest in him beyond his teaching her English and her numbers. They understood each other. He wanted Mena and to be left to his garden and books. Betty wanted enough to eat so that her belly wouldn't growl, and to live in a warm house that wouldn't slide off the side of the mountain when the earth shook.

For a long time, Betty thought Mena's invitation to come to America was a miracle--- one brought, according to Mena, by her Jesus. But that was before she knew loneliness, before she knew longing, and before she knew Caretaker with his dirty hands and foul breath. Now, Betty believed Caretaker was the price she paid for her miracle, the balance on the scales for a full stomach and a dry, clean bed. With Jon gone, would Mena send her back to

Taiwan? Would Taiwan be better than Jekyll Island, better than living in fear of Caretaker? Soon, Betty learned Mena had no intentions of sending her back to Taiwan. Mena still needed her to cook and to clean Sparrow Cottage.

Caretaker returned to the island two days after Jon died. He told Mena that he took the steamer because he was so upset about the boy going missing that he went to ask help from the Glynn County Sheriff. He brought the older boy back from Brunswick with him, and for weeks afterwards, Betty saw the brother walking the beach, searching. When no sheriff came to the island to look for the boy, Betty knew Caretaker had lied about asking for help.

They buried Jon in the island cemetery with the help of two men from Brunswick who brought a pine casket over by boat and stayed to dig the grave. Neither Caretaker nor the older boy attended the graveside service, but the old, black man and his daughter came driving a squeaking, worn out wagon pulled by an equally worn out mule.

There, in the back of the wagon, was the chair. The one that had washed ashore after the Germans sank a tanker. The one cursed by angry Japanese gods---the akuryou, the evil spirit. Betty told Mena when she'd first seen the chair that she'd known a chair like that in her village. It belonged to a wealthy Japanese man whose household was plagued by sickness, murder, and suicide. Better to leave it to the sea. But Mena thought the carved chair was beautiful---said it reminded her of happy times in Taiwan. She insisted they bring the chair to Sparrow and put it in the library. Then, soon after that, there was a fire in the library, destroying many of Jon's precious books.

And finally, one morning as Betty was cleaning the garden room where the chair was moved after the fire, she drew back the drapes to let in the sun. A rattlesnake was coiled in the seat of the chair, its darting forked tongue tasting the morning breeze drifting through the windows. Betty killed the snake, and Mena agreed to banish the chair. That's when Caretaker took the chair home, and the young boy became attached to it as any other boy would a dog. In his own garbled little voice, he told his older brother that the chair sang to him. He sat in the chair, ate in the chair, and would have slept in the chair if his mother had allowed it. Then the yellow fever came to kill the boy's mother, and now the boy and Jon were dead.

And the chair was back. "Washed ashore again," the black woman told Betty over Jon's open grave. "This very morning," she said in a hushed voice. "Now ain't that something? The same chair that little drowned boy loved to sit in. What you think about that, Betty? You reckon Miss Mena wants her chair back?"

Betty didn't answer. She looked away from the twisted faces carved into the back and along the arms of the chair, tried not to think about the snake she'd found sitting on it. She closed her eyes, trying to hear only Mena's prayers for Jon's soul to rest with Jesus, but the chair kept crying out to her, calling her name---*Betty, Betty.*

Now, so many years later, in Aileen's hospital room, Betty looks down at her wrinkled hands. She knows she is old and that Jon's funeral was over sixty years ago, yet she can still smell the sour, turned earth of his grave. She also knows that her daughter would not be sleeping so close to death if the chair had not called her name again, had not called her back to Jekyll Island.

What does this evil spirit want in exchange for my tiger daughter's life?

CHAPTER NINE

There is a singular stillness when the tide is out, almost as though the ocean has released a long, intimate sigh and is holding its breath to savor the moment. Daniel and I stood barefoot on the wet sand and watched gulls catching early evening thermals. We had about thirty minutes to spare before meeting Susan and Sam for supper down in the village, and I didn't want to squander one single second of it arguing about Garland Wang.

Daniel asked me twice, after we drove away from Jekyll that afternoon, if I was going to "jump in the mess with Aileen." Now he was bringing it up again. I didn't have any intentions of playing detective, but I wasn't going to lie and say I wasn't interested in who shot Aileen and why.

Without thinking very hard, I could name two or three political players in Atlanta who might want to shut her up enough to send a calling card delivered by a sniper. One of them was already under indictment for allegedly giving the nod to a staff member to hire a thug to put the fear into his ex-wife---the politician's ex-wife, that is. It was all over the papers when the wife called the thug's bluff and then beat the living crap out of him with a sock full of rocks before calling 911. Trust me. The thug must have been dumber than the rocks to take this woman on. I've met her---think Conan the Barbarian in very expensive drag. Who knows what dirty secrets the ex-wife was threatening to spill. Must have been potentially pretty damaging. Maybe she was talking to Aileen about going public with what she knew, and Aileen hadn't gotten the memo that the ex had reportedly taken three million dollars and skipped the country for parts unknown.

I tried to assure Daniel that I didn't intend to get involved with who shot Aileen. "We could go by the hospital and pay our respects to Betty Wu and Garland later tomorrow, maybe after the wedding and lunch. Or we could drop by before supper tomorrow night. How about that? No sleuthing. I'm just curious. But don't fuss if I ask what the GBI thinks about the shooting. Agreed?" Daniel nodded yes, but the frown lines in his face said no.

I decided since he was already aggravated, I might as well clear the air. "And one last thing: don't be telling anyone what you do or don't want your wife to do. That sounds so...so proprietary. That statement you made to Garland sounded like I was your new truck, and you didn't want some neighbor kid driving me off through the mud getting me dirty."

The frown lines deepened into a grimace. "I don't know why the hell you'd use a ten dollar word like *proprietary*. You mean I think of you as property? Where did you come up with such an insane idea? I want you safe. What's so all-fired wrong with that, *Dr. Promise McNeal*? And more importantly, I'd never liken you to a new truck."

Daniel took a couple of steps away from me and then fired his final salvo. "A new Maserati sports car, maybe, but never a truck."

He ducked, dodging the shoe I threw, and then being the gentleman that he is, he picked it up and carried it for me back to the hotel.

Supper was at the Blue Water Café overlooking the ocean at St. Simons. Daniel and I had fried green tomatoes served with the house special horseradish sauce and a delicious piece of grouper. Susan and Sam had flounder stuffed with crabmeat. None of us mentioned that Blue Water was where Paul and Barkley had eaten the night before when Aileen was shot.

After dinner we walked across the parking lot to the pier and watched enthusiastic would-be fishermen and women throwing bait lines for crab off the railings. We didn't see anyone hoist anything up on deck, though everyone seemed to be having a good time. We had a half-hearted discussion about taking the walking ghost tour of the village, but honestly, I was toured out from our morning over on Jekyll Island and voted to amble around people watching. The nays for the guided tour having carried the vote, we headed for the lighthouse with Susan reading us a brief history of the 104 -foot tall building as we walked. According to Susan's brochure, the lighthouse was built in 1810, dynamited by Confederate troops as they abandoned the island to the Union army during the Civil War, and then rebuilt in 1872.

The lighthouse boasts its own ghost, a former light keeper who shot his assistant one morning in a fit of anger. We stood on the front lawn looking up at the darkened windows of the light keeper's residence where several people have seen and photographed---according to the brochure---unexplained, ghostly lights. My cell phone rang. It was Paul. He and Barkley were at the hospital. There was no change in Aileen's condition and they would be staying on the island for an extra day to answer questions from the GBI agent who'd arrived to take over the investigation. An investigation, Paul said, into attempted murder.

I asked Paul if the agent had said they had evidence, or just suspicions, the shooter wasn't a poacher? He answered that there was evidence and then added he would give me the details later. I said something to the effect that it was a good thing the GBI had sent someone down to investigate, and knowing Garland, he'd probably pulled some strings to get one of the best agents.

Paul replied, "Well, yesss, you could, maybe, say that."

The way he dragged out the yes and added the maybe made me think he wanted to say more but didn't. I supposed I'd get the rest of the story when we saw him again. I extended a wedding invitation again and hung up encouraged that Garland was happy with his GBI agent and probably wouldn't press the idea of me getting involved.

"I was hoping that call would be from Mac," Daniel said. "Maybe that he couldn't get my cell to connect and called yours."

I shook my head, said I was sorry, and gave them the news about Aileen.

Daniel's mind was still on his cousin. "Mac should be here by now. Do you mind if we go back to the hotel? We can wait for him in the bar. Catch him as he comes in."

Susan and Sam decided to revisit the village and check out a bar we'd strolled past earlier, where music and good looking young men and women spilled out onto the sidewalk. Daniel and I walked back to the Subaru and I drove us to The King and Prince. We checked with the front desk to inquire whether Daniel had any messages---he didn't--and then claimed a table in the bistro within sight of the hotel entrance---just in case Mac arrived.

Once our drinks arrived, Daniel fidgeted with his brandy, moving it around on the tiny marble table like a chess piece. Every time someone came through the door, his head jerked up at attention. It didn't take long for me to have enough of his silence and my watching him watch the door.

"Daniel, why are you so antsy about Mac getting here? You know how he is. He probably left the office late and isn't calling because he doesn't want a tongue lashing from you." He nodded an acknowledgment but didn't answer my question. Finally, he finished his brandy in one swallow, made the pronouncement that Mac was a big boy and could take care of himself, and suggested we go up to bed.

That was a little after eleven o'clock. I fell asleep as soon as my head hit the pillow but woke about three a.m. to see Daniel, wearing his jeans but no shirt, standing in front of the glass doors looking out at the ocean. I propped up on one elbow and asked him if he was okay. When he said, "I'm fine, Babe. Go on back to sleep," I did. The next time I woke the bedside clock read five-thirty. Daniel was asleep on top of the covers, still wearing his jeans, and a phone was ringing, ringing, ringing.

CHAPTER TEN

I couldn't quite reach over Daniel to grab the phone. When I dragged myself out of bed and walked around to his side, I realized the noise wasn't the room phone but my cell phone. Stumbling back across the carpet, still groggy with sleep, I snagged the cell from atop of the dresser and punched answer.

"Dr. McNeal here. What is it?" My sleep-glazed mind thought I was back in my therapist days. One of my clients was probably in the ER under suicide watch.

The voice on the other end wasn't St. Joseph's Hospital ER. "Promise, put Daniel on the telephone." It was Fletcher Enloe. When I heard my neighbor's voice, I was confused about why he would be asking for Daniel. Then my confusion bloomed into fear that something terrible had happened to my house or animals.

My already racing heart lurched in my chest as I followed orders and crossed the darkened room to where Daniel now stood beside the bed. Before I gave him the phone, I pressed the speaker button on so I could hear. There had to be a good reason for Fletcher to call at five-thirty in the morning on our wedding day.

"Son, you awake?"

"I am now, Fletcher. What's up?"

"I need you to listen up. Let me tell it all to you before you say nary a word. You hear me?"

Daniel replied, "Yes, sir," and we both sat down on the edge of the bed.

Fletcher exhaled and then cleared his throat. "Two hours back of this, that skinny good-for-nothing deputy Pate Hoag was a-knocking on your MaMa Allen's door. She allows as how she let him in the house and he tells her..." Fletcher stopped in mid-sentence. I could hear his dry swallow.

He waited a moment and then continued. "Well, it's Sheriff Mac, son. Hoag told your MaMa that somebody put a bomb under Mac's patrol car late yesterday afternoon. The explosion pretty much blowed him all the way to God's Kingdom. Son, you mark what I'm saying?"

Daniel sucked in a sharp breath. I took his free hand in mine and held on tight. "What? Fletcher, are you telling me Mac is dead?"

"Yes, son. That's the sad truth. I'm as sorry as a man can be. I know how close you two boys were. Your MaMa was wanting me to tell you on account of her being so upset and all."

Daniel was silent. In a second or two Fletcher continued. "Now here is the rest of it, just so I get it all told to you like your MaMa wants me to do. Pate Hoag is a-thinking you was in the car with Mac. Course, Honoree knowed you wasn't but her being a Melungeon woman, and her people being swayed twixt the whites for four hundred years, you know she always bides her tongue to see whose shooting afore she stands up to wave howdy. Besides, she allows to me she don't trust Pate Hoag, and fact is I don't neither. That's how come she didn't tell him you wasn't in the car with Mac. You following what I'm saying, son?"

Daniel's hand gripped mine so fiercely that my knuckles cracked with pain. When he spoke, his voice was rapid, full of questions and disbelief. "Did you say bomb? How the hell could anyone wire the sheriff's own car with a bomb without him or somebody else seeing it? I mean, sweet Jesus on a bicycle, what's happened to Perry County? Our people don't... we're hay farmers and cattlemen..." Daniel stopped to calm himself and then asked the one question Fletcher might be able to answer. "Why would Pate Hoag think I was in the car with Mac?"

"Well, son, here's what I understand from Honoree. The explosion blowed as Mac was pulling out of your driveway onto the blacktop. Deputy Hoag told Honoree your truck was parked around back of the house, and you wasn't at the house, so I reckon he thought...." Fletcher didn't finish his sentence.

Daniel was probably thinking the same thing I was. His message from Mac in the early afternoon said that he had one stop to make and then he would be leaving for St. Simons. It now seemed that stop was at Daniel's house. But why? And why would anyone put a bomb in Mac's car? Perry County is not some big city crime area. Everyone loved Sheriff Mac. Well, apparently not everyone.

The idea that Mac had been snuffed out of existence with no chance to say goodbye seemed impossible. Daniel had talked to him the day before. His voice message was still on Daniel's phone. He couldn't be dead. He and Daniel were more like brothers than cousins. Because Mac, long ago divorced, didn't even have a child to knit into family, he and Daniel talked or saw each other nearly every day. They were the last of the Allen men with no other living kin, except Susan and MaMa Allen, nee Honoree Mullins, who'd come from East Tennessee to marry their grand daddy---twenty-five years her senior--- when Mac and Daniel were small boys.

Fletcher picked up the thread of Mac being in front of Daniel's house when the bomb went off. "Why you reckon Mac was over to your house? Wait. Hang on. Honoree is telling me something else."

I broke into the conversation. "Fletcher, is MaMa Allen there with you?"

Fletcher answered with the disdain he reserves for my flatlander brethren and me. "Well, god-a-mighty, girl. You think I'd leave Honoree over to her house alone with all that's happened? Of course I went over there and brung her over here. She'll be safe with me, don't you worry about that."

Safe? Why is he saying safe? Why wouldn't she be safe?

Fletcher continued from where I'd sidetracked him. "Daniel, Honoree is saying to tell you Pate Hoag kept asking her what business Mac had over to your house today. He also wanted to know if she'd talked to either of you boys yesterday. I reckon he means before the... explosion. Hoag mentioned he was a-looking for Susan to tell her what happened, but she wasn't at the house. He was pressing Honoree about would she go over to your house with him since he couldn't find Susan and see if anything was missing or out of place."

Daniel frowned, plowing deep furrows in his forehead. "Hoag wants to search my house?" he said aloud.

Fletcher went on. "I guess. That's what it sounds like. I ain't for sure what's going on, but I know for certain whoever is acting as sheriff would've called in the state boys by now, and they wouldn't be sending little Pate Hoag out to investigate nothing but a dog bite."

I believed Fletcher. He knew what he was talking about. His occupation during the thirties and forties had been outsmarting the local law and the federal agents who were sent into the mountains to wipe out bootlegging. The story is that, back in the day, he and his brother held the distinction of making the most whiskey runs from Perry County to Atlanta without being caught.

After serving in Korea and giving up hauling shine---at least we thought he'd given it up---my irascible neighbor had been pressed into service on more than one occasion by Sheriff Mac to work on the right side of the law. Nobody knows the Western North Carolina Mountains or the local folks like Fletcher Enloe.

I might also mention this is that same Fletcher Enloe who had saved my life up on Fire Mountain last year. The man doesn't hesitate to take care of business.

"What'd MaMa tell Pate?"

"Well, son, like I said. Honoree is a smart lady. She didn't say yea or nay. She told him she'd appreciate being alone with her grief and asked him to leave her be until she could see about funeral arrangements."

Daniel and Fletcher were quiet, no doubt each of them trying to wrap their minds around a tragedy that made no sense at all.

Daniel took his hand from mine and stood up to pace the floor space between the bed and the glass doors to the balcony. "I need to think for a few minutes here, Fletcher. I appreciate you going for MaMa. She needs to stay over there until I get back and figure out why Pate is so interested in getting into my house. That okay?"

"Well, sure it is. Pate ain't the smartest hound on the hunt. It'll take him a day or two to come around to realizing where she is. I figure by then the state boys will be all over Perry County like syrup on a biscuit. None of them cotton to one of their own being…" Fletcher let the rest of his thought trail off. No need to finish his sentence. We knew.

"Thank you, Fletcher. Let me get my mind in gear. Maybe have a cup of coffee. I'll call you back in about an hour. Can you hold the fort until then?"

"Well, hell yeah---me and my Winchester. Soon as it gets daylight I got to go on over to Promise's to see about the animals---milk her nanny goat and all. Honoree can listen out for the phone."

"Sounds like a plan. You're a good man. Can I talk to MaMa before I hang up?"

"Sure, I'll put her on."

There was a pause of the phone being passed, and then MaMa Allen spoke. "Daniel, you still there?"

"Yes, Ma'am. How you holding up?"

"I'm bent most to the ground, son, 'bout same as you, I reckon. Torn twixt hunting down the bastard that killed Mac and hanging him from the highest tree and falling on the floor with a good cry. Right now my anger is keeping me standing."

There was a long sigh from her end of the line. "Course, I know we both gonna have to get past the anger. Being mad won't do no good. We got to hold on to the blessings Mac left us. He was a smile to my face and a sweet soul. All he ever wanted was to be a good sheriff---take care of this county and his people."

Her voice broke and I think Daniel was also fighting back tears. I wasn't doing as well and felt hot tears spilling from the corners of my eyes.

MaMa Allen continued. "I'll be all right, Daniel. I got faith those that done this terrible thing will be punished." She sniffed and then said, "Listen here, son. I know Mac would want you and Promise to go on and have your wedding. And that's what I want you to do. It won't make no never mind if you get home tomorrow or the next day. Oh," her voiced raised on the last word. "There's something I most forgot to tell you."

"What's that MaMa?"

"Well, I didn't tell the deputy, but Mac did call me yesterday---sometimes early afternoon. I think he was mostly calling to tell me he was going home to get his truck so he could come on down to the wedding, but then he commenced to chuckling over the telephone saying he'd broke into your house and reckoned you'd call the law on him once you got back. I reckon he thought it was funny, him being the law and all.

"I told him he'd no reason to tear up your house since I had a key, if he needed something that all-fired bad. He just laughed and told me not to worry cause he didn't make a mess, that the mudroom window out to the back porch was open a little bit, and he'd pried off the screen with his pocketknife and stepped through as easy as pie."

Daniel didn't say anything for a few seconds. Finally he said, "Hmmm. Well, you know Mac. He was probably leaving Promise and me some funny just married signs around the house, but I'm glad you told me. We'll talk to the state folks when I get back. You stay with Fletcher and don't go over to my house. When it comes out that you knew I was down here, you say that you were too upset to think straight. That's why you didn't tell Pate when he came around. You understand?"

"Yes Daniel, I understand. You be careful coming home and give my love to Promise and Susan."

"Yes, Ma'am," Daniel said and hung up. He turned his back to me, thwacking the cell phone against the palm of his left hand as though he was driving a nail into a piece of wood.

I reached out and rested my hand on his shoulder. All I could think to say was: *I'm sorry. I'm so sorry.* Daniel nodded his head but said nothing. I didn't blame him. What could either of us say that would matter?

When he tossed the cell phone onto the dresser and went to shower, I drew back the drapes at the glass doors in time to see the growing dawn crouching low over the ocean, reaching out from the eastern sky with god-sized fingers of nectarine pink, white, and gold. It would have been a beautiful day for a wedding.

Once we were dressed and downstairs in the restaurant with our coffee in front of us, I asked Daniel, "What would Mac be looking for at your house?"

"I don't know, but it seems like Pate Hoag is looking for the same thing."

"So you don't think Mac was over there to hang up just married posters for us?"

Daniel frowned at my question and answered with a question. "Do you?"

I shook my head no and then sipped my coffee. I couldn't shake the feeling that Daniel knew more about why Mac was murdered than he was telling me. Maybe his anxiety with Mac making it to St. Simons was about more than his best man showing for the wedding. I toyed with the idea of asking Daniel but nixed the thought. Daniel being Daniel, he'd only tell me when he was ready to talk.

"Course, we don't know that Mac breaking into your house had anything to do with him being killed, do we?"

Daniel's voice was low, firm. "No, we don't. But we do know that Mac didn't trust Pate Hoag, and Hoag seems to be a little too interested in what Mac might have wanted at my house. That tells me Hoag is connecting Mac's death to something at my house. I don't have any idea whether he's right or wrong at the moment."

"How do you know Mac didn't trust Hoag?"

I got a condescending look from Daniel. It was a dumb question. The two men were like brothers. Of course Mac talked to Daniel about what went on in the Perry County Sheriff's Department.

"All right," I said, "I guess we'll know more when we get back. Right now, we need a plan for today. You tell me what you want to do."

After a short banter back and forth, we decided the wedding would go ahead as planned. We would wait to tell Susan about Mac's death until the ceremony was over. Early afternoon, Daniel and I would check out of the hotel three days early and head back to Perry County. Susan and Sam were booked at the Village Pub until Sunday. They could decide whether to leave with us or stay. One way or another, we didn't think there would be a funeral until the following week.

Daniel went outside to call Fletcher from his cell. I stayed in the restaurant to have another cup of coffee. When I reached over to pour a fresh cup from the carafe, a shadow fell over my left shoulder and moved across the white linen tablecloth. I looked up, saw no one, but had the feeling that Mac was there, looking for Daniel. The shadow drifted away from me. I followed it to the semi-circle of windows that made the large bay facing the ocean. Was I meant to see something?

Outside on the beach, silhouetted by a sunrise of blue and white-pillowed sky, two couples wearing shorts, sweatshirts, and billed caps strolled along the spume-pocked sand picking up shells. An older, very thin, deeply tanned man with a yellow lab in tow jogged past them. As he and his dog trotted into the distance, I noticed his white tee shirt had a black thunderbolt symbol on the back.

Nothing seemed out of the ordinary. I turned back to the restaurant looking for the shadow. It was gone, replaced by a prism of blue, red, and yellow sunlight flickering on the green, carpeted floor.

The waitress stood beside our table ready to take our breakfast order.

CHAPTER ELEVEN

Life changing events seldom, if ever, play out exactly as I envision them. For instance, when my son Luke was born. I did the Lamaze classes and was committed to natural childbirth. I visualized the birthing experience as a mountain I could climb with determination and dignity. I was ready, or so I thought. Wrong. By the time the last stages of labor had me slamming into a solid wall of pain, I was hollering like a banshee and begging for something to knock me out. Thankfully, Luke's father was not at the hospital to witness my fall from the pinnacle of the perfect birthing mother. But that's another story.

I don't know why I was thinking about Luke's birth as Daniel, Susan, Sam, and I stood before blooming scarlet peonies in the Crane Cottage garden. Maybe because I was missing Luke, concerned about him, prayed he was safe, wherever he was. Luke was my by-the-textbook normal, reasonably cheerful, well-educated child. Why in the world would he work for a government agency demanding total secrecy? That decision didn't sound normal to me. And more than that, I'm his mother, but I had to learn by accident that his position with Acadian Oil was not really as he'd described.

RB Barnes---may be choke on a peach pit---was the answer to my question of why Luke would work for the government. Luke is a son trying to gain an absent father's respect. Damn Randall Barnes. Damn his selfish, sorry hide.

A flush of guilt washed over me. Thinking about an ex-husband during your wedding had to be extremely bad luck. Besides, cussing RB was a waste of energy and was sure to give me more wrinkles. I was marrying a man nothing like Randall Barnes. Daniel was a man I loved and respected, for goodness sakes. Forget Barnes.

I fought to focus on the joyful reason we'd gathered in this beautiful garden.

But then my mind jumped to Aileen Wang being shot less than a city block away from where we stood and to the predawn phone call that brought news of Mac's death. Puff---a candle extinguished with no warning. Just gone. How would Daniel deal with the loss? What would he do with the anger he must feel? Such a tragedy and such a painful reminder of our tenuous hold to this earth. I thought of my son again. Be safe Luke. I love you. Be safe.

An ocean breeze huffed landward across the wide, green lawn beyond the garden, stirring the peony bushes and lifting the hair along my neckline. I could hear the faint shush, shush of waves. The tide had turned. A sweet fragrance catching a ride on the breeze brought me back to Reverend Sam Quinn, her white robe and pale red hair shimmering in the glare of the midday sun.

I concentrated on her voice and felt her words rising from somewhere deeper than her throat, tumbling into the air and walking on the sunlight surrounding her. I know it was just a trick of the light, but it felt magical. Her prayer was for Daniel and me to walk with God and with each other. This was not the wedding day Daniel and I planned, but it was ours, and I wanted to savor every minute of it.

Sam took our wedding rings---mine a gold band with five brilliant, demi-sized diamonds---and blessed them. After we'd exchanged rings, Sam joined our left hands and rested her hand on top. All too soon the vows Daniel and I pledged were said and Sam let her hand fall away. Daniel held on. His gentle brown eyes told me he would never let go, never let me fall, never leave me. His unspoken words took my breath away. After a few seconds, we hugged and I heard myself say, "I love you, Daniel Allen."

His reply was: "That's all I need to know."

Susan stood beside us, smiling a more somber version of her usual bubbly grin. Could it be that even Susan felt the gravity of what had just happened between Daniel and me? The Reverend Sam Quinn's voice called us back to the ceremony. "And Ruth said, 'whither thou go, I will go; and where thou lodge I will lodge; thy people shall be my people, and thy God my God.'"

After a pause, Sam prayed, "Oh God who has known us before we were, and from whom no hearts are hidden, look mercifully upon these thy servants that they may love, honor, and cherish each other, and so live together in faithfulness and patience, until death do they part. Amen."

Sam's quote from the Book of Ruth was a surprise. I made a mental note to ask her about it. We repeated, "Amen" and the ceremony was over. Susan hugged her dad and then me, whispering in my ear that I would not be sorry. Daniel retrieved his Stetson from the garden wall and set it solidly on his head. My Daniel---hat and all.

Suddenly I felt unmoored, wanted to cry out, "No, wait. There must be more. Don't let it be over, not yet." Daniel reached over, drawing me into his arms, and I was okay again.

"You gonna take your robe off?" Susan asked The Reverend Quinn.

Sam gave her a sheepish look. "Well, tell you the truth, I was so excited about doing the ceremony that I forgot about our fancy lunch and slipped my robe on over my running shorts and tank top. Sometimes that's what I wear when I think the church is going to be really hot. So I guess you guys are stuck with me looking like a real priest over lunch."

Susan did the Allen eye roll and then smiled. "Don't worry about it. You look great. Maybe you'll get to christen a baby over iced tea and crab salad."

Daniel escorted us beside the fountain and out of the garden to the front of Crane Cottage where we entered the restaurant through the courtyard. I think it was when the maître d' welcomed us as Mr. and Mrs. Allen that I woke from the words spoken in the garden to the reality that we were truly married---husband and wife.

I remember thinking: *Okay, old girl, you have put your bare feet on the rocky road. Hope you're up to the trip.*

A bottle of Chandon Brut champagne, chilling in a silver bucket, waited for us on our table. A small white envelope leaned against the bucket. Daniel passed the envelope to me; I opened it and read aloud. "Dear Promise and Daniel, We wish you a lifetime of love and happiness. Sorry to miss the party, but we are off to Atlanta. Someone must hold Aileen's empire together. Enjoy the bubbly. Warmest Regards, Barkley and Paul."

"Perhaps this means Ms. Wang is improving," Sam said.

"Maybe," I replied. "I'm sure Aileen wouldn't want her production assistant and one of her regular guests lolling around the hospital when they could be back in Atlanta soothing sponsors and chatting up the local press."

Daniel agreed with me, then added, "Whatever the case, champagne is a nice gesture. We'll have to write them a thank you note when we get back home."

It was my turn to do the eye roll thing. *We would have to write a thank you?* Daniel plays a soulful fiddle and grills the best steaks in North Carolina, but write a thank you note? I didn't think so!

Our waiter appeared and asked Daniel if he should open the champagne. Daniel looked uncertain. My guess was that he was thinking of Mac. I answered for him, "You know what? I think we'll save the champagne for later. Will that be all right?"

The waiter smiled. "Certainly, ma'am. I'll wrap it for you when you leave." Shortly, our water glasses were filled and we were left to the lunch menu.

Daniel took a sip of water. "Susan, sweetheart, we've had some sad news this morning and Promise and I felt it was best to tell you after…"

Susan reached across the table and took her dad's hand. "I know, Daddy. That's why you don't feel much like champagne. I called the restaurant just before we came over here, to see how things were going, and Ben told me about Sheriff Mac. I wasn't sure if you knew. How did you find out?"

"Fletcher called us about 5:30 this morning. MaMa Allen is with him, so you don't need to worry about her. I wonder how Ben found out so quickly?"

"His sister Rochelle works dispatch at the sheriff's department, remember?"

"Oh, yeah, I remember. When he applied for the assistant manager's job, he listed her as a reference. Lord, oh Lord, another advantage of living in a small town." Daniel lowered his voice. "Honey, did Ben tell you what happened? The details?"

Susan looked down at the table and nodded yes. Her eyes clouded up with tears and Sam put an arm around her.

Daniel continued, "I don't want to talk about the details right now, not until I'm home and get some straight answers from the state boys. I'm sure they will be handling the...the...situation. Talking about it won't do any good, anyway. Nothing can bring Mac back. The fact is something ugly has set down in Perry County--- something evil---but it will be sent back to whatever hellhole it crawled out of. I can promise you that. That's what Mac would want."

I think Daniel realized how angry he sounded because he paused and studied his clenched fists resting on the table. After a few seconds, he uncurled his fingers and said, "Fact is, I've never had a world without Mac in it. He was my cousin, but y'all know he was also the brother I never had. I can't seem to get my mind to thinking about a world without him." Daniel was quiet again. Under the table, I kept my hand firmly on his knee.

Sam broke the silence by asking quietly if Daniel would like her to say a prayer of thanksgiving for our meal, our marriage, and for Mac's life. I felt the tension in Daniel's leg relax a little as Sam prayed.

Lunch was delicious, though our little foursome was understandably subdued. Daniel thanked Sam for conducting the ceremony and for being a good friend to all of us, especially Susan. Sam responded that she was honored and that we had made her feel a part of the family. *The family.* I looked around the table. *Yes, the family.* My family. I was happy to be counted among these good, loving people and sad that Luke was not with us.

When our dishes were cleared and coffee poured, Susan fidgeted in her seat. Finally, she couldn't contain herself any longer. "All right, Daddy. You're calling the shots. What do we do now? Pack up and head back home this afternoon?"

"We'll talk about that in a few minutes. Right now I'm happy drinking this delicious coffee and savoring the company of the women I love."

Sam excused herself to find the powder room. I watched her small frame, white robe skirting the stone floor, cross the restaurant. Several guests waiting to be seated lowered their heads and gave her a wide berth. What was this? Do folks think priests don't have to eat? Susan was saying something to her dad.

"I hear you, but I know we need to get on back to North Carolina. There's a funeral to organize, MaMa Allen to see to, and Mac's killer could be a thousand miles away by the time the state investigators get their butts in gear. We can't just sit here and do nothing."

Susan is what you might call pugnacious. Like Fletcher Enloe, she is not given to letting the moment for action slip through her fingers. Being six feet tall and knowing how to deliver a good punch probably help her confidence, though I suspect she would be just as ready to defend herself and her own if she were a foot shorter. Susan simply will not be bullied. I like that about her.

This time though, I suspected Daniel would be reluctant to let Susan plow into the fray. We were talking about murder, an obviously well planned murder of a respected county sheriff. There had to be a lot at stake for someone to risk such a high profile crime, in broad daylight no less.

Our waiter came over to the table with our check. Daniel looked at it and stiffened up. "I don't understand," he said, frowning. "What is this?"

The scrubbed and polished young man wore an inscrutable smile. He stood patiently beside Daniel, but didn't immediately offer an answer.

Sam returned to the table. "What'd I miss? Is something wrong?"

Daniel held up the check as though it was on fire. Susan took it from him and studied it before she shook her head and handed it back to her dad. "Don't look at me, Dad. I have no idea."

"Somebody paid for our lunch," Daniel announced and looked at the waiter. The waiter's face remained pleasant, but silent. "Who was it?" Daniel asked.

He handed Daniel our champagne, nicely wrapped in a burgundy linen wine bag. "I don't know, sir. I really don't. The maître d' gave me your check and told me it was taken care of, including the gratuity. We hope you enjoyed dining with us at Crane Cottage today, and that you will return often. Have a wonderful day."

As the waiter walked away, Daniel turned to me. I answered before he could ask. "Wasn't me. You know that. How come you sound all grouchy about it? I think it's a lovely gesture. Maybe the restaurant comped our lunch as a wedding gift."

"Come on. No way the restaurant would do that and not let us and everyone else here know about it. Good advertising is worthless if you hide it. Do you think Paul and Barkley did it?"

I shook my head. "I doubt it. They would have said something about it in the note they left with the champagne. No, it wasn't them. I'm sure of that."

After a short silence, Sam offered a possible explanation. "May be a coincidence, but when I was looking for the ladies room, I saw your friend Garland Wang out in the reception area."

I do not believe in coincidences, nor do I believe that Garland Wang gives a gift unless he expects something in return. I wondered how much our lunch would eventually cost me.

CHAPTER TWELVE

Daniel held my hand as we crossed the drive in front of Crane Cottage, walked past a manicured redbud tree, heavy with magenta blossoms, and followed the sidewalk around Faith Chapel to the parking lot, empty now, except for my Subaru and Susan's Jeep.

Susan jingled her car keys in her hand as she and Sam walked ahead of us and then paused with one hand on the Jeep's door handle, waiting for us to catch up. "Okay, Daddy. Sam and I will go check out of the Inn. Why don't we meet in about an hour in the public parking lot down by the pier? We can follow you back to North Carolina. Or you can follow us---whatever."

"Hold your horses, Susan. I've been thinking about the best thing to do, and that isn't it. Hear me out."

What did Daniel mean: he'd been thinking about the best thing to do? He and I had already agreed on driving back to North Carolina today.

We paused our conversation while a yellow VW Bug pulled into the parking lot, and a pleasant looking, sun-blond, young woman, wearing a knee length black skirt and white blouse got out. She waved, called out a cheery hello, and entered Faith Chapel through a rear door.

Sam smiled. "One of my breed, I do believe," she said.

I wondered for a second if Sam was talking about the fact that she and the young woman in the black skirt both drove VW Bugs. Before I could sort out Sam's comment, Daniel made his announcement. "Here's what I've decided. Susan, I want you, Sam, and Promise to stay down here until I call you to come home."

Susan's reaction was loud enough to scatter perching crows. "No!" she bellowed. "No way are we staying here lolling on the beach while you ride into Perry County like the Lone Ranger after the bad guys."

"You know," said Sam, "I think I'll mosey into the chapel and introduce myself to my fellow girl-priest, maybe get a little tour of the chapel while you guys are ironing out this family issue."

"Oh, come on Sam," Susan pleaded, "Don't jump ship on me. You don't want to stay at St. Simons, do you? Not after what's happened."

"Look, I'm technically on leave until a week from Saturday, so I'm fine with whatever you guys decide. I didn't know Sheriff Mac, but I think I understand how much he meant to your family. I also understand Daniel must have his reasons for wanting you to stay here, at least for a few days, until he can get a handle on what's going on up there. Like I said, I'm not taking sides. I'm fine either way."

Sam headed for Faith's front entrance and Susan turned to Daniel. "Look Daddy, I don't see there's anything to get a handle on. It's pretty simple; Mac's been murdered and we need to be in Perry County. If Pate Hoag is the best they have to catch the killer, they have nothing."

I wanted to tell Daniel I had no intentions of letting him leave St. Simons without me, but knowing how hard-headed both Daniel and Susan were, I felt it was better to let father and daughter argue around the issue for a while before I got into it.

Surprisingly, Daniel didn't raise his voice to match Susan's. He stayed calm. "Sweetheart, I know you want to get up there and light a fire to find Mac's killer. So do I. But think about what happened. Planting a bomb under a sheriff's car is not the way our small-time, coun-try bad guys deal with the law. We're pretty much get along kind of folks. Our usual criminal types would just lay low or move on over across the county line if they felt Mac was crowding them. Plus, the bomb went off just as Mac backed out of *our* driveway, and Mac was at *our* house looking for something. Maybe the two are related, maybe not. But I need to check around a bit to find out."

"What do you think Mac was looking for?"

"I don't know. I really don't. Like I said, maybe it has nothing to do with him being killed, but Pate Hoag is way too interested in why Mac was over to our house, so I have to consider that the killer might also be interested. I don't even understand why Pate is asking questions. I have to believe the State Bureau of Investigations will take the lead on a case like this. One way or another, I don't want you and Promise anywhere near Perry County until I know it's safe. Just give me a couple of days to check out the whole story, and I'll call you to come home. Besides, you and Sam have already paid for your rooms at the Village Inn until Sunday. Just stay put and chill out. I'll call you, I promise."

Susan balled up her fists, as though looking for something or someone to hit, before she stalked off across the parking lot.

Daniel drew me into his arms. "Oh Babe, I'm so sorry things have gone this way. I wanted our wedding to be perfect and our honeymoon to be…well, you know, perfect, too. Shoot. We haven't even taken any beach pictures to show the grandkids when we're old and gray."

What was he talking about? I was pretty much already gray under my L'Oreal light auburn. "What grandkids? Do we have grandkids I don't know about?"

"You know what I mean. Surely between Susan and Luke, we'll get at least one."

I stepped back to look up at Daniel. "I know you, mister. You're making jokes because you're worried. Do you know more about why Mac was in your house than you're telling?"

After lowering his eyes for a second, he shook his head no. As well as I thought I knew him, I had no idea if he was telling the truth or not. Then he held me by my shoulders and said, "I know we discussed leaving together after the ceremony, but the more I thought about it, the more it bothered me. I need to check out a couple of things first, and then I'll call y'all home in a couple of days. Stay on over at the hotel and relax. Take the boat cruise you were talking about; hunt for antiques; visit Aileen. I know you're popping a gut to find out what happen with her."

Well, I wasn't exactly *popping a gut*, but I was curious. "I'll hate staying at the King and Prince without you. Somehow a honeymoon isn't as good if you're alone."

He hugged me again. "I know, but it'll be okay. We'll have our honeymoon, that's for sure. I just need you to stay down here with Susan for now."

"So, I figure here is your logic---correct me if I'm wrong: if I go back with you, Susan will absolutely not stay here, and you're worried that she'll stir up a hornet's nest back home. If I stay, maybe I can keep her occupied for a few days."

"Exactly. You are a smart lady. One of the reasons I married you."

"Oh Daniel, what in the world is happening to our quiet little county? What would be worth killing a sheriff? Who would think they could get away with that? I mean, they would have to think the…"

Before I finished my sentence, Susan returned from pacing the parking lot. "Okay, Daddy. I've thought about it. You win. You've got three days to satisfy yourself that we'll be safe at home, and then I'm on the road to North Carolina. We've got a new restaurant to run. It isn't fair to expect Ben to keep doing his job and ours. And I'm not letting anybody run me out of Perry County. Speaking of which, it may not be safe for you at our house right now, not until we know what's going on."

"That's a good point, Daniel. Why don't you go on over to my house? MaMa Allen is next door at Fletcher's, and we were planning to move you over anyway."

"Okay. I'll do that. Now you both give me a hug and let's say goodbye here. I'll swing by the hotel and pick up my bag. Promise, call me and let me know if you're staying at the King and Prince or not."

Susan got the first hug and then said, "Promise can stay with us over in the Village Inn, if she wants. I think we need to be together at a time like this."

Since we first met---me as the new owner of Granny's Store and Susan as my manager, inherited from the previous owners---Susan has called me Ms. P. This was the first time I'd heard her call me Promise. I liked the sound of it.

What I didn't like was standing in the parking lot of Faith Chapel waving goodbye to my new husband, who, incidentally, was driving my beloved Subaru. I was left feeling alone sans husband and sans car. I was also afraid---afraid for Daniel. He was too determined to keep Susan and me away from Perry County not to know more than he was sharing. Daniel's words to us at lunch came back to me. Mac was the brother he'd never had. Brothers tell each other things, secret things they don't tell their mamas or their wives. What had Mac told Daniel?

I took a deep breath and tried to convince myself that I was overreacting, assuming a lot because we knew so little. The only thing we really knew was that Mac was dead and he'd been at Daniel's house just before he was killed. But Mac went over to Daniel's often. Maybe what Daniel said to MaMa Allen was correct; he'd get back home and find Mac had decorated the house with good wishes for our marriage. I wanted to will that to be so, for it to be true.

Sam came back to us as Daniel was pulling out of the parking lot. He waved and we waved back. "So, we're staying?" she asked.

"For now," answered Susan. "Did you get your tour?"

"Short one. Made a new friend, a fellow parson. Hey, did you know Faith Chapel has a tiny room in the back, a library of sorts, full of ledgers chronicling marriages, baptisms, and deaths on the island? They even keep what they call Prayers of the People journals. I didn't notice it, but Rev. Sloan says there is a red book in the narthex for visitors to leave written requests for prayers. The idea is that when someone visits, that person can read the requests in the book, light a candle, and say a prayer. Rev. Sloan says the records go back to 1904 when the chapel was built."

Susan's response to Sam was polite, though unenthusiastic. I don't think I said anything at all. My eyes, and my heart, were following Daniel as he turned onto the main road leading off Jekyll Island.

"Well," Sam said in a lowered voice, "I wrote a prayer request for Daniel in the book and lit a candle. You guys want to go back inside and do the same?"

Susan reached out and hugged Sam.

I managed a wan smile and followed them back into Faith Chapel. My mind was already calculating. What was the driving time to North Carolina? About eight hours? Daniel should call me by eleven tonight.

Even as I was on my knees praying for Daniel a safe trip home and peace for Mac's soul, my mind was talking to me, saying I should have left with Daniel. What was I thinking? I should not have agreed to stay behind.

CHAPTER THIRTEEN

Long legs crossed, aviator sunglasses hiding his pinched, angry eyes, he sits on a wrought iron bench facing the Hanover Square fountain, in Old Town Brunswick. He rolls his unlit cigar in his mouth between thumb and forefinger and thinks about the meeting. How would he rate its success, from one to ten? A five, maybe a six. It was hard to tell. How many more damn useless meetings would he have to sit through before they either sold him the leases or sent him packing?

If there weren't so much money to be made, he probably would have told all of them to go screw themselves long before now. Though it really isn't about the money. He has plenty of money. It's all about winning, about being the first to bring oil up off of the coast of Georgia. That is, if he can get past the red tape and bull crap. He wonders how the federal government can find so many useless bureaucrats to push around so much paper. Not like the army he remembers. The army was efficient---a good career. The brass outlined the goal, no need to know the politics of the target. You go in, do your job, get out. No bull crap.

Tightening his grip on the cigar, he replays moments of the meeting. *That pompous, bald-headed geek from the Department of Interior didn't do me any favors. What a piss-ant. Looking down his fat nose at me.* He hears the man's Northern, nasal voice in his head.

"Mr. Coleman, I believe T. Boone Pickens has been quoted as saying he doubts the coast of Georgia will give up much crude. Do you have evidence to contradict Mr. Pickens?"

What was my answer to that stupid question? Oh yeah.

"That's the point, now isn't it, sir? None of us has any actual evidence or experience off the coast of Georgia. Pickens has an opinion. I have an opinion. They are different opinions. But, I'm the one who is willing to risk my considerable investment here in the Golden Isles to see which one of us is right. Without the oil leases, we'll never know, now will we?"

He wonders if his answer was strong enough to sway the other Department of Interior guys. *I'd be a fool to outright disagree with Pickens. He's got more street credibility than the frigging President.*

At least some of the Glynn County representatives were willing to vote with him. But how many? He isn't sure. In the end would there be enough to carry an approval for the leases? "Crap shoot", he says under his breath. "A frigging crap shoot."

What he is sure about is this has not been a good week. First there was the business with the Atlanta TV woman and her stupid idea of restoring Sparrow Cottage and donating that horrible chair to kick off the fund raising. And, of course, just his luck she'd announced she was writing a book about Sparrow---lots of history, lots of old photographs. His stomach turns over at the thought of the faces of Mena Simpson, Betty, all of them, staring back at him from the pages of a book.

How long would it take for the TV woman to add him to the stories in the book? *Not very long*, he thinks. *I had a fairly easy solution to turn my luck, except I botched the job. I'm getting too fucking old. Losing my touch.*

His mind jumps to the note, delivered early that morning by the chauffeur, no less. The Peterkin sisters, requesting that he call on them at his earliest convenience. *Well*, he decides, *that answers the question of whether old Pris and Paula recognized me at the party. And why do they want the pleasure of my company? Reminisce about old times? I doubt it.*

He bites the tip off his cigar, spits the head into a flowering crepe myrtle, and stands. His right hand goes up to smooth his neatly trimmed mustache. The Peterkin house is a couple of blocks away on Halifax Square. He decides to walk it. Pull himself together. Be ready for old Pris and Paula.

Both women are standing at the open, leaded glass, front door of the Queen Anne, two-story when he mounts the porch steps. "We saw you coming down Halifax," says one of them. "Knew it had to be you."

He can't decide which is Pris and which is Paula. They are nearly identical. The same screw curled gray hair, heavy rouged cheeks, and little, spidery bodies.

He notices the blue paint on the house is about ten years past needing a redo, and responds to their greeting with an uncommitted, "Ah."

They wave him into the dark, cypress-paneled foyer, and he removes his sunglasses, his eyes adjusting to the shadowy inside. The house smells of musty, old rugs and last night's shrimp gumbo.

"Let's sit in Daddy's parlor," says the other Peterkin sister, and they lead the way.

Daddy's parlor? He's thinking, *Daddy has probably been dead since about 1960.*

The sisters motion for him to sit on a small Victorian sofa---a peach colored, velvet monstrosity with fruit carved all along the back rail and arms. It's scarcely deep enough for his tall frame to perch during the short time he's decided he would tolerate the sisters. They take matching, spindly looking chairs opposite him. An oval, polished wood table, as ugly and ornate as the sofa and chairs, separates them.

One of the sisters reaches for a box of assorted candies on the table. Most of the flat, gold-foiled box, still bearing a red poinsettia Christmas decoration on top, is empty, but she rearranges the remaining pieces and offers it his way. "A Russell Stover chocolate candy, dear? Sister and I do love a sweet treat now and then."

He says no thank you, and the sisters gobble down four pieces each while he watches. The sister who offered him the candy wipes chocolate from the corners of her mouth with her fingertips and prattles, "Well, you can just imagine how surprised we were to see you at that little soiree on Jekyll Island. I would have recognized you anywhere, though. I do declare you look the same, only a little older, of course. And then, you certainly didn't have a mustache in those days. Sister Pris wasn't so sure it was you. She said we should march right up and ask if you really were Freddie."

At least now he knows which one is Paula and which is Pris. The speaking one, Paula, is the one in the purple dress. Pris is in light gray. Name tags, he's thinking. They should wear nametags.

Even when they were much younger, visiting Sparrow to drink Mena's apple brandy and eat the pecan pralines Betty made, he couldn't tell them apart. Betty had said she couldn't either, and didn't care to. *The chicken women*, she called them. *Always pecking at anything under their noses.* Now they were pecking at him.

"But I said no, sister. If he really is Freddie Coleman, he may not want everybody in the world to know who he is. So

I asked that gentleman from the Chamber of Commerce your name, and he said Clip Coleman. Now imagine that, little Freddie Coleman is now Mr. Clip Coleman. He says you are quite the successful businessman these days. But why ever are you called Clip, dear?"

Pris reaches over and pats her sister's hand. "Now Paula. That's none of our business. Freddie surely has his reasons for changing his name."

He clenches his jaw and then works at relaxing it again. "Why, my dear ladies, I haven't changed my name. Clip is simply a nickname from my army days."

"Is that so?" says Pris. "The army. Imagine that. Would you care for some tea, dear? We no longer have a house-keeper, but I'll be happy to make tea myself."

"Oh, no thank you Miss Peterkin. I have to be leaving shortly, business in Brunswick. While I was in town, I thought I'd respond to your note, call on you. By the way, how did you locate the address for my summer lease over on Jekyll?"

Paula chuckles into a wrinkled hand. Pris answers, "Oh, the Chamber of Commerce person was very helpful. He seems to know a lot about a lot of things. A lovely man, really. Though sister and I did think he was a little tipsy on all that champagne at the party. And oh my, my, isn't it awful what happened to Ms. Wang? She seemed like such a sweet person. Didn't you think so, Freddie? Can you imagine someone in our quiet little town sneaking up and gunning her down like a common rattlesnake?"

"Oh Paula, don't be overly dramatic. We don't know what happened. Maybe she was shot by accident. We all know that can happen. Don't we, Freddie?"

Coleman feels a band of anger tightening around his chest. He's not sure what game the sisters are playing, but he's sure he'll snap if he doesn't get out of *Daddy's parlor* pretty soon. *Always were useless old biddies,* plays in his head.

"Still, they say she's near death…" Paula says and lets the question of Aileen Wang's survival hang in the stale air.

He rises to his feet and attempts a smile. "It's been wonderful to see you ladies again, after all these years, but I really must go."

"Oh don't go yet, Freddie," whines Pris. " We need to discuss the matter of the roof with you."

He continues to stand, determined to be out the front door in ten seconds or less. "The roof? You mean your roof?"

They say yes in unison and stand to face him.

"Sorry ladies," he says. "I know nothing about roofs. I suggest you ask around for a reliable contractor if you're having roof problems."

"Oh, we have a well-recommended roofer, dear," says Paula.

"But you see," adds Pris, "it's a tile roof. Daddy built it the old way, the best way."

"Twenty thousand dollars," says Paula.

"Yes," Pris agrees, "I'm afraid it's twenty thousand dollars. That's how much it will cost to replace it, and we want you to pay for it. Cash would be nice. Checks are so bothersome."

He feels blood throbbing behind his eyes and the pain of a migraine clawing up the back of his neck. "And why would I do that?"

"Well," says Pris, "perhaps because you are our dear little Freddie Coleman, gone from Jekyll Island so mysteriously and so soon after all that tragedy."

"Hush, Pris. We agreed not to talk about that. It's unseemly. Freddie doesn't need to be reminded of any of that. It was long, long ago. Wasn't it, Freddie?"

Before Freddie, aka Clip, Coleman leaves the Peterkin house on Halifax Square to retrace his steps east to the Old Town District, he has agreed to return the next morning with financial assistance for the sisters' leaking roof.

Before he's reached his black Range Rover parked along Newcastle Street in front of a trendy coffee shop, he has a plan to take care of Pris and Paula Peterkin.

Amazing what you can order off the web these days. A little Bute painkiller, a generous helping of headache power, a little sweet treat…

CHAPTER FOURTEEN

By the time we drove from Jekyll over to St. Simons Island for Susan and Sam to change out of their wedding clothes, and they ferried me over to the King and Prince to do the same, it was after four o'clock when we arrived at the St. Simons Island hospital. The good news was that Aileen was out of the coma and somewhat conscious. The bad news was that, as we stepped off the elevator, I saw Garland in the hallway deep in conversation with RB Barnes.

The Shoulda-woulda girls' committee quickly convened in my head, shook their long collective finger at me, and scolded. *We tried to tell you thinking about your ex-husband when you are busy marrying husband number two is bad luck.*

You speak the devil's name and up he jumps. You should know that by now, Miss Smarty-pants.

Getting back in the elevator seemed like a winner of a plan. Unfortunately, before I could corral Susan and Sam, Garland disappeared into what was probably Aileen's room, and Barnes spotted us. Naturally he swaggered down the hall in our direction. I hadn't seen him since the episode at Paul Tournay's house about three years ago, and that wasn't nearly long enough for me. As I worked to keep a neutral look on my face, I couldn't help but wonder why the fates had chosen to cross my path with my ex-husband's on the day I married Daniel. Perhaps the Shoulda girls were right.

RB Barnes looked pretty much like the snake in paradise he'd always been. Rock solid work-hard-at-the-gym, white bread kind of macho. Clean-shaven, angular face. Graying blond hair with a military cut, except for a narrow patch of kicked up bangs in front that made it seem he was giving the third finger salute to everyone he approached. Knowing Barnes, the hair message was no accident. Expensive navy slacks. White dress shirt. Red silk tie with white pin-dots. A smirk you wanted to slap off his face.

And immediately out of his mouth, "Well, if it isn't Dr. Promise McNeal. Garland tells me you're down here getting married to that redneck, North Carolina cowboy I met in Atlanta a couple of years back. Is that true, or is Garland shit'n me?"

"You know Randall, your immaturity never ceases to amaze me. You've been married and divorced three times since we split, and I've never made one single tacky comment like that about any of your wives." I should have added, "to your face," but I didn't.

Before RB could decide if my remark was an insult or not, Susan stepped forward and held out her hand for him to shake. Since she's taller than he is, he had no choice but to take it. "Hello," she said pleasantly. "You must be Promise's ex-husband, Randall Barnes. I'm Susan Allen, the redneck cowboy's daughter." Susan hesitated two beats for her words to sink in and then continued, "You know, I've met your son, Luke. He's a really nice guy. Takes after his mother, I guess." RB dropped his jaw and Susan's hand.

Then, preempting a response from the newly encircled enemy, Sam offered RB a huge smile and a little wave. "Hi there, Mr. Barnes. I'm The Reverend Sam Quinn from Asheville. I'm here to say prayers over those fallen in verbal battle."

RB gave Sam a what'd-you-say look and frowned. The man has never had a sense of humor and was always a little slow on the uptake.

What a team we were. I suddenly felt like Wonder Woman with a posse. RB Barnes was speechless. I had the urge to click my gold bracelets together and throw the net of truth over the guy. Well, actually the urge was more like throwing him out of the third floor hospital window into the salt marsh below.

Reality returned when I remembered I was a grown-up person and we were here at the hospital because of a serious tragedy. I tried for being nice. "So what brings you down to St. Simons, Randall?" I always call him Randall, and not RB, to his face because I know he absolutely hates it. I visualized his toes cringing inside his high-polished loafers and smiled. Okay, so I'm not totally a grown-up person.

Barnes finally had his turn to speak. "I'm with the Georgia Bureau of Investigation now. I'm down here on the Aileen Wang case."

Ah, so RB was the agent Garland had personally requested. "The GBI? Really?"

"Absolutely. Why does that surprise you? The GBI is always looking for a few good men."

"I believe you mean the Marines, Randall dear."

"Well, hell, Promise, same difference."

It probably was, especially where RB Barnes was concerned. His leaving the City of Atlanta Police Department and moving to the Georgia Bureau of Investigation really didn't surprise me. RB is ambitious and hardworking, at least at being a cop, if not at being a faithful husband. I had to admit, my *issues* with RB aside, he's one tenacious bulldog when he's on a case.

Garland, guiding Betty Wu with a firm hand on her elbow, came out of Aileen's room and joined us. He motioned to the end of the hall where a small sofa and two plastic chairs made up a mini waiting area.

We followed behind them, with Betty shaking her ivory-handled cane at her son-in-law and fussing. "Why should I leave? Who you think you are? She's my daughter. I belong here. You want to go, go. Call your fancy office; get a haircut; find a Starbucks. You no help, anyway. I try to tell you it's that akuryou. Evil curse. You make that chair go away, send back to ocean and my daughter will be well."

Garland lowered his voice, "I hear what you're saying Mrs. Wu, but you are upsetting Aileen with all that talk about a curse. She's hardly awake and doesn't even remember why she's in the hospital. She doesn't need to hear about…." He fell quiet when Susan, Sam, RB, and I stopped near them and formed a semicircle in front of the sofa.

Betty noticed our little group and diverted her cane shaking from Garland to us. "Who all these people?" she demanded as she rapped Susan on the chest with the ivory dog's head. Under normal circumstances Susan would have probably taken the cane away from the old woman, broken it into two pieces, and returned it with a smile. I was relieved when she only grimaced and looked my way for moral support.

RB interrupted with his own question. "Garland, can I go in and talk to Aileen for a few minutes?"

"You can, I guess. But like I told Mrs. Wu, Aileen is only semi-awake. She remembers nothing about being shot. She seems to have the cocktail party confused with a party we attended at least a year ago while on a cruise to the Bahamas. She's very clear about strings of lights hanging from the trees while we danced, but that's about it. The doctor says that's pretty normal with a head trauma. She may remember what happened later on, or she may not."

"Yeah," replied RB, "I've worked trauma cases before. Doesn't leave us with much to go on if she doesn't remember." He turned and walked back down the hall to Aileen's room.

So far, Garland hadn't answered Betty Wu's question. I extended my hand to her. "Hello Mrs. Wu, I'm Promise McNeal. I'm a friend of Aileen and Garland." She ignored my hand. I let it drop to my side. "We've met a couple of times at the TV station."

Betty looked suspicious. I wondered if she didn't believe I was who I said I was, or if she didn't think Aileen and Garland had a friend. Knowing Betty, probably both. I introduced Susan, who kept her hands by her side, though nodded politely. Then I turned to Sam. "Mrs. Wu, may I introduce you to our friend, The Reverend Sam Quinn, Assistant Rector of Christ Church in Asheville, North Carolina."

The tip of Betty's cane went back on the floor where it belonged. Sam held out her hand. Betty shook it quickly and gave Sam a quizzical look. "You a lady priest?"

With a tolerant smile, Sam said, "Yes, ma'am."

"You a Jesus priest?"

"Yes, that's right, a Jesus priest."

Betty reached out, took Sam's hand again, and pulled her aside. "Good, you come with me. I have to talk to you about life and death matter."

I'm not sure if Sam followed Mrs. Wu willingly, but she did follow her down the hall and through the stairway door. I turned to Garland. "You don't suppose Mrs. Wu would…"

Garland broke in before I finished my question. "I have no idea what Betty Wu would do. I'm afraid The Reverend Quinn is on her own. We are all on our own when it comes to Betty Wu. I can't tell you all the ways she drives me crazy. She's like a snake. You never know when she'll strike, but you know she will. And you know what else drives me nuts?"

I shook my head no, and he leaned in closer to me. "Betty Wu has been in this country since 1938 and still refuses to speak proper English. She can. She just won't. It's embarrassing. Leaves out verbs and pronouns like the rest of us are wasteful for putting them in a sentence. Aileen ignores it, of course, but then she ignores most of what her mother does. Can we talk while she's occupied?"

"Sure, I'm listening."

Susan scratched an eyebrow and looked over Garland's head toward the stairs. I had the feeling she wanted to follow Sam, just to make sure she was okay. "Hey, you want me to walk around for a few minutes while you two talk?"

"No, no, that's all right. Stay. I need all the help I can get."

"But Garland, you have help," I reminded. "Barnes is here. You know he will stay on the case until whoever shot Aileen is found."

RB walked up behind me and broke back into the conversation. "I can't talk to Aileen; she's asleep. Promise is right. I'll find the guy. And I'll find him or her by solid investigative skills, not by amateur sleuthing. So you, Dr. McNeal and Miss Allen here, can go back to North Carolina."

Garland was quick to interject. "Except you told me earlier that your boss wants you back in Atlanta. How is going back to Atlanta going to find the shooter?"

"Holy crap, man, don't try to make me feel guilty. Yes, I have to be in Atlanta late tomorrow on another case, but I'll be back as soon as the lab sends me a report on the bullet we recovered at the scene. I should have that by day after tomorrow at the latest."

"You found the bullet that shot Aileen?"

"Yes, Dr. McNeal, we found a bullet. It may be the bullet or maybe not. So don't get so excited about it. Lab tests will tell us more. Remember, you amateur, me cop. Go away and let us cops do our job."

"Well for heaven's sake, Randall. I was just asking. You are so pompous."

"Pompous? I am not pompous. You're butting in where you don't belong and where you and your new step-daughter could get hurt."

I heard RB but I was thinking about Daniel saying the same thing to us. *We could get hurt.* Now Daniel was on his way back to North Carolina without me. He could get hurt. Whoever killed Mac could kill again. I should have gone with him.

"What time is it?"

RB Barnes looked at his watch. "Five, straight up. Why?"

"Hmm. Just wanted to know. No reason."

Susan stepped closer to me. "He's not there yet. He's hours away."

I nodded.

Barnes rubbed his eyes and shook his head. "You see, Garland, this is why I don't like working with women. They make no sense. No sense at all."

Garland removed a folded sheet of paper from his inside suit pocket. "Okay, RB. Let's stop wasting time. I want Promise to look at this guest list from the party and see if any of the names ring a bell for her. Then she can do some checking on the names while you're in Atlanta."

"Did you say: ring a bell for her? Oh cripes, Garland, are we talking about that psychic crap again? Looking at the names on the list isn't going to find the shooter. A bullet match is what we need. Believe me, Promise is not psychic. I lived with her for seven years, I know. Half the time she couldn't even find her own car keys."

"Nine years, Randall. Nine years. Not seven. Let me see the list." Garland handed me the list and I unfolded it. "It's in longhand. Who wrote it out?"

Garland looked over my shoulder. "Not Aileen's handwriting. She probably dictated it to Barkley. Why?"

"Well, it's just that I notice a few of the names have stars beside them. Wonder what that means?" RB eyes perked up at the mention of some of the names being starred, but I knew he wouldn't say he was interested.

After studying the names for a few seconds, Garland answered, "Knowing Aileen, the stars are meant to show the prime suspects for big donations to the Sparrow restoration project. She is really hyped about restoring the cottage."

Remembering Paul Tournay had mentioned Aileen's mother lived in Sparrow Cottage as a young woman, I looked up from the list. "What does Betty Wu think about the Sparrow project? Does she want Aileen to revive the old cottage?"

"Aileen didn't tell her about the project or even that she was coming down to Jekyll Island. I tried to explain to her about the cottage restoration when I got down here, but by that time Aileen had been shot, and Betty was hysterical."

RB was paying attention. "But wait, you told me Mrs. Wu was here at the hospital when you arrived from Atlanta. If she didn't know Aileen was here, or about the Sparrow project, why was she here?"

Garland rubbed his temples and squeezed his eyes shut for a moment before he responded. "That's the hysterical part. As soon as I got the call from the hospital I drove down here. The hospital didn't call Betty, and neither did I, yet she beat me here by two hours.

"According to the ER nurse, Betty came storming into the emergency room ranting and raving that she knew her daughter was here because of a premonition she'd had. Something about the wind wailing outside her windows the night before, and a neighbor's cat leaving mouse entrails on her welcome mat. You can imagine how well that story went over with the ER folks.

"When I got here Aileen was in surgery. Betty was pacing the hospital corridors looking for a fight. After Betty dressed me down for not returning her call from earlier in the morning, she announced that Aileen was shot because of a curse on the carved Chinese chair that once belonged to Sparrow Cottage. Is any of this relevant?"

RB shook his head as though the effort would make sense of what Garland was saying. I don't think it helped much. "Okay, Garland, back up," he said. "What's Betty Wu's connection to Sparrow Cottage and this curse thing? And, why wouldn't Aileen tell her about the restoration project?"

A nurse approached and asked Garland to step back to the nurses station. She assured him Aileen was okay; they only needed additional information from him. "I'll be right back," he said and scurried off following the nurse.

I knew RB couldn't wait on Garland to have his question answered. The man is not wired for waiting. He glared at me and then asked, "I suppose you know what the hell he's talking about? Not that I think Betty Wu shot her daughter, but it does seem odd that she would hightail it down here from Atlanta because of some chair."

Susan, quiet much longer than I thought possible, answered him. "According to Barkley and Paul, Betty Wu lived at Sparrow Cottage with the Simpson family during WWII. When the carved Chinese chair washed ashore after a German U-boat torpedoed a cargo ship off the coast of Georgia, Betty got it in her mind that the chair was cursed."

RB threw up his hands. "Well, sure, who wouldn't think that? Makes perfectly good sense to me."

"Come on, Randall. You asked. Just let Susan finish."

Susan looked satisfied. "Anyway, as I was saying, apparently she'd told Aileen stories about the chair and even had a photograph of it from way back when. That's how Aileen knew it was the same chair when she saw it at an antique auction in Atlanta---because of the old photograph. Maybe Aileen didn't tell her mother about the chair or restoring Sparrow because she figured her mom would go ballistic if she knew---because of the curse and all that. I mean it stands to reason that Aileen knows she can't change her mom's mind about the chair being cursed, so better to keep quiet about it."

Garland rejoined us and picked up Susan's commentary. "That's right, Betty loves to tell the story of the cursed chair. We've all heard it a million times: how the chair started a fire in Sparrow's library; how it had snakes living in it; how it screams at night when the wind blows. Crazy stuff like that. Who knows where she got the story. Maybe something she heard as a child back in her village.

"Betty was only fourteen when she came over here from Taiwan in 1938. Only I think it was still called Formosa back then. Or maybe the Japanese had occupied it by that time and were calling it Taiwan. I don't recall. Betty says her people were Han Chinese and had lived on the island since the seventeenth century. When the Dutch arrived about a hundred years later, they named the island Formosa---because Formosa means beautiful island in Dutch.

"Anyway, Betty and her husband, a schoolteacher, were brought to Jekyll Island as employees by a Methodist missionary, Mena Simpson, after an earthquake destroyed their village. The Simpson family owned Sparrow Cottage until the state took it by condemnation about twenty years ago. Course Betty had left Jekyll Island long before that."

I perked up. "Did you say Betty had a husband at fourteen, and he was a schoolteacher? I thought her husband was a diamond merchant."

"Aileen's father was a diamond merchant. He came into the picture years later. In 1938 Betty was married to a man named Jon---I forget his last name. He was her paper-husband and died on Jekyll Island around 1950."

"What's a paper-husband?" asked RB

Susan spoke up. "Oh, I know what that means. In college, I read a couple of books about early Chinese immigration into the United States. Back then it was next to impossible for a Chinese woman, or a man for that matter, to immigrate. The US laws actually excluded the Chinese in most circumstances. So sometimes a Chinese man already in the US would say a boy who wanted to come into the country was his son. But he wasn't. He was only a son on paper---for the immigration forms only--- to get the boy into the country. I guess Garland means Betty wasn't really married to this Jon person. The marriage was a sham to get Betty into the country. Is that right, Mr. Wang?"

"Something like that. Mena Simpson being a missionary and her husband being a wealthy businessman must have made the immigration easier. But yeah, for some reason the marriage arrangement was thought necessary. From what Betty has told Aileen, she and Jon didn't live together as man and wife. They both worked for Mena Simpson at Sparrow, and Betty had her own room separate from Jon.

"After he died, and Mena Simpson passed away, Betty caught the first Greyhound bus headed away from Jekyll Island. For a time, she worked as a clerk for a dry cleaners in Atlanta. That's how she met Aileen's dad, George Wu. George was a merchant of many things, mostly diamonds, and when he and Betty teamed up, it was *Katie bar the door.* They were a very successful team. Today, Betty Wu's net worth makes mine look pitiful."

I listened to Garland's story and wondered what life on Jekyll Island had been like for Betty Wu. She worked for Mena Simpson for about fourteen years, a long time for a young woman in a strange country without family or friends who even speak her language. As I remembered from my Georgia history, the millionaire members of the Jekyll Island Club who'd built cottages there before the turn of the century had stopped spending winters on Jekyll in the 1930s. The hotel closed, and then the war years followed, and visitors were prohibited due to a fear of German invasion by sea.

Likely, the only outsiders Betty saw during the war years were the few soldiers stationed on the island to watch for enemy sea traffic. Then, when the State of Georgia bought the island in 1947, it was closed to visitors while the state made repairs and determined how to reopen it as a public state park.

My point being, Betty must have been lonely on the island. She had a paper husband, a missionary employer, and not even a bridge to the mainland. I wondered how many other permanent residents were on the island? Maybe a few workers stayed when the hotel closed? Still, Betty must have felt isolated.

CHAPTER FIFTEEN

We chatted in the hallway for a few more minutes. RB asked Garland if he knew of anyone who might dislike Aileen enough to drive from Atlanta to Jekyll for the express purpose of shooting her. Garland made some glib comment. I think he asked RB if he wanted Aileen's enemies in numerical or alphabetical order. I wondered if earning enemies was the price you paid for top ratings on late afternoon TV.

RB peeled off a stick of Juicy Fruit chewing gum, folded it in thirds, and stuck it in his mouth. Why did the man have to chew gum when he was thinking? And why did he always fold the damn gum before he put it in his mouth? I'm a psychologist; I'm supposed to understand these things. Actually, I do understand these things, but when RB Barnes does the gum thing, I still get pissed off. And what's more, he didn't even offer us any Juicy Fruit.

"I hear what you're saying," RB said to Garland. "The woman does know how to expose a nerve, but taking a potshot at her when it's nearly dark, in an unfamiliar location, doesn't sound smart for a shooter who's been hired by some Atlanta big shot. I mean that's really kind of amateur thinking. If it were me, I'd want to do the job where I felt comfortable, knew the surroundings."

Susan looked at her watch. "Sam's been with Mrs. Wu for over half an hour. Promise, you ready to go? Maybe we should catch up with her."

I nodded---grateful for Susan's excuse for us to leave---stuffed the party list in my purse, and promised Garland I would call Barkley later about the starred names. Talking on the phone with Barkley wasn't exactly what I'd hoped to be doing on my wedding night, but I would do it anyway and not whine.

I was grateful for Daniel and the possibility of other nights together. Mac had no more nights. Who would be brazen enough to blow up a county sheriff's car? Too bad RB Barnes was such a jerk. He's a good cop. I would have liked to tell him about Mac and ask his opinion. Instead, Susan and I left to rescue Sam from Mrs. Wu.

When we didn't find her talking with Mrs. Wu in the stairwell, we took the stairs down two flights and exited the hospital into a lower courtyard overlooking a peaceful salt marsh. Sam was sitting on a wood bench, alone, looking out at two very long legged birds standing in the shallow water. She spoke as we approached, "Watch what they do. Look, first one bird lifts a leg and bobs its head up and down, and then the other bird does the same thing. It's like they are copying what the other is doing."

We watched for a few seconds; she was right.

"Do you suppose it's some sort of mating ritual?" Sam asked.

Susan patted her friend lightly on the back. "Everything is some sort of mating ritual, sweetheart, everything."

Susan might be correct. "Where's Betty Wu?" I asked.

Sam's shoulders slumped as she exhaled a long sigh. "She said she was going for a quiet supper and then come back and sit with Aileen."

I walked around in front of Sam so I could see her face--- try to read what emotion her long sigh signaled. "What did she want to talk to you about?"

Sam looked up at me and sighed again. "Well, it's complicated."

"Hmm. You sound exasperated. From what I know about Betty Wu, she can often be exasperating."

Susan made a little harrumph sound that reminded me of my neighbor Fletcher Enloe. Was this one of those Western North Carolina native things? I wasn't sure I could duplicate the sound even if I tried.

"Exasperating?" Susan said. "The old lady seems pretty much loony tunes to me, girlfriend. I mean chairs with curses, come on."

For some reason, I felt I needed to defend Betty Wu. "I'm not sure I would say loony-tunes. Let's just say Mrs. Wu is complicated."

"Well, okay, complicated. So Sam, what did the old broad want?"

Sam stood up, cocking her head to one side and pursing her lips like a little girl who was about to say: no, I will not take a nap. "At the risk of making you both angry, I have to say that I can't tell you what Mrs. Wu and I talked about."

I was puzzled. Susan was indignant. "And why not?"

Sam picked up her purse from the bench and brushed down wrinkles from the front of her denim skirt. "Because she talked to me as a minister, in confidence, and I'm not sure…" She let the sentence hang and began walking away from us.

We followed, Susan asking, "You're not sure what?"

Sam kept walking.

"Are you going to answer me or not?" Susan barked.

Sam didn't reply until we reached the parking lot and were about to climb into Susan's Jeep. "Look, you guys. This is new territory for me. I usually spend my days visiting sweet little old ladies in nursing homes, new mothers, or parishioners recovering from surgery. Mrs. Wu is---well---she's different. And I have to think, and pray, about what I do next. Please don't ask me again."

Susan threw up her hands and slid into the driver's side to start the car. Sam climbed into the back seat and I sat up front with Susan. I had a feeling that Sam felt safer from Susan's questions in the back seat.

Boy, what a day this had been. I hadn't a clue what Betty Wu told Sam, but honestly, at that point I was too tired to care. It was only six o'clock, and I felt like crawling under the covers. After a brief discussion, we decided to stop for an early dinner in the village at a cafe serving home cooked vegetables. Afterwards, they would drop me off at my hotel. Just as the waitress placed my macaroni and cheese with sides of fried okra and fried apples in front of me, my cell phone rang. I grabbed it from my purse, and quickly said hello, hoping the caller was Daniel. It wasn't.

"That you, Promise?"

"Yes, Barkley. It's me. I was going to call you a little later. By the way, thank you, and Paul for the champagne."

"You are quite welcome."

I couldn't hear Barkley's next comment over the noise in the restaurant. "Hang on and let me get outside where it's quiet." I mouthed to Sam and Susan that the call was Barkley and went outside.

"Okay, I can hear now. What did you say?"

"When I got back here to the office, I checked my Aileen email. That's the private account Aileen uses to send me memos, reminders, and queen orders---you know like, pick up my blue suit from the cleaners or fire that incompetent make-up person. So in the inbox were a couple of memos about the Jekyll Island project. One has to do with you."

"Do you mean Aileen is sending emails from her hospital bed?"

"No, no, though if anyone could do that, it would be Aileen Wang. They are from the night of the cocktail party. I guess she sent them after Paul and I left the party to get some supper. Maybe she was afraid she would forget to tell me later on."

"Okay that makes sense. What are the messages?"

"The first one is telling me to call T. Boone Pickens' office and set up a phone call appointment for her to talk to him."

"He's the oil billionaire, right? What does he have to do with restoring Sparrow Cottage?"

I heard a dramatic moan from Barkley. "Oh who knows? Last week Aileen had me check out about a thousand web entries about him, and I didn't find any reference relating to Jekyll Island. The only thing remotely connected was a comment he made in a television interview that he doubted the Georgia coast had much crude oil. When I told her that, a couple of days before we left for Jekyll, the only comment she made was: *how interesting.*"

"But now Aileen wants to talk to Pickens on the phone?"

"Right."

"Okay." I had no clue what T. Boone Pickens had to do with Aileen's scheme to become the cottage restoration darling of Jekyll Island. Did she plan to ask him to underwrite the venture? In time, maybe Aileen would remember more about her Jekyll project, but right now, according to Garland, she hardly remembered even being at Jekyll. "What is the message relating to me?"

"Do you have something to write on?"

I dug for a pen from the bottom of my purse, withdrew it along with the party list, and turned the list over to the back. "Go ahead, I'm ready."

"Let me just tell you what she wants. Then I'll give you some information I found."

"Okay."

"All right. What Aileen's email says is that I'm to call you and ask you to research a man named Garr Lemley who lived on Jekyll Island in the 1940s and maybe early 1950s. Her email says that you and your family used to vacation down there, and you might remember what happened to him."

"Geez Barkley, that's a little before my time. I wasn't born until the mid 1950s and we never stayed at Jekyll Island. It was always on St. Simons. Actually, Aileen's mother would have been on Jekyll during that time. Wonder why Aileen didn't just ask her?" As soon as I said that, I knew it was a stupid question. We'd already been told by Garland that Aileen was hiding the Jekyll Island project from her mother. "Strike that last question."

Barkley laughed and then said, "I will. You know Aileen would rather die than ask her mother anything."

I wondered if Barkley's comment wasn't a bit prophetic, since Aileen had almost died.

My right ear was beginning to numb from pressing the cell phone against it in an effort to hear above the street noise outside the restaurant. I switched ears as Barkley continued. "Well, here's the thing: unlike dear Aileen, I know when you were born, so I figured you probably didn't know anything about the guy. Thus, being the curious pussycat that I am, I ran Lemley though some of my nifty background searches. Here's what I found. Now you can take notes?"

"Go ahead."

"An article in the Brunswick News dated November 11, 1951---very short. Just says the death of local fisherman, boat captain, and island caretaker Garr Lemley remains a mystery. Then the article has one sentence recapping the fact that Lemley was found a couple of days before, dead on the beach at Jekyll Island, shot in the back. Did you write down the name and dates? Garr has two rs, by the way. What kind of name is that, anyway?"

"Yes, I wrote it down. Garr? Isn't that a Southern slang term for alligators?"

"Oh my God. I am from Nashville, and we *do not* have alligators there, unless they are part of some country sing-er's boots. But Promise, I have to say, you are a wealth of information."

"Hmm. No doubt. So why would Aileen want me to research the Lemley guy when you could do it from your computer?"

"I have no idea. That is odd. Maybe she thought I'd be too busy hunting down T. Boone Pickens?"

"Maybe so."

I was thinking that I did do occasional research for Garland, but the only time Aileen had ever called on me for research was when she thought her daughter Sara was dating a sometimes student and full time con man. Her request had been simple: give her enough information to bury the man, send the bill for my time to her personally, and don't tell Garland. She was specific that what I found out was for her ears only. I wondered if she'd meant Lemley to be handled the same way.

"Well, that's all from Atlanta, and the queen's court," said Barkley. "How's Her Highness doing, by the way?"

"Garland says semiconscious. I haven't talked to her yet. I guess you know Garland called in a favor and the GBI sent RB Barnes down here to investigate?"

Barkley hummed a few bars of the theme song from the old TV show *Dragnet*, and then teased me. "I'll just bet you were thrilled to see good old Randall again?"

It seemed Barkley was less enamored with RB Barnes than I was. "Let's don't even go there."

"Oh, sweetheart. Believe me I do not want to go there, or anywhere with Barnes. Do you know he grilled Paul and me like criminals when he got down there? As if one of us had shot Aileen. Lord knows, there have been times when I'd like to kill her, but I wouldn't do it. I mean really, if we'd shot the Queen, why would we call 911 when we found her slumped over in that damn chair? What is it with Barnes anyway? Do you think he's one of those macho homophobic men?"

I didn't tell Barkley what I thought, which was that RB was probably still smarting from the Atlanta incident. He thought Paul should have been criminally responsible for the stolen artifacts hidden in his basement, but the DA refused to charge him with anything. According to Garland, she told RB there was no evidence against Paul, and that he should get a life and move on to the next case. Plus, three years later, he was still trying to get the DA to pursue murder charges against the person he believed killed Paul's ex-lover. Knowing RB, just seeing Paul again would aggravate his frustration.

"Oh no, I don't think that's the case," I told Barkley. "RB has a lot of faults. But that isn't one of them. Can we talk about the party list? I was planning to call you later about it."

"Later? Aren't you on your honeymoon, girl?"

"Well, sort of. But that's a long story and my fried okra is getting cold. Let me fill you in next time we talk. Right now, can you tell me why some of the names on the party list have stars beside them?"

"Oh sure. That's an easy one. As I added the names, Aileen had me look up each person's net worth. If they were wealthy enough for her to cultivate as a donor for the cottage restoration, I added a star by the name."

"And I believe you said there was no one at the party who is not on the list?"

"Well, that's not totally accurate. We phoned up a few people at the last minute when Aileen got paranoid that the crowd might not be big enough to attract attention from the press. And then we had those old sisters Pris and Paula Peterkin from over in Brunswick, who came uninvited."

The Peterkin sisters' names kept surfacing. I thought perhaps I should talk to them. "Why weren't the sisters on the list?"

The line was silent for a few seconds. Barkley must have been thinking. "Well, I don't recall Aileen mentioning the Peterkin sisters until they showed up at the party. I guess Aileen didn't know them, or maybe she knew they didn't have the big bucks necessary to be of use to her. You know Aileen. She doesn't believe in *casting her pearls before swine.*"

Yes, I did know Aileen, and the more I thought about someone taking a shot at her, the more I realized those who would probably wish her harm would be many in number. Aileen was high in the TV rating, but decidedly low in the beloved ratings.

Another thought crossed my mind: from what Garland said, the Peterkin sisters had been frequent guests on Jekyll in the early years. I wondered if Aileen had asked them about Garr Lemley's death at the party. Yes, I would definitely make a trip to Brunswick and visit with Pris and Paula Peterkin.

Somehow all of this---Aileen being shot, her determination to restore Sparrow Cottage, the ugly carved chair, Lemley---must be connected, not just coincidences. Aileen might not be well loved, but she was brilliant at making connections and ferreting out a juicy story. My bet was that whatever story Aileen was working had something to do with her being shot. Pity she remembered little about why she was at Jekyll Island. Course, the doctors told Garland that Aileen might remember later, but what about now? Would whoever shot her be content that she was temporarily in the St. Simons hospital and out of the picture? Was a little revenge all the shooter was after?

I looked at the list again. "Barkley, have you thought any more about who the person was that Aileen was keen to snare for restoration money? I see seven names with stars next to them. "

"No, I really haven't a clue. I do remember most of the seven are local businessmen or retirees known for supporting worthy causes. One I think was new to the area. Aileen already had a commitment from several of them---she didn't say who or how much. You know Aileen, she likes to keep her secrets."

When I couldn't think of anything else to ask, Barkley and I agreed to talk again the next day, and I went back to my vegetable plate.

By eight-thirty I'd had a shower and was trying to hold my eyes open long enough to talk to Daniel when he called. If I was tired, I could only imagine how exhausted he must be after starting the day with the news of Mac's death, getting married, and then driving four hundred miles home to North Carolina. Around eleven o'clock, I was in that nether land between anxiety and sleep when my cell phone rang.

"Hey, Babe. You awake?"

"Sort of. I'm so relieved you called. I was beginning to worry. How was your drive?"

"Long. Glad it's over. I'm at your house and about to call it a day. Alfie says hello, by the way. I think he misses you. Looks like he's been sneaking in and sleeping on your bed."

"Oh no, please don't let him get used to being on the bed. He's so hardheaded we'll never get him back on his own bed. You know where the clean sheets are, right?"

"I do, but I'm too tired to worry with it. I just need to lie down. Is everything all right down there? Susan behaving?"

"Oh yeah, we are fine. I just miss you and regret letting you go without me."

"I miss you, too."

Daniel seemed to be skirting the issue of Mac's death. I hesitated bringing it up, but my need to know the whole story of something is always a tripwire to my mouth. "Did you go by your house? See if Mac took anything?"

After a pregnant silence, Daniel offered, "Just quickly, I couldn't see anything obvious."

Daniel neglected to tell me that someone who was not very good at covering up the search had ransacked his house. I had to find that out later, along with several other bits of information. "Have you talked to anyone at the Sheriff's Department?"

"No, I figure I'll go down there in the morning after I talk to MaMa. I want to see the look on Pate Hoag's face when I show up."

"So we don't know any more about what happened than we did this morning?"

"No, not really. I had a lot of time to think driving home. A couple of things I want to check out, but no, I don't know anything more."

"Anything you want to share?"

"No. Not now, except…"

I waited. After a couple of seconds I heard Daniel clear his throat. "What is it, sweetheart? Except what?"

After more silence, he finally said, "It's the white pines where the drive turns onto the blacktop…you know, there are about twenty or so tall trees in a tight thicket along the road. The whole corner at the drive is burned… ground looks black, scorched, like someone took a torch to it… trees look like skeletons…reminds me of something I've seen before…maybe in Nam…I can't quite recall."

His voice trailed off, as though his mind was struggling to catch a dandelion seed of memory before the wind blew it away. I finally realized he was trying to tell me the charred trees along his property line were from the bomb that killed Mac. My mind scrambled for something comforting to say. But what was there to say? *Don't worry, we can replant trees?* Anything I said would be useless.

"Daniel?"

"Yeah, Babe, I'm here."

"I love you."

"I love you, too."

"Listen, maybe it's a mistake for me to stay down here. Why don't Susan and I pack up and head home tomorrow."

He answered quickly. "No, I want you to stay there. Don't come back here until I have a chance to follow up on a few things."

Once Daniel and I said our goodbyes, I was wide-awake, more anxious than before he'd called. After a few restless minutes, I got out of bed and stood at the French doors to stare at the tide pull and push the sand on the moonlit beach below the balcony. In and out, in and out, again and again, the sea gathered the world into its watery arms and then abandoned it to the shifting shore.

CHAPTER SIXTEEN

I ordered my coffee and Danish in the hotel dining room---sitting at the same table Daniel and I shared the day before. Was that only yesterday? How could that be? It seemed like a week. And what was I doing sitting here looking out at the Atlantic without my new husband? Well, certainly not enjoying myself. And the dark circles under my eyes were a testimony that I certainly wasn't sleeping well. I looked at my watch---eight-thirty---and wondered if Daniel was on his way to the sheriff's office.

Who would be appointed acting sheriff to finish out Mac's term? Would the county commissioners make the appointment, or would there be a special election? Maybe the sheriff's position was what Pate Hoag was after with all his questions to MaMa Allen. Maybe he thought he could rush in and solve Mac's murder---be the hero---and be first in line to be named sheriff. Though I couldn't imagine Pate being offered the job considering his young age and limited experience. But then, Pate struck me as the kind of kid who valued himself far more than others did, so maybe he thought he had an excellent chance at being the new sheriff.

Who else might want the job? I didn't think Mac's senior deputy would be keen to move into the position. He'd announced before the last election that he had no interest in taking Mac's job and wouldn't run against him, regardless of the rumors. I thought Hazlett was his last name. Couldn't remember his given name. Something like Alvin, or Alton. As I remembered, Mac once said that Hazlett was close to retirement age and was looking forward to keeping his head low for the rest of his time, and then traveling around the country with his wife in their RV.

Susan and Sam walked into the restaurant, interrupting my speculations. As usual, Susan got right to the point. "We saw Betty Wu outside navigating that monster Cadillac of hers into a parking space. Is she staying here?"

"Yes, good morning to you too. I have no idea if Betty Wu... here she comes. You could ask her."

Betty, business-like in a black linen sheath and oatmeal colored London Fog raincoat, hesitated for a moment, tapped her dog-head cane on the floor a couple of times, and then made a beeline over to us. While she ignored

Susan and me, she spoke to Sam, "Aren't you that Jesus priest from the hospital?"

Sam extended her hand. Betty shook it once and then let it drop. "Yes, ma'am. Sam Quinn. How are you today?"

"Fine," she answered. "You look different today. Yesterday you have long red hair all over everywhere. Today you hide under ugly ball cap. Not attractive. Are you looking for me?"

'No, ma'am, we're just having coffee with Promise. She's staying here at the hotel. Are you also a guest?"

Betty squinted as though Sam's question gave her a headache. "Where else would I stay? Best hotel on island. Why you want to know that?"

Sam offered a slight, non-threatening smile. "No reason Mrs. Wu. Just making small talk. "

Betty frowned and said, "Ha. I see. Small talk."

"How is Aileen this morning?" I asked.

She looked at me as though she'd only just noticed I was sitting at the table. "My daughter a tiger. She soon will be well. You wait and see."

"Ah, I'm sure you're right. Would you like to join us for coffee?"

Susan moved aside and offered Mrs. Wu a chair across from me. She looked down at the chair and then up at Susan. "Who are you?"

"I'm Susan Allen. We met at the hospital yesterday."

She gestured to me with her cane. "You this lady's daughter?"

"Well, yes ma'am, I am now. Would you like coffee? I'll get it for you if you like."

Tapping her cane again on the floor, Betty replied, "No coffee. Hurrying to change clothes and see my daughter." Then she nodded, turned, and walked away.

I observed two things about Betty Wu. There was a sagging bulge in the pocket of her raincoat, something far heavier than car keys or sunglasses. And the heels of her straw espadrilles were dark with moisture and coated with sand and grass.

Sam and Susan sat down. Susan remarked, "So, Betty hasn't been to the hospital this morning. Where do you suppose she's been? It isn't even nine o'clock. Too early for a shopping trip down to the village."

"Hmmm, I wondered that myself."

Sam shook her head. "You guys are so suspicious. Maybe the woman went for a walk on the beach."

"In a linen dress, raincoat, and espadrilles? And did you notice her shoes were wet and grassy?" Susan doesn't miss much.

Sam shrugged. I called the waiter over to order coffee for them, and we turned our attention to our plans for the day.

"I mean I don't even know why we are having this conversation. We should be at home with Daddy, not helping that pompous, self centered attorney figure out who shot his wife," Susan said while the waiter poured our second cup of coffee.

She took a long sip and fired her next comment. "Garland Wang has your obnoxious ex-husband jumping like a trained bear. Why does he need you on the case?" Her eyes widened. "Oh, I get it. You want to find out what happened before Barnes does to prove you're as smart as he is."

My jaw clenched. If Susan's fractious attitude this morning was any indication, she hadn't slept any better than I had last night. "I'm already smarter than RB Barnes. That has nothing to do with it"

Susan waved my reply away with her hand. "I know you're smarter than that overage jock. But really, think about it. The shooter probably figures he made his point and is long gone by now."

Sam stirred more cream into her coffee and then pointed the spoon at Susan. "I can't believe you aren't curious."

Susan crossed her arms over her chest. "Curious? I'll tell you what I'm curious about---what Betty Wu told you at the hospital yesterday. You must have talked to her for thirty minutes."

"Listened. I listened. Didn't do much talking."

"Okay, whatever. What was she bending your ear about?"

I was as curious as Susan about what Betty Wu had told Sam and hoped she'd give up at least a tiny bit of information, but she didn't. "I told you. I can't share what she told me in confidence. It's a priest thing."

"Okay, okay, enough of that subject. Please." I ended the Betty conversation and turned to Susan. "I think we should be in North Carolina, too, but this is what your dad wants, so we need to give him a day or two. And in the meantime, I'd rather be busy asking questions about who shot Aileen than trying to sit still on the beach. I just don't think I can do that right now. I'm way too anxious about your dad. Could you really spend the next two days lying on the beach or sightseeing?"

Susan shook her head no.

"I didn't think so. However, if you don't want to go with me to Brunswick and call on the Peterkin sisters, I can drop you two in the village and drive your Jeep. I will be very careful not to bend it."

"Well, actually," Sam interjected, "I have an appointment with the priest I met over at Faith Chapel yesterday. As it turns out, she's pastor to a congregation here on St. Simons, down in the village. So if y'all will drop me somewhere near the Inn, I can walk over to her church. Then we can meet up later, after y'all get back from Brunswick."

"Why didn't you tell me this before now?" Susan sounded hurt.

Sam sounded equally wounded when she replied, "I'm telling you now. It isn't a world-changing event. I just want to get to know her, ask her opinion about a couple of issues. I'm new at all this you know. Asheville is my first post since seminary...."

I wondered how we three crotchety women would get through the next couple of days without losing our collective tempers.

We dropped Sam in the village and drove off island headed for Brunswick. Susan was uncharacteristically quiet. As soon as we were on the causeway, salt air from the open windows cleared my head, and the sight of the Marshes of Glynn filled my view. I felt better, more in control of the day.

The marshes are a calming, sweet chamomile tea for the soul. Stretching to an unbroken blue horizon on either side of the highway, this four-mile wide apron of tidal salt marsh connects Georgia's barrier islands to the mainland. It is the nursery for unseen shrimp, crabs, oysters, raccoons, and fish---a multitude of creatures punctuated by birds fishing in the tall, undulating grass. Today, as we drove over the marshes, I watched sunlight play like tinkling glass above cornfield-sized hummocks, surrounded by high tide, and breathed in the beginnings of life.

Brunswick is only a short drive from St. Simons, and since I'd easily found the address for the Peterkin sisters in the phone book, all we had to do was locate Halifax Square on the local map I'd picked up from a kiosk of maps in the hotel lobby. Piece of cake. We passed by the house slowly, to verify the address. Susan asked me, "So, once we get the old sisters to invite us in, then what?"

"Hmmm. I guess we'll begin a conversation with the obvious: did they see anyone at the party who looked suspicious, or notice anything that might point to who shot Aileen? And I want to know if Aileen asked them about this Garr Lemley person. There must be a good reason why Aileen wants me to research him. I'm thinking the sisters have been around forever, so they might remember him being shot."

"But if they don't know anything, how will you find out about Lemley---I mean the guy was shot back in what, 1951, or something like that. Barkley already said he only found one reference to him on the web."

"Yeah, I know. We are so used to instant information from the web that it makes it tough to go back to the old fashioned way, but that's what I'll have to do, I guess. Probably start with the local newspaper's archives, maybe locate somebody who remembers…"

"Crap, you should have asked Betty Wu about Lemley this morning."

Susan was right. I should have, though Betty's attitude hadn't seemed amenable to questions. She'd snapped at Sam for even asking if she was staying at the King and Prince Hotel, so I doubted she was in the mood for a trip down memory lane. In fact, this morning Betty had reminded me of a person who'd been caught at something she'd rather you hadn't seen. Where *had* she been so early in the morning? Susan pulled into the short drive beside the Peterkin house and stopped the Jeep a respectable distance behind the closed doors of a dilapidated clapboard garage.

We rang the front bell several times, and then Susan knocked. When no one answered, we followed the wide porch to the right and found French doors leading into what seemed to be a parlor set with a Victorian settee, two matching chairs, and various bric-a-brac nesting on tables and book cases. As my mother was fond of saying, "The room was so crowded you couldn't sling a cat in there."

Susan knocked on the glass door and it opened slowly on its own. I stuck my head in and called out, "Hello," several times. No answer. I think I commented that perhaps the sisters were in the backyard.

Susan frowned and pointed to an expensive looking black leather handbag on the floor, leaning against a carved leg of the velvet settee. "Isn't that like the purse Betty Wu was carrying around at the hospital yesterday? It's an Yves St. Laurent tote---look at the clasp. Betty's had the same black and red silk scarf tied through it."

The black bag did look like Betty's. "Doesn't look like the kind of purse two little old ladies from Brunswick would have, does it?"

Susan agreed and then said, "Come to think of it, did you notice Betty carrying a purse when we saw her earlier this morning?"

I had to think about that. I was so focused on Betty Wu's damp shoes and the bulge in her raincoat pocket, that I'd failed to notice if she had a purse or not.

Susan answered her own question. "No purse. I'm sure she didn't have a purse this morning. Let's tiptoe in there and look inside. Check out the billfold. Look for a driver's license."

"Oh yeah, and maybe get arrested for trespassing and trying to steal Miss Peterkin's purse."

"Promise, I'm telling you, that's Betty Wu's purse. She was probably coming back from here when we saw her at the hotel. Maybe she left in a hurry and forgot the purse. Why do you suppose she was visiting the Peterkin sisters?"

"Good question. We'll ask the sisters when we find them. Let's go back around to the front door and knock again."

Back at the front door, Susan knocked more forcefully. When no one came, she turned the doorknob and opened the door partway. "Hello, hello," she called.

A radio at low volume played classical music somewhere in the house, but there was no sound of feet on hardwood to answer our call. My eyes dropped to the Oriental rug just inside the front door. Was I looking at pink fingernails?

"Susan, push the door open a bit more." Susan did, and the rest of a small hand appeared palm up and pale against the worn, multi-red color of the rug.

Susan pushed again and the door met resistance from the body attached to the pale hand. We stepped sideways into the foyer of the house and looked down at a very dead Peterkin sister. Susan said, "Holy shit."

I knelt down and pressed her neck for signs of a pulse, though from what I saw, the effort seemed useless. "We need to call 911."

Together, because neither of us wanted to stay inside with the deceased, we retraced our steps to the driveway to make the call. Susan was remarkably calm when she gave the address and reported what we'd seen to the operator. No surprise, the operator told us to stay in the yard and wait for a sheriff's deputy to arrive. She hung up and we stood silently, anticipating the siren that would surely follow.

"What do you think? Did the old lady have a heart attack? I wonder where the other sister is?"

"I don't know what killed her. She was still somewhat warm to the touch when I felt for a pulse, so she couldn't have been dead long. Less than three hours, maybe."

"How do you know something gruesome like that? You learn that as part of your psychology degree?"

"No, I guess I read it somewhere, maybe in a Patricia Cornwell novel. Depending on the outside temperature, a body cools and rigor mortis sets in about three hours after death. Maybe the other sister is out for a walk. I mean we are only about three blocks from downtown Brunswick, she could be anywhere."

"True," Susan replied. "Why do you suppose Betty Wu was over here?"

"Not sure, but she doesn't strike me as the kind of person who would pop in to get reacquainted with women she hasn't seen since she worked for Mena Simpson sixty-years ago. She must have wanted something. Maybe she's thinking the sisters know something about who shot Aileen."

Susan nodded and we went back to waiting. I noticed the Halifax Square neighborhood was unusually quiet for a late spring morning---no sprinklers swooshing water over azalea bushes, no dogs barking or children whooping in backyards. Then I heard one sound above the silence. "Susan, is the Jeep's engine running?"

"No, of course not."

"Do you hear that drone sound, sort of like a car engine idling?"

Instinctively, we looked up and down Halifax Square---no cars stopped at the curb, no people parked in drives ready to back out into the empty street---then together we looked at the closed garage door.

Susan's dark eyes grew wider and then she bounded for the garage. She tugged and pulled at the handle to raise the door but it wouldn't budge. While I was running around to the side of the building in hopes of finding another door to the inside, I heard a yell, "Ah-ei." Then I heard a whack, whack and wood splintering.

I ran back to the front. "You kicked the door in?"

"Well, hell yeah, " Susan said as she pulled up the broken, but now unlocked, garage door. "What else?"

Inside was an old, green Lincoln limo, the engine now sputtering to a stop. I took a deep breath of outside air and went to the driver's side of the car. The back of a tightly curled gray head, attached to a small woman wearing a lavender dress, slumped over the steering wheel. That's when I heard sirens wailing and saw two Glynn County Sheriff units pull up to the curb.

"Stand back," one of the deputies ordered. Susan and I gladly went back to wait by the Jeep. By now, the quiet neighborhood of five minutes ago was alive with curious people coming out to stand on their front porches, or crowding onto the sidewalk to gawk at the excitement. An ambulance, red light whirling on top like a county fair ride, swerved around the corner at the far end of Halifax and jumped the curb in front of the Peterkin house to park on the small lawn between the house and the garage. Two EMTs jumped from the back of the ambulance and ran for the front door. The driver stayed in the ambulance, saying something into the radio unit he held against his cheek.

An elderly lady left the porch next door and walked over. She asked me what had happened, what we'd found at the house. I didn't answer her, but my guess was we'd found the Peterkin sisters.

CHAPTER SEVENTEEN

Three hours later Susan and I sat at the Dairy Queen on St. Simons Island wolfing down juicy cheeseburgers and telling Sam about our morning. Sam had eaten lunch earlier with her new, gal-reverend friend but ordered a small caramel dipped ice cream for dessert. She was full of questions and I was happy to eat and let Susan make a dramatic show of our sad discovery at the Peterkin sisters' house.

"Susan, that is so bizarre. Except the part about you kicking the garage door in. I can totally see that happening. Do the police think the one sister had a heart attack and the other was so distraught that she committed suicide?"

Susan shook her head while she chewed, swallowed, and took a sip of iced tea. "No. They won't tell us what they think. We don't even know if the one sister had a heart attack. Could have been a stroke. Jeez they both had to be ancient. Didn't Garland Wang say that Aileen told him the sisters used to visit Sparrow Cottage back during WWII?"

I nodded yes, reminded them that the Peterkin sisters and Betty Wu were about the same age, and continued to devour my cheeseburger. I know it was probably irreverent to be so hungry after the morning we'd had, but it was after two o'clock and my little breakfast Danish had worn off hours before.

Sam licked her ice cream around the edges. "Yet, it does seem unlikely that one sister would find the other dead and then run right out to the garage and rig up a carbon monoxide suicide. Even the Cohen brothers would probably think that too outlandish to write into a movie script. What do you think, Promise?"

I rested what remained of my burger in its basket and wiped my greasy fingers. "I'm thinking that here we are poking around trying to find out who shot Aileen, and two people we wanted to talk to about it end up dead. Way too coincidental, and you know how I feel about coincidences. Hey, look over there." I motioned to a stocky, blue-uniformed woman coming into the restaurant. "Isn't that the Georgia trooper we met over at Sparrow Cottage?"

We watched as Olean Hopper ordered an ice cream and turned to leave. I rose and followed her outside.

"Officer Hopper, excuse me, excuse me," I called after her. She stopped, turned around, and took a generous bite from the side of her large chocolate dipped cone. "I'm Dr. Promise McNeal. We met the other day...over where Aileen Wang was shot."

She swiped her mouth with the back of her hand and said, "I remember you. What can I do for you?"

"Could I ask you a quick question? I know you're busy, but..."

"Actually I'm not all that busy right now. I'm done for the day. Had to come over here to St. Simons to interview a couple of college kids who swear they saw a big cougar over on Jekyll last night. Course, they were probably stoned and wouldn't know a cougar from a tomcat. What's your question?"

"Cougar? Really? We heard some folks talking about cougar sightings at Barbara Jean's restaurant the other night."

Hopper laughed. "So now the cougar is hanging out at Barbara Jean's. Ordering crab cakes to go maybe?"

I shared her amusement at my misplaced words with a smile, and then continued, "You know what I mean. What I wanted to ask you is if you've always lived in this area?"

"Yep, except for a tour in the army. Do I get a prize for being a local?"

I was amazed at how chatty Hopper was today. She certainly wasn't this friendly when we met at Sparrow Cottage. Guess it was being off duty, and the ice cream. "Sorry. No

prize. I just wondered if the name Garr Lemley meant anything to you. It would seem he was shot and killed on Jekyll
sometime in late 1951. The killer wasn't found. At least I
don't think so."

Hopper braced back and gave me a puzzled look.
"Why are you interested in Lemley? Are you thinking the
same person who killed him also shot Ms. Wang? From
what you're saying, the guy was killed over sixty years ago.
Kind of far fetched, don't you think?"

I hadn't put the facts into exactly that framework, but
when Hopper repeated it back to me, the connection did
sound foolish. She ate the rest of her ice cream while I
explained about Aileen wanting information on Lemley.
I told her that, at this point, I was only wondering how, or
if, her curiosity about Garr Lemley was somehow linked to
the reason someone might want to kill her. But the same
shooter? No, I wasn't thinking that.

Olean Hopper listened while I finished my story. Then
she was silent for a few seconds before she replied. "Well,
Garr Lemley doesn't ring a bell for me right off. But then
the shooting would have been before my time. I'm not
even sure who would have investigated the incident back
in 1951. You may know that the State of Georgia bought
Jekyll Island a few years before that, but the development
and management of the island was pretty spotty and full of
problems until about the time the bridge was completed
in 1954. You're reaching back to a kind of murky time period for Jekyll. A lot of stuff probably happened over there

that went under the radar because of the confusion about who had jurisdiction. Could be Glynn County Sheriff's Department handled the case if Lemley was a resident. Maybe. Do you think Lemley was a visitor to the island or a resident?"

I thought back to the short newspaper article Barkley located on the web. "The Brunswick News wrote he was a local fisherman, boat captain, and caretaker."

"Well, that doesn't really tell us, now does it? Local could be Brunswick or even Darien. Not necessarily Jekyll Island."

"No, I guess not."

I was ready to say thank you and walk away when Hopper added, "But hey, you mentioning the Brunswick News reminded me of someone who may know about Lemley. His name's Sid Balfour. He's a volunteer at the Jekyll Museum and a retired newspaperman---used to be with the Brunswick News. Wrote a history of the island. Go ask him, and if you turn up any connections to the Wang shooting, be sure to let me know. I'd love to show up that conceited, pretty-boy GBI agent working the case. Did you get a load of his inflated ego?"

I smiled but refrained from telling Olean Hopper that I'd gotten the full load of RB Barnes' ego years ago.

Susan and Sam were chatting, smiling at each other, when I got back to our table. I hoped that meant the earlier tension between them had relaxed. Looking at the two young women, I felt a motherly urge to have a talk with

Susan about her feelings for Sam, but knew better than to act on my urge. After all, Susan was a grown woman and I was the new stepmother. Still, the Shoulda-woulda-coulda girls' committee meeting in my head reminded me: *You are also good friends. Don't good friends bring up sticky issues with good friends?* I told the committee they were talking about me putting my nose where it didn't belong---always a bad idea--- and sat down beside Sam. If Susan wanted to talk to me, she would talk.

"So, what'd I miss?" I asked.

"Not much," Susan replied. "What'd you find out from Olean Hopper?"

I filled them in while we collected our trash, deposited it into a receptacle at the door, and walked out into the warm afternoon. "Bottom line is she doesn't know anything about Garr Lemley, but suggested a volunteer at the museum by the name of Sid Balfour might remember the story. I'd like to go over there, if y'all are up to it."

"Jeez, Ms. P, tell you the truth, I've had my fill of the Aileen Wang drama for today. Sam and I want to walk down to a shop across from Barbara Jean's. She wants to look for a couple of outfits, and I need a pair of flip-flops."

"Are you talking about Go-Fish?"

"Yes, that's the shop," Sam said. "We noticed some really cute dresses in the window---not too beach like, but not stuffy either, and lots of color. Black and white robes go with everything, but sometimes I need color to cheer me up."

It was decided I would take Susan's Jeep and go to Jekyll. They would shop up and down Mallery Street in the village and we'd connect later at their inn. As I was driving over the causeway for the second time today, it occurred to me that I'd spent more time away from St. Simons Island than on it during this trip. Next year, I told myself, Daniel and I will come back alone and practice chilling out on the beach.

I took my time driving over to Jekyll, thinking about why I was so intent on solving the mystery of who shot Aileen. Was I trying to prove something to RB Barnes? No, I didn't think so.

The truth is, I'm just wired to have to know the rest of the story, no matter what story it is. Not seeing the whole picture makes me crazy. Give me a 1,000-piece picture puzzle and you can bet I'll sit down and put it together in one sitting. Put me in a cheesy movie and I'll still stay until the end just to know how it turns out. I am, if nothing else, tenacious. And tenacity was a helpful personality trait when I was a counselor. I was comfortable sitting with clients, picking and picking at life stories, tugging on that one thread leading to the truth of their life's story. Sadly though, sometimes tenacity isn't enough to untangle the stoking lies and heal the wounds crippling a human soul. I had my share of failures.

I turned left on Stable Road, drove a short distance to the building that once housed horses and carriages for the millionaire members of the Jekyll Island Club, and parked

Susan's Jeep in front of the museum. A young woman behind the reception desk directed me to my right and down a short corridor where she said I would find Sid Balfour. He was on his knees with his back to me, half inside a glass display case when I approached. The title above the case said: King Cotton and Jekyll's Early Economy. I waited until he'd stacked a small basket full of mini cotton bales into a pyramid shape on the floor of the display case before I spoke.

"Excuse me, are you Sid Balfour?"

He extricated himself from the case, got to his feet, and turned to look down at me from his large, gentle face. "I am unless you have a complaint. If you're unhappy, then I never heard of the guy." His smile filled the space between his beard and nose---a beard, the same white as the cotton he was so carefully making conspicuous for museum visitors. I noticed he was even taller than Daniel and looked oddly familiar to me.

"Hello." I extended my hand. "My name is Dr. Promise McNeal. Olean Hopper gave me your name as someone who is an expert on Jekyll Island history." He shook my hand like a big man afraid of crushing my knuckles and continued to smile. "She said you've even written a history of the island."

"Well, written but not published. Not yet, anyway. I keep finding more little tidbits that beg to be included. I may not have the darn thing completed until I'm too old to remember why I started it in the first place. Did you know a German U- boat sank three ships off the coast of Georgia during WWII? When the Germans torpedoed a tanker headed north from Florida the explosion rattled windowpanes as far away as Brunswick and washed up a lot of stuff on Jekyll. Are you a Jekyll Island history buff? Dr. McNeal, did you say?"

"Please, just Promise. I don't know why I added the doctor, force of habit I guess. I hold a doctorate in psychology. I did have a counseling practice in Atlanta but I'm retired."

"Me, too. Retired, that is, a couple of years ago. I hold a doctorate in being a snoopy newspaper reporter, but nowadays they let me hang around here and bother the visitors a bit."

It finally dawned on me why Sid Balfour looked familiar. "Has anyone ever mentioned to you that you look a lot like Monty Woolley?"

Now he laughed. "Good Lord. I doubt there are five people on the island who remember Monty Woolley. But yes, it has been mentioned a time or two. Probably it's the bushy, white beard. You know Woolley was nicknamed 'The Beard' by the composer Cole Porter. As I remember, the two were in school together and remained close friends for life. You can't be old enough to have seen Monty Woolley on the great silver screen."

"No. Well, maybe I did as a kid, but I don't remember. It's that I'm fond of the classic movie channels on cable. I saw *The Man Who Came To Dinner* a couple of weeks ago---very funny movie. Woolley was a wonderful actor. He played such a loveable cad."

"Yes, he did. Won an academy award I believe. But I doubt you came looking for me because you heard I love old movies. I'd say you are a lady on a mission. What can I do for you?"

Sid Balfour listened patiently while I told the story of Aileen being shot, me being friends with Aileen and Garland Wang, and Aileen's interest in finding out about a man named Garr Lemley. I was honest with him and said I had no idea if Lemley was related to what happened to Aileen or not.

His smile disappeared as I told my story. "Yes, I know a bit about the Wang lady being shot. Terrible thing. Terrible thing. You see, I'm retired, but my contacts at the paper still keep me up to speed on the local goings on. In this case, I attended her cocktail party with a friend from the Chamber of Commerce, though after we did a minimum of polite mingling we left to have dinner at the hotel."

"Ah, really? Did you notice anyone suspicious at the party? Anything out of the ordinary?"

"No, the most out of the ordinary occurrence was my friend being grilled by two little old ladies from Brunswick. They were extremely curious about a man neither of us knew."

My face flushed. I hoped he didn't notice. He had to be talking about the Peterkin sisters. "What did the ladies want to know?"

"Oh, they pointed out a man in the crowd---wanted to know his name, where he lived, and if we had a phone number for him. My friend knew the guy's name and that he's new to the island, but that's about all. Well, I take that back. I think he also gave them the name of a realtor he thought had leased the man a house. I really wasn't paying very close attention. Tell you the truth, I was more interested in the lobster I intended to order for dinner."

"This new guy in town, did he look suspicious?"

Balfour smiled again. "Come on, Dr. McNeal, you sound like a cop show on TV. I mean, what does suspicious look like? Back in my reporting days I saw serial killers who looked like the nice kid next door. This guy looked like most of the successful residents on the island. Older man. Tall. Mustache. Well kept. No paunchy belly like mine. I saw him chatting with Ms. Wang at one point. He was elegantly dressed. I'll tell you that. The rest of us were dressed in polo shirts, cotton slacks, and blazers. He was decked out in a summer tuxedo."

"Anything else you remember about him? Do you recall his name?"

"No, sorry. Don't recall his name. If I were you, I'd locate the ladies from Brunswick and ask them why they were interested in the guy. If it's any help to you, I'm pretty sure I recognized them---Pris and Paula Peterkin---old money, Brunswick society family. The old Peterkin house is near the historic area of Brunswick. On Halifax Square, if I'm not mistaken. The sisters are sort of local characters in Brunswick. Used to be in the society section of the News a lot."

"I tried to call on the Peterkin sisters. Unfortunately, they both passed away earlier today."

He frowned. "What do you mean? Both sisters died today?"

"Yes, I think so."

"On the same day?" Balfour stroked his bearded chin and raised an eyebrow. "Interesting. I smell a story. Maybe I'll call my buddy at the paper later, ask what happened."

I nodded and asked him again if the name Garr Lemley meant anything to him.

He repeated the name a couple of times to himself and shook his head. "The name sounds familiar. I mean, once you hear a story about some guy called Garr, it sort of stays with you. But I'm drawing a blank on the details. I tell you what. Leave me a number where I can reach you. I've got notes on the island going back four hundred years. Surely I've come across Garr Lemley somewhere."

I thanked Sid Balfour, gave him my cell number, and went to collect the Jeep, wondering what I should do next. Driving from Stable Road, I took a right on Old Plantation, another right onto Riverview Drive, and headed north toward the Jekyll Island fishing pier where I planned to walk out over the ocean and think. Instead, when I saw the Horton House ruins, I pulled over to the verge, stopped, and crossed the road to du Bignon Cemetery.

CHAPTER EIGHTEEN

I couldn't remember if the small cemetery looked the same as it did when I was a child. From reading a visitors guide narrative, I'd learned no recent graves had been added, but my memory of the Spanish moss draped oaks and the low tabby wall encircling the cemetery was fuzzy.

Perhaps we hadn't visited du Bignon when I'd vacationed with my parents. Unlike my mother, my father didn't find old cemeteries entertaining and avoided anything related to death or dying. He refused to make a will or participate in Mother's decision to purchase burial plots for the their final resting place. I think his words on the matter were that he didn't intend to be idle for eternity, so a piece of ground to lie down in was useless.

I pushed through the rusted, iron gate into du Bignon Cemetery and then walked across crushed shell and rock to stand before two knee high grave markers.

These markers, my visitors guide noted, are in memory of two young men---employees of the original Jekyll Island Club who drowned off Jekyll on the same day in 1912. The above ground brick tombs to the left of the markers are in memory of three du Bignon family members whose remains have not been located, though their graves are believed to be near the present cemetery site. In other words, if I understood the guidebook correctly, the tombs are here but the bodies aren't. While I pondered the question of whether that information made the du Bignon site a cemetery or a memorial, my cell phone rang.

"Hey. I'm so glad you called." It was Daniel. "What am I doing?" I reached out for something plausible to tell Daniel rather than I was wandering around a cemetery looking at empty tombs. "Oh, just following up on a couple of leads in the who shot Aileen saga. She's doing better, by the way. What did you find out today?"

"Hmmm. Not much really. Went to the sheriff's department this morning. Alton Hazlett is acting sheriff until the county commissioners appoint an interim person. Then there will be a special election in November. Alton was real nice to me and introduced me to the state team investigating the...what happened, but my feeling is that he will pretty much tread water until someone else takes over."

"Yes, I remember Mac saying that Hazlett was close to retirement and was keeping his head down and his nose out of controversy."

"Exactly. But in fairness, the state team seems sharp and determined to find the son of a bitch who killed Mac. I sat down with them and answered a long list of questions about what Mac had been doing lately."

A white SUV pulled over and parked behind the Jeep on the grassy shoulder of the road. When a young couple sprinted across and began taking photographs of the cemetery, I ambled back through the gate and crossed the road.

"That sounds like progress. What had Mac been working on?" There was a long silence from Daniel's end of the line. "Daniel, are you still there?"

"Yes, I'm here. I'm thinking. Mac didn't tell me everything, you know. He was pretty professional about not involving civilians in police work." Meaning that was the press line Daniel gave the state investigators. However, I knew Mac relished sharing war stories with Daniel. I considered if this was the time to call his hand about how much he knew, and decided, no.

Daniel continued to ramble. "And then, Mac being Mac, you never knew where he might show up shaking hands and politicking for his next term. Case in point: I stopped at the feed store today to pick up a bag of goat chow for you, and after Roger told me he was real sorry about Mac, he said he'd seen him Monday night at an auction out on Louisa Chapel Road. He said Mac was busy slapping backs and making small talk."

"I didn't know Mac liked to go to auctions. Do you suppose he was there to bid on something or just making an appearance?"

"You've got me there. Mac at an auction was a surprise to me."

"Maybe he had a date and the lady likes auctions."

"Nah, the auction was for big equipment like road graders and that kind of stuff. Not many women get excited by road graders. Besides, Roger said Mac had Pate Hoag tagging along."

"Really? I didn't think Mac and Pate were exactly pals."

"They weren't. Now that I think about it, Mac must have been there on business. I'll call the state team and tell them about the auction thing. It's probably nothing, and Pate probably already told them about it, but who knows?"

"Speaking of Pate Hoag, how did he react to finding out that you weren't in the car with Mac?"

"Turned out he already knew. Remember Ben Owens' sister?"

"Rochelle. Works dispatch for the sheriff's department."

"Right. Susan talked to Owens. He talked to his sister. She'd told Pate already. His sorrow about Mac did seem pretty genuine though. I didn't get a chance to ask him why he was so interested in Mac being at my house. I'll save that for later."

Looking back across the street to the du Bignon cemetery, I asked Daniel, "Any news on when you could have a funeral for Mac?"

"Hmm. Probably the best plan is to have a memorial service in a week or so. I'm headed over to Fletcher's house to talk to MaMa Allen about that now. As far as family, it's just her and us. Though I expect a lot of Perry County would like to come to pay their respects to Mac. So, where are you now, and what's Susan up to?"

"Susan and Sam are shopping over at St. Simons. I'm checking out something on Jekyll that may tie in with Aileen being shot." I left out the part about Susan and me stumbling over the deceased Peterkin sisters. Daniel had enough problems; he didn't need to worry about us finding bodies. I heard what sounded like a repressed snicker coming from the phone. "Are you laughing at me?"

"Lord no, not at you. Couldn't stay out of the Aileen mess, eh? Never mind, don't comment. Just be careful, okay? Hey, wasn't the GBI sending an agent down to investigate?"

I figured I might as well go ahead and tell him. "Yes, and the agent turned out to be RB Barnes, newly employed hotshot for the Bureau."

Another laugh from Daniel bellowed in my ear. I didn't think it was *that* funny.

"You've got to be kidding. Is that what you and Susan call karma? Don't suppose you're following leads on the shooting to prove something to Barnes, are you?"

I was glad Daniel's sense of humor was in tact, but I didn't want to hear that question again. "Susan mentioned the same possibility, and the answer is no. My looking into a couple of things has nothing to do with Barnes. I'm just curious, and it keeps me busy while I'm waiting for you to give the sign we can come home. I miss you, Daniel, and I feel like a unmoored ship without you."

After hanging up with Daniel, I decided not to linger on Jekyll. The mention of RB was a wakeup call that he probably needed to know about the Peterkin sisters and my conversation with Sid Balfour. I wasn't sure exactly what the information had to do with Aileen but had a clear sense that it was all related.

Garland had mentioned RB would be back in Atlanta today and then return to St. Simons in a couple of days. I'd go to the hospital and see Aileen. If Garland was there, he could call RB and fill him in for me. That way, I didn't have to talk to him.

Just before I drove off the island, I pulled into the visitor center parking lot and called Susan to ask where they wanted to have supper. Interestingly enough, Susan said they'd met a couple of girls from Macon, and hoped I didn't mind if they "hung out" with them and had dinner at a bar and grill in the village. I could keep the Jeep until the next day if I wanted to. I think Susan offered the Jeep because she felt guilty closing me out of the party plans, but really, I was fine with my own company.

And, too, I wanted to catch up with Garland at the hospital.

CHAPTER NINETEEN

It was suppertime when I arrived at St. Simons Island Hospital. I stepped off the elevator onto the second floor and into a traffic jam of staff delivering food trays trolleyed on huge, stainless steel, rolling racks and nurses navigating around the trolleys to ferry meds up and down the hall to patients. By the activity at the nurses' station--- some nurses packing up to leave and others settling in---I must have also arrived during shift change. I navigated my way through the uniforms and knocked on Aileen's door.

She answered, "Enter."

Sounded like the old Aileen to me. She was sitting up in bed, an IV drip taped to her right hand, a sizeable bandage affixed to the left side of her skull, and the local telephone book across her lap. Garland stood at attention beside her.

"You know they shaved off half of my hair on the side where the sniper's bullet almost killed me," she announced to me as though I'd been in the room all along. "God, what am I going to do? I look like a Shriner's clown. I can't very well tell the cameraman to shoot only from my right side. That would be *amateurish*. Boring. I need a wig. That's what I need. I've been looking in the yellow pages, but of course, no wigs anywhere south of Savannah. Garland, go call Barkley and tell him to find me a wig in Atlanta and have it over-nighted down here."

Garland and I exchanged sympathetic looks as he stepped around me and left the room.

"Glad you're feeling better. I must say you gave us all a scare."

Aileen's small face looked vulnerable for a second or two as she peered up from her dais of white pillows, blankets, and sheets. Then her moment of insecurity passed and she was Aileen again. "This place is freezing all the time, Promise, and they have nothing decent for a vegetarian like me to eat. If I weren't so damn tired I'd get up and walk my ass out of here."

I nodded my understanding. "I would think it's normal for you to be tired. Your body's been through a lot…"

"I know, I know---rest, rest, rest. But really, I can rest in Atlanta. I've told Garland to get me out of here tomorrow, or else. If I could remember where my car keys were, I'd leave on my own. By the way, what are you doing here? Surely you didn't come all the way to Jekyll Island to see me imprisoned in the hospital."

"You're at St. Simons Hospital. There's no hospital on Jekyll. I was already down here--- getting married."

Aileen perked up. "To that tall, good looking man with the Stetson hat?"

"Yes. Daniel Allen. We finally took the plunge. You seem to remember him pretty well. How's your memory of the night of the cocktail party?"

"If you mean do I remember anything about being shot, then the answer is no. I understand Garland has RB Barnes down here to find the guy who shot me. I assume it was a guy, though plenty of my enemies are women." Aileen's dark eyes danced with a hint of wickedness. "Hmmm. By the way, speaking of RB Barnes, it must be very uncomfortable for you to see him again while you're marrying someone else?"

I could almost hear the meow, meow in her question. I looked up at the ceiling---not at her--- so I could lie with a straight face. "Not really. He's ancient history. Barnes doesn't get to me any more." Then I changed the subject. "I won't exhaust you any more than you already are. Just wanted to say hello, and ask you a quick question."

Aileen sat up straighter. "Shoot," she said and then groaned. "Bad pun, sorry."

"Humor is good. Here's the thing: Barkley gave me a message that you wanted me to research a man named Garr Lemley who lived on Jekyll during WWII. Is there anything you can tell me about the guy that would help?"

Aileen frowned, her forehead furrowed. "What did you say the name was?" Just then Betty Wu walked into the room.

I repeated the name. "Garr Lemley."

Aileen seemed puzzled, as though trying to retrieve the memory. Betty Wu looked startled. "What you say?" Betty blurted out.

Aileen looked at Betty Wu and parroted, "Garr Lemley, Mother."

Betty cocked her head and fixed her daughter with a look of such ferocity that the skin on the back of my neck tingled. Aileen held her mother's gaze like the dutiful child waiting for the slap she'd learned to anticipate. For a couple of seconds, unspoken words passed between them.

Finally Aileen said to me, "Whatever message I gave Barkley, just forget it. I'm sure it wasn't important. Don't bother yourself with it."

I couldn't make up my mind if Aileen remembered giving the message to Barkley, or if she remembered why she was interested in Lemley. I did decide Betty Wu knew the name. I told Aileen I was glad she was improving so rapidly, wished her well, and excused myself from the room. Garland was pacing around the tiny waiting area at the end of the hall.

"Ah, the dutiful husband," I said, in an effort to get him to smile and relax a little. "I'm glad you're still here. Did you reach Barkley?"

"Yes. You can imagine his reaction to Her Highness's directive to find her a wig."

"What'd he say?"

"He asked if she wanted a Marie Antoinette or an Elvira."

Barkley is so good at making me laugh. Garland, on the other hand, was not as amused. "I tell you, Promise, this whole thing is about to give me a nervous breakdown. Having to deal with Aileen and her mother is more than any sane man can handle. Speaking of Betty, now she's obsessed with posting a guard at Aileen's door. I mean is that reasonable? What do you think? Maybe I should call Barnes and ask him." Garland took out his cell phone.

"Hang on a second. I need you to relay something to Barnes." I looked back down the hall and saw Betty come out of Aileen's room. She was carrying her black designer handbag with the red and black silk scarf tied through the silver clasp. "Garland, has Betty Wu been here at the hospital all day?"

"No, she just got here. Told me she'd been out running errands all day."

My bet was that one of Betty's errands was to the Peterkin house to collect her purse. I'd also bet she'd had to explain to a Glynn County sheriff's deputy why her purse was in the parlor. Why had Betty visited the

Peterkin sisters at all? I wanted to ask her but remembered the scathing look she'd given Aileen when Garr Lemley's name came up. Betty turned away from us and walked to the nurses' station, tapping her dog head cane on the floor every few feet as she moved. She spoke with a nurse behind the desk and then turned our way.

"Here comes Betty. I need you to tell Barnes that the Peterkin sisters were found dead this morning---probably not natural causes. Remind him they were at Aileen's party and were cousins of Mena Simpson, who owned Sparrow Cottage. Tell him to call the Glynn County Sheriff's Department for the details."

Garland nodded and walked to the far end of the waiting area where through the wall of windows, sunset was spilling the last red and gold colors of the day onto the white tile floor.

Amid the scurry of light blue uniformed hospital cafeteria staff, and darker blue clad nurses and doctors in the hallway, Betty Wu stopped. I had a cheery thought that perhaps she wasn't coming my way, and that I could leave without talking to her. As I was warming to the idea of catching the elevator and putting Aileen's issues aside for a walk on the beach, Betty rapped her cane on the tile floor, made an about face, and hurried back into Aileen's room. No more than two seconds later, I heard her---the whole hospital probably heard her.

"*What you do? Stop. Stop,*" Betty screamed. I ran for Aileen's room. So did two female nurses.

Then I heard glass breaking, metal clanging on the hard surface of the floor, and Aileen hollering, *"Mother!"*

I pushed my way into the room just as a tall man in dark blue scrubs and a surgical mask shoved past me and ran for the stairwell. The two nurses came right behind me. Betty hollered, her cane thrashing into empty space. "Call police. *Hurry.* Get that tall man."

One of the nurses asked, "What happened, Mrs. Wang."

Aileen raised both hands to cover her eyes and shook her head back and forth. Garland suddenly appeared in the room and went to Aileen's bedside, taking her hands away from her face and holding them. "Oh God, Garland," she cried, "Mother attacked a male nurse. I think he was about to put medicine in my IV and she started beating him with her cane. She must have hit him a dozen times. Just look at this mess."

The room was indeed a mess. Aileen's IV stand was sprawled across the bed. Shards of glass lay on the floor, and a stainless steel pan sat cocked against the wall in the corner.

Betty stepped over the broken glass to Aileen's side and leaned within inches of her face. "You foolish girl. Not nurse. He want to hurt you. I save your life. You act like I shame you, you ungrateful tiger daughter. What's wrong with you?"

Garland spoke calmly to Betty, using his best court-room attorney's voice. "What makes you think he wanted to harm Aileen?"

"What? Not thinking. I'm for sure. He had big needle. About to put poison in her medicine tube. He's not a nurse. You see those fancy leather loafers? Italian, easy cost seven hundred dollars. Also hospital pants too short. You see chino slacks under blue hospital pants? Call police. You want him to get away?"

"Betty," Garland began and then changed his mind and asked the nurses, "Was my wife scheduled for meds?" The nurses shook their heads no. "Did you get a good look at him?" Both nurses shook their heads again. "How about you, Promise?"

I thought for a second. "Just that he was tall, not heavy, and wearing a hospital mask. He was wearing a hospital cap also, so all I could see of his hair was a little gray at the temples. Though, when he pushed past me, I did look down at the shoes. I don't know about Italian, but they did look expensive. And Garland, if he were a nurse, why run like hell for the stairwell?"

Garland tapped his head with the heel of his hand just like the guy in the *I could have had a V8* commercial. The taller nurse said, "I'll call 911," and ran from the room.

After talking with Glynn County's sheriff department for the second time in twelve hours, I wanted to go back to the hotel and crawl under the covers. I must have explained ten times why I'd been at the Peterkin house earlier, and why I was at the hospital when the mysterious tall man chose to make his grand entrance.

The deputies told us that if the man had some type of poison with him, there were no signs of it in Aileen's room. Betty Wu commented that of course not, because she'd knocked the syringe out of his hand with her cane and then hit him several times about his head and face as he was picking it up from the floor. A nurse volunteered that one of the LPNs had reported his scrub uniform missing from his locker.

It seemed Betty Wu was right about the man, but there was little to go on that would help find him. Four additional deputies arrived, searching the hospital for anyone matching his description. Though, realistically, if you locked up every tall, sort of slim, white man with close cropped graying hair, you'd have half of St. Simons Island in custody.

Once the deputies took statements from all of us and posted a uniformed officer outside Aileen's door, they left. Garland called Barnes again. This time it was to tell him about the incident in Aileen's room. RB said he would follow up with the Glynn County Sheriff's Department by phone and return to St. Simons on Sunday. Then he asked to speak to me.

Reluctantly, I took the phone. "Hello."

"Promise, what the hell is going on down there?"

I was shocked that RB would ask me such a question. Either he was only venting his frustration, or he actually thought I might have some insight into the matter. I'd go for the frustration factor. "Can you be more specific, Randall?"

"Don't Randall me. I already talked to Glynn County after Garland called the first time, so I know you and Susan Allen were the ones who found Pris and Paula Peterkin dead. Now you just happen to be at the hospital when the perp shows up to try and finish the job on Aileen. Like you always say, Dr. McNeal, you don't much believe in coincidences. Neither do I. You are stirring up something down there, meddling in police business again, just like the Tournay case in Atlanta. You need to stop it.

"I mean what the hell are you even doing down there? I heard your new husband left already and went home. What kind of deal is that? Why don't you go home? Stay out of trouble. I'm ordering you to cease what you're doing. We've got a match on the type of rifle used to shoot Aileen, and when I get down there on Sunday..." RB broke off in mid-sentence. There was silence on the other end of the phone.

"Randall, are you still there?"

"Yes. I'm thinking."

Well that was a rarity---RB thinking in lieu of ranting at me. I waited. Certainly didn't want to disturb history in the making.

After a short interval, RB was a changed man. He was calm, not on a tirade. I suspected one of the conditions of his new job with the GBI was a crash course in people skills---but maybe not. "Okay. Let's back up," he said in an amicable voice. "On the off chance you may have found out something useful with your nosing around, let me begin again. Can we cooperate on this thing?"

"Sure." I think of myself as a cooperative person by nature.

"Good. Why were you at the Peterkin house this morning?"

I explained that the sisters were at Aileen's party. I figured someone at the party was the best candidate for being the shooter because that person would know when Aileen would be alone. The sisters were described as busybody types. They might have noticed someone suspicious. And also, they were lifetime residents of the area and were often on Jekyll during the 1940s and 1950s. I wanted to ask them if they knew a man named Garr Lemley who'd been shot and killed on Jekyll in 1951."

"Promise, what in the hell would a 1951 shooting have to do with Aileen?"

I told him I didn't know the answer to that yet. I also told him about Barkley's message from Aileen regarding wanting me to research Lemley. Then I told him about Aileen's and Betty Wu's reactions when I mentioned Garr Lemley to them.

"So, you think Aileen stumbled on something about the Lemley killing while researching Jekyll and Sparrow Cottage, and somehow that ties in with someone wanting to shoot her?"

"Yes." After I said yes, I felt an even greater conviction that yes was the right answer. "And Betty Wu must remember something about Garr Lemley. Otherwise, why the shut-up look at Aileen?"

"You mean when you asked Aileen what she already knew about him?"

"Right. That's when Betty Wu gave Aileen the totally withering look. Then Aileen said to drop the Lemley subject, that it wasn't important. For me to forget it."

"Well, maybe it isn't important. Maybe you're making a big leap into thin air with your suspicions."

"Hmm. Maybe. But my sense tells me Betty Wu knows something about Garr Lemley."

"Your sense? Right. So tell me this: if she knows something that relates to who shot her daughter, why isn't she sharing it? Why would Mrs. Wu protect him or her, whatever the case may be, if she thought that person was trying to kill Aileen? You'd think she'd tell what she knows, want to catch the bastard, especially after what happened today. It doesn't make sense. And besides, if you're trying to make a case that the same person who shot Lemley shot Aileen, he'd probably have to be Betty Wu's age at least---that's over eighty years old. Did the guy you saw running out of Aileen's room look eighty to you?"

I thought for a second or two. "Well no. He didn't run like an eighty-year-old. But he wasn't a young man either. I saw a bit of graying hair."

"So there you are. Sounds like the Lemley connection is a dead end to me. Who knows, maybe Lemley was Betty's boyfriend way back when and she's embarrassed about him. I mean, with a name like Garr, he probably didn't travel in the social circles Mrs. Wu is accustomed to at this point in her life. Let's get back to the Peterkin sisters.

"Glynn County Sheriff's Department tells me they are investigating both deaths as suspicious, which means the GBI will probably be called in, and I'll get the case. Who do you figure would want to off two old ladies? Glynn County's deputy says both sisters had a reputation for being pretty snarky and major gossips, but there's nothing from the neighbors to indicate why someone would kill them. It doesn't look like robbery. They didn't even own a computer or big screen TV.

"In fact, the neighbor next door told Glynn County the sisters recently sold the family silver, and you know Southern women don't part with the silver unless they are down to the last grain of rice. According to the same neighbor, the sisters had a roofing contractor out this past week who told them they needed a new tile roof---at a cost of twenty thousand dollars. The sisters told her they would have to 'consider their options' about the roof---meaning they probably didn't have the twenty grand. The point being, Pris and Paula had money troubles and probably didn't have anything worth stealing. Plus Glynn County says the house didn't look like anyone had tossed it looking for goodies."

"Wait. Did you say they needed twenty thousand dollars for a new roof?"

"That's what the neighbor told the Glynn County deputy."

"Aileen told Garland that the sisters pitched her to hire them as consultants for the Sparrow restoration. They wanted twenty thousand dollars in advance."

RB laughed. "Well, sounds like the old girls were resourceful, if nothing else. Maybe Aileen was one of their options."

"Except Aileen turned them down. Wonder what their other options were?"

"I can hear your brain making another big leap into open space…"

Before I could point out RB's poor choice of metaphors, he cut the conversation short. "I gotta go; the boss is buzzing me. Call you later."

"Okay."

"By the way, are you armed?"

"Armed? What do you mean?"

"Armed. As in are you carrying a weapon?"

"You mean like a pistol?"

"Lord no, how about a *sling-shot*? That ought to scare the bad guys…of course I mean a handgun."

"You know I hate guns. Don't own one."

"Well, get one, doctor. You may need it before this is all done."

With that RB hung up and I was left considering where a person actually carried a gun, unless you were like RB and had a cool, leather shoulder holster.

Another possibility occurred to me. You could put a small hand gun in your pocket, if your pocket was big enough, like the deep pockets of, say, a London Fog rain-coat---a raincoat just like the one with the bulging pocket Betty Wu was wearing earlier this morning when we saw her at breakfast.

CHAPTER TWENTY

What a day. I drove to the Harris Teeter from the hospital, picked up a large salad and a cold bottle of mountain spring water from the deli, and then stopped by a shady, public park off Ocean Boulevard near my hotel. Though darkness marched our way and deep shadows already gathered under the oak trees, I noticed one family lingered in the park---the young parents packing up beach chairs, a cooler, and the remains of a picnic into the back of a light green mini van, and two children pumping swings high into the warm evening air.

Choosing a table outside their family space, I opened my *dinner in a box*. All I wanted was to be still for a few minutes, listen to the surf churning in the distance, and feel the comforting crunch of crisp lettuce, cucumbers, and carrots in my mouth. After eating my salad, I planned to go back to the hotel, take a long shower, and look for something non-threatening on TV while I waited for an update from Daniel. Reruns of the Andy Griffith Show would be a perfect distraction from all the drama playing in my life at the moment. Yes, what I needed was three back-to-back episodes of Andy, Opie, Gomer, Aunt Bea, and Barney.

When I dropped my trash in the receptacle near the street and the park security lights powered up, casting an eerie yellowish glow up into the outstretched arms of the oaks around me, it occurred to me that I was a woman, alone, in an unfamiliar, dark place. Maybe RB had a point about being armed. I should probably carry pepper spray or something.

Shoes slapping on pavement pounded toward me. I flinched at the sound and turned to see a skinny, older man wearing running shorts and a white terry sweatband low on his forehead, jogging down the sidewalk. He sped past me, raised a hand and called out, "evening." As his white tee shirt receded into the shadows, I saw the black thunderbolt on the back and realized this was the same runner I'd seen Thursday from the hotel restaurant. I returned his greeting and tried to place the symbol of the thunderbolt. I knew I'd seen it before, but where?

Later, lying in bed and flipping through TV channels looking for Andy Griffith, I thought of the thunderbolt symbol again. I wished I'd had my laptop. Google would no doubt tell me its significance. No computer and no Andy Griffith. I settled for Fred Astaire and Ginger Rogers on the classic movie channel and was enjoying the pair glide across the dance floor when Daniel called.

"Hey, Babe. What's going on?"

"Not much. I'm relaxing with Ginger and Fred. Susan and Sam are in the village carousing with some new friends. Missing you…"

"You and your old musicals. Does it ever strike you that the plot lines are usually pretty simplistic? Not a lot of variation on human nature with old Fred and Ginger."

"Absolutely. That's why I love them so much. Though I'm surprised to hear you say that. I didn't realize you spent time thinking about the variations of human nature. But don't tell me you don't like Ginger Rogers and Fred Astaire; cause if you don't, I'm not sure I should have married you."

"Oh no, don't say that. I love Fred and Ginger. Can't get enough of the dancing duo. Those guys are my all time favorites. Fred wears greats duds. Love the top hat."

I almost laughed. "Duds? Did you say duds? Good Lord, maybe you really are a cowboy."

"Yeah, but I'm your cowboy, and you're stuck with me now."

"I'm not complaining. Hey, I've seen a jogger a couple of times with a thunderbolt symbol on the back of his tee shirt. Do you know what it means? I can't place why it looks so familiar."

"Does this somehow relate to Ginger Rogers or to Aileen Wang and the mysterious gunman?"

"Neither. You know me. When I can't remember something I get obsessive until I do remember." I went on to tell Daniel about the incident at the hospital and he interjected several you've-got-to-be-kidding responses.

Then he asked, "When is Barnes coming back?"

"I talked to him today and he said Sunday. He also said the GBI had a match on the rifle that was used to shoot Aileen."

"Good. Stay out of it, please."

"I'm not in it. But knowing the type of rifle doesn't catch the shooter. What are they going to do, knock on every door on Jekyll Island and ask to search the house for the rifle?"

"You sound like you're in it."

"Please. I just happened to be at the hospital when the guy showed up. Let's change the subject. Any news from your side?"

"No, not really."

"Why do I think there is more to your *not really*?"

"Hmm," answered Daniel. Which really wasn't an answer at all. I let a long silence fill the space and waited. My much-used counseling technique worked and Daniel spoke again. "I wouldn't say I have news, but I did come across something odd today. I drove over to Mac's place late this afternoon to check on the house and bring in the mail. Also, I wanted to see if he had any bills that needed to be paid. That's why I opened his bank statement from today's mail---to make sure he had money in the account to cover the bills."

"So, are you saying you can write checks out of his account?"

"Yes, he put me on the account after his divorce. Just in case...well you know, in case something like this happened."

"Okay. Go ahead. What about his bank statement? Is something wrong?"

"Everything looks okay on the statement, except he has a lot more cash in there than I thought he would have, and there was a thirty-thousand dollar deposit to the account last week."

"Thirty thousand dollars? Where would Mac get that kind of money?"

"That's just it. I have no idea. His county paycheck was an automatic deposit, just like always, and it sure wasn't thirty grand. Mac didn't have anything that I know of that he could have cashed in or sold for that kind of money. Anyway, the deposit bothered me so I looked at last month's statement. There was another thirty thousand deposited about the same time last month. Mac---I guess it was Mac---had circled the deposit in red on the bank statement."

I considered several reasons why Mac's account would have an extra thirty thousand dollars in it. None of them seemed plausible, but I offered the most likely scenario. "I can see why that amount worried you, but maybe, since Mac circled the amount on last month's statement, he saw that the deposit was an error. He probably called the bank about it. Can you call the bank and ask them?"

"I'm not sure. Maybe. Since I'm on the account. But if Mac called last month and told the bank they'd made an error, why would another deposit show up? Plus this month's statement doesn't show the first thirty thousand going out of his account. You know, like the bank was correcting an error and debiting his account for the funds."

Good question. I didn't have an answer. "Go to the bank tomorrow. Talk to one of the managers and clear it up. Then you can stop worrying about it."

Daniel said, "Uh-huh."

"What's wrong with going to the bank?"

"I don't know, Babe. You know how you have your *feelings* sometimes? Well this is one of those times for me. I'm not sure I should talk to anyone about it right now."

"You think there might be some connection between the money and Mac's death?"

"Maybe."

"Then maybe you need to tell the state investigators about it?"

I got another non-committal response from Daniel. His mind was clearly processing something that he wasn't ready to share with me, and I could understand that. After all, I hadn't told him about Garr Lemley, yet, for probably the same reason. I had a suspicion that Lemley's death was related to Aileen being shot but nothing to tie the two events together. And Daniel had nothing to tie the money to Mac's death. At least I didn't think he did. I was still unsure if my new husband was telling me everything he knew about his cousin Mac.

As we said goodbye, Daniel added quickly, "Wait a second, Babe. Remember that jogger you saw---the one with the thunderbolt on his shirt?"

"Yes."

"How do you know it was a thunderbolt and not a lightning bolt? I think, technically, what you see is a lightning bolt, and what you hear at the same time as the lightning is a thunderbolt. Or is it if you hear the thunder at the same time as you see the lightning, then the electrical charge you see is called a thunderbolt? Oh hell, I don't know. Which is it?"

I thought for a few seconds. "Well, now that you say that, I'm not sure which is correct---thunderbolt or lightning bolt. Except, what I saw on the shirt was black, not silvery white like you'd expect lightning to be. For some reason, the symbol in black makes me think thunderbolt. Why do you ask?"

"Oh, no reason. Sleep well. I love you."

"I love you too."

CHAPTER TWENTY-ONE

My mind refused to shut down for sleep. I watched the rest of the Fred Astaire movie and played about ten games of solitaire with a deck of cards I found in the dresser drawer, but the thirty-thousand dollar deposit made to Mac's checking account continued to prick at me. Daniel was right. Maybe the bank made one deposit error last month, but the chances of them making the same error twice were pretty slim. There had to be a logical explanation. Maybe Mac had stocks or other investments that he liquidated. But, if that were so, wouldn't he tell Daniel?

Finally, about ten o'clock, I threw on some clothes, grabbed my purse, and headed for the newsstand in the hotel lobby. Why didn't I bring a book to read? Remembering the reason was that our trip to St. Simons Island was meant for a wedding and honeymoon didn't make me smile. Our lives would be forever altered by Mac's death---divided from now on by the before and after of the day he died. Yet, being so far from North Carolina, I felt I couldn't grasp the true shape or size of what had happened. I needed to be there.

At this time of night, the hotel newsstand was deserted except for the college aged sales person who looked as though she was anxious to close the shop and join friends in the village for a cold beer. She tidied items in the glass case by her register while I perused the one revolving rack of paperbacks and picked out an Ellen Hart mystery I didn't think I'd read.

As I scanned the back cover for a clue to the plot, I heard a tap, silence, tap, silence, tap, crossing the tile floor of the lobby. I looked up to see Betty Wu---her dog-head cane in hand--- walking slowly but purposefully toward the front of the hotel. She was wearing the raincoat with the bulging pocket again. I replaced the book in the rack and walked out into the lobby. Betty exited the brass and glass double doors to the covered entrance and turned right into the parking lot. I stepped outside and watched from behind a potted sago palm while Betty got into her Cadillac and started the engine.

For no good reason, I hurried to where Susan's Jeep was parked, jumped inside, started it, and watched the rear view mirror for Betty Wu's Cadillac to move under the security lights of the parking lot and drive past me. She turned left out of the parking lot toward the village and I followed. Visiting hours at the hospital were over at nine, so she wasn't out to check on Aileen. Maybe she was going over to the grocery store for antacids or aspirin for a headache. When she continued on through the village and didn't double back to the shopping center, I knew she was up to something else. I kept my distance and followed her off the island. She took a left at the main highway intersection, and I knew she was going over to Jekyll Island.

Even on the well-lighted highway, I lost sight of the Cadillac in the traffic and didn't spot her again until we both slowed down in the line of cars passing through the visitors checkpoint onto the island. There were two cars between us as we were waved through. All of us made the same turns until the two in front of me veered right into a residential neighborhood. I dropped my speed back hoping Betty wouldn't recognize me behind her. She drove through the historical district, slowed down by the millionaire's cottages, and then pulled out onto the main drag again, driving the speed limit up Riverview Drive. After we passed the pier, I realized she was circling the island. Was she only out for an evening drive and would head back to St. Simons?

When she made a turn for the second time on the road leading to the historical district, it occurred to me that her destination was the ruined Sparrow Cottage, sitting apart from the other restored homes at the end of the district. I figured she hadn't stopped earlier because she'd seen my headlights in her rear view mirror and was waiting for me to turn off at my destination. I made a quick turn onto a neighborhood street, pulled into the first driveway that looked like it belonged to an empty house, and cut my lights. I'd give her time to get to Sparrow, then double back over there and see what she was up to.

After counting to a hundred, I backed out of the drive and traced what I hoped was Betty's route. There were no other cars on the road when I reached the historical district, so I cut off my headlights and navigated at a snail's pace down the two-lane asphalt strip. Betty's shiny champagne colored Cadillac was easy to spot where she'd pulled off the road nearly behind Sparrow. All the other cottages were dark, closed up for the night. The nearest lights shone from the hotel off in the distance. About a hundred yards from the cottage, I backed into an oak grove on the opposite side of the road and killed the Jeep's engine.

Under a low hanging moon filtered to a dull glow by Spanish moss, I watched the cottage for Betty. No lights burned inside, no ghostly shadows moved across the tall front windows. My mind went down a list of possible reasons for Betty Wu to be wandering around in the dark at Sparrow Cottage. The most logical one was that she felt a need to visit the house where she'd spent so many years, so long ago. But if that were true, why come at night?

Something to my right stomped in the dry leaves. Three young does, spooked by something I couldn't see, bolted from behind the trees and sprinted across the road, their hooves making clomping sounds as they ran.

They moved to the left of Sparrow, plucking leaves from head-high bushes, methodically nibbling as they foraged farther into the darkness of the side yard.

I had no idea how long I'd been sitting in the Jeep, but pretty soon I came to the conclusion that whatever Betty's reason was for being in the abandoned, dark cottage, it wasn't good enough. A woman over eighty years old had no business being where snakes and alligators were fond of taking up residence when humans moved out. I'd better go check on her.

As I rummaged in my purse for the penlight I thought was somewhere at the bottom of the mess, I caught movement out of the corner of my eye, to the right of Sparrow near Betty's car. Oh good, I thought, she's leaving. But it wasn't Betty. The figure was tall, lean, wore a dark sailor's cap, and moved along against the cover of Sparrow's tabby walls. I decided to forget the penlight and call 911. Except, since I'd intended to make a quick trip downstairs to the newsstand for a book---not skulk around Jekyll Island---I'd left my cell phone in the hotel room.

That's why I found myself getting out of the Jeep, fast walking across the road, and following the figure as he turned the corner of the house and dropped out of sight. I kept to the same route as the figure and worked my way to the rear corner of Sparrow where I stopped and peeked around the side.

The man wearing the sailor's cap had his hands in the air. Betty faced him, and stood beside the antique carved chair that Aileen would donate to the Sparrow Cottage restoration project. An anemic start of a fire flickered on the ground under the seat of the chair and then gave up with little fanfare. Did Betty have grass-covered shoes this morning because she'd been at Sparrow looking for the chair? Had she made plans this morning to come back tonight and set fire to it?

My mind went back to the man with his hands in the air and I noticed the gun Betty pointed was aimed roughly at his midsection.

He laughed a low smug laugh. "Well, well. It is you. I thought that was you today. That cane of yours packs a mighty whack, old woman."

"Don't call me old woman. You almost as old as me."

"Not true. You've got ten years on me, at least. So, now that we are here, enjoying our little reunion, what're you going to do? Shoot me? Go ahead. I don't think you can do it."

"What you doing here anyway? I thought you dead long time ago."

"Crashed in the middle of the godforsaken jungle. Missing for a long time, but not dead."

"I should shoot you dead for hurting my daughter. Like Mena's Bible say, 'an eye for an eye.' Why you want to hurt my daughter?"

"I didn't know that foolish TV woman was your daughter until today. Why do you want to burn up Mena's chair?"

"Chair has curse on it. You know that. Bring only bad times. When chair is gone, curse is gone. You tell me now why you want to hurt my Aileen? Then maybe I won't shoot you."

He laughed again and let his hands drop.

"Hands up so I can see what you do."

"Okay, okay." He raised his hands again. "But I still don't think you have the guts to shoot me outright. Not unless I turn my back. I know you---remember."

"Ha. You fine fish to talk. So what Aileen ever do to you that you want to kill her?"

"It's not so much what she did, as what she can do. It's nothing personal, just business. Anyway, I wouldn't think you'd want your daughter resurrecting Sparrow memories any more than I would."

Headlights cut the darkness beside Betty and the man. Someone had pulled into Sparrow's driveway. I looked over at the approaching lights. When I looked back, the man was gone; Betty no longer held the gun---maybe it was back in her raincoat pocket. She took off walking toward her car.

I heard a female voice call out, "Georgia State Patrol. Stop where you are."

I leaned around the corner a bit more and saw Olean Hopper gaining on Betty Wu. Olean called out, "Ma'am, I said stop. You'd best do what I say."

Betty stopped and turned to face Hopper.

When Olean Hopper asked Betty for her driver's license and quizzed her about what she was doing on Sparrow property, I could have stepped out of my hiding place and told her about Betty and the burning chair. Perhaps I should have. And perhaps I should have said something about the tall man whom I believed to be the man Betty had beaten with her cane earlier in Aileen's hospital room.

And maybe I should have mentioned the gun in Betty's raincoat pocket. But for all I knew, maybe she had a permit for carrying the gun. Whatever the case, there was no doubt in my mind that I would be the one who sounded a tad unbalanced when Betty denied a man being there. And I was sure that she would do just that. Then there was the matter of why I was sneaking around in the dark, hiding in the shadows. How would I explain that?

I stayed hidden until Hopper had instructed Betty Wu to follow her to the highway patrol office and both vehicles eased out onto the road. As I watched their taillights recede into the distance, fear crawled up my scalp. Was I alone? Where was the tall man?

I heard a voice in my head saying: *Bad idea to stay here. Run for the Jeep. Run. Just do it.* For once, the committee in my head was giving sound advice.

CHAPTER TWENTY-TWO

S aturday morning breakfast at The King and Prince was a mouthwatering buffet of Georgia shrimp and grits, crab puffs, fluffy pancakes, stacks of bacon, crisp little sausage links, fresh fruit, eggs prepared four different ways, plain grits, biscuits, a two foot tall pyramid of cinnamon sweet goodies, and--- I don't know what all else. I couldn't make up my mind where to start, so I poured myself a cup of coffee, laced it with cream, and sat down at a table for two.

No surprise that after last night's adventure of playing detective over on Jekyll, I hadn't slept well---too much going on in my head. From what I'd overheard between Betty Wu and the tall man, it would seem he was the person who'd shot

Aileen, and Betty knew him---or used to know him. I wondered: does Aileen know the guy? Is he from Atlanta?

I should have stepped out when Olean Hopper showed up, told her what I'd seen. Though, for some reason, I was still certain Betty Wu would deny everything. Still I should have said something. Finally, my guilt got me out of bed at six thirty and I called RB Barnes. Not that I wanted to talk to him, but since he was officially in charge of the investigation, I figured he needed to know. His cell rolled over to voice mail and I left a message.

Now, I sat drinking my coffee and going over what I'd learned from Betty's conversation with the man---other than the fact that she knew him and looked serious about shooting him. He said he didn't know Aileen was her daughter until he saw Betty at the hospital, so he probably hadn't seen Betty in a long time, hadn't kept up with her married name, and didn't know she even had a daughter.

One thing was certain: the man seemed to be afraid Aileen would uncover something that would impact his business if she continued with the Sparrow restoration project. That's what he said--- *Nothing personal, just business.* What kind of business would be worth killing for? I shook my head and chided myself for asking such a dumb question.

Maybe when RB returned my call he'd have some answers. After all, I could be wrong; Betty Wu might have told Olean Hopper about the man. Surely she would want her daughter's attacker caught? But RB might not call back for hours. I dialed Garland's cell number. He might know something.

"Good morning, Mrs. Allen."

For a second I didn't connect who Mrs. Allen was. Daniel and I hadn't discussed the question of me using his name or keeping McNeal. Or should I use both names? I must have hesitated a little too long because Garland added, "That's you, Promise. Remember?"

"Well yes, of course I remember. How could a person forget getting married?"

"Oh that's easy. I think Aileen forgets on a regular basis."

I probably didn't want to go there with Garland. "How is Aileen this morning?"

"She's improving, doing great actually. Better than I am."

"Why is that? Are you coming down with something?"

"Yeah, a terminal case of the Betty Wu disease. That Georgia trooper we met over at Sparrow the other day got me out of bed at midnight to come over to Jekyll and bail Betty out of her latest craziness."

"You mean Mrs. Wu was in jail?"

"No, no, it didn't come to that. It seems Betty was lurking around Sparrow Cottage last night trying to start a fire. Olean Hopper just happened to be out patrolling and caught her red handed---pardon the bad pun. She didn't arrest Betty for trespassing because she's bright enough to know that Aileen's little foundation owns the cottage, and she probably wouldn't want her mother locked up. Better to call me in the middle of the night and haul me over there to explain why Betty would be trying to set fire to that damn chair she thinks is cursed."

"Oh, I see," I replied, and of course, I did see because I was there. "So no harm was done? Nothing else happened and Hopper released Betty?" I was fishing to find out if Betty Wu had volunteered any information about the tall man.

"Yeah, after I got there and confirmed she wasn't really trespassing---not technically anyway---Hopper let Betty leave. She did give her a stern lecture about starting an unpermitted fire on the island, but I'm sure that warning bounced right off Mrs. Wu's hard head. And I haven't told Aileen about her mother's late night escapade---in case you are wondering. Though who knows? When Aileen finds out she may only laugh and include Betty's fixation about the chair in her book. Might make for scintillating copy."

"Book? What book?"

Garland groaned. "Oh, Aileen has some nutty notion that if she writes a book about the history of Sparrow Cottage---you know, the life and times of Jekyll and all that---the money to restore the old place will come pouring in. While we were talking about something totally different last night, writing the book suddenly came back to her, and she rattled on about the idea as though I knew all about it---which I didn't. Never heard anything about a book on Sparrow until last night. Course you know Aileen, she won't actually write the book; she'll get someone else to do the hard part after she brags awhile about coming up with the brilliant idea."

Ah, how interesting. That might explain why Aileen sent Barkley a memo about me researching Garr Lemley. She must be thinking about using the Lemley killing in the book. "Garland, who else knows about the book idea?"

"I have no clue. Well, actually I do have a clue. Aileen said she announced the book at the cocktail party the other night. You know how big she is on promotional, pre-show marketing---better known as TV hype."

"Hmm." My mind was whirling. So, Aileen announced a forthcoming book at the party. Perhaps the tall man was there and decided a book about Sparrow would…would what? What could Aileen possibly find out about an old, dilapidated house that would threaten his business? Who was this guy anyway? "So, anything else from Betty since the chair incident?"

"Not yet, but it's only eight thirty in the morning, Promise. Give the old bat a couple of hours to wake up and start making trouble. I tell you though, seriously, her superstition about this chair being cursed needs to stop. You are a psychologist. Can't you talk to Betty? Maybe if she talks to someone about it…"

Garland's remark reminded me that Betty had talked to someone---our own Reverend Sam Quinn. Was she talking to Sam about the cursed chair? No, I didn't think so. Betty had told the story of the cursed chair to anyone willing to listen. Her topic had to be more private than the chair for Sam to insist the conversation was privileged information.

"You know I can't force myself on Betty. If she wants to talk, I'll listen." All the while I was giving Garland my little professionalism speech, my mind was reaching for ideas to get Betty to fess up about the tall man. Not very professional, but hey, I wasn't wearing my counselor's hat at the moment.

Three slices of bacon, two poached eggs with hollandaise sauce, and a cinnamon bun later, I waved to Susan as she walked into the restaurant. Her dark curly hair was freshly spiked with mousse. She wore white jeans and a black and white nautical print shirt---very beach looking--- and she was smiling. That was good. The relaxing evening out with new friends must have been just what she needed. She helped herself to a cup of coffee from the buffet bar and sat down across from me.

"Hey. You look cheerful this morning. Where's Sam?"

Susan frowned. "Sam went back to bed. Said she felt like she was catching a cold, or allergies, or something."

"Oh, I'm sorry. Nothing serious I hope."

"No, I don't think so. She'll probably rebound with a couple of hours extra sleep."

"Guess you came over to get your Jeep? Hey, how did you get down here from the village?"

"I walked--- gave me time to think. Sam and I had a long talk last night after we got back to the Inn."

Waiting for the long version of the story, I only replied, "Hmm."

"You have your counselor face on. Don't do that."

I tried to change my expression but probably failed. I'm sorry, but I have one of those generic, neutral faces even when I try to smile and show I'm happy. "Is this talk something you want to share?" I ventured.

Susan offered a shy smile. "Well, duh. Why else would I bring it up?"

I set my coffee cup down in the saucer and prepared myself. Why did I have the strong feeling that I was about to get a clue as to why Susan turned down every male in Perry County who pursued her?

"It all boils down to three things. The first is I've been acting jealous and bitchy and I need to stop it. That's not me and *I* don't even like that person. The second is that I've been trying like crazy to push Sam into a relationship that she isn't ready for right now---or may never be ready for---and I need to back off before I run her off. I know I'm in love with Sam, but I have to accept the possibility that she doesn't feel the same about me. That old song, *I Can't Make You Love Me*, is spot on."

I was thinking that must have been some talk they had last night. I was also amazed that Susan was sounding so mature about the whole thing. Geez, when I was her age I would have probably...well, I don't know what I would have probably done. I was married to RB Barnes when I was her age, and obsessing about ways to make myself more attractive to him so he wouldn't run around on me. Lord, was I stupid, or what? Well, maybe not stupid, but certainly immature, and unaware that I had absolutely no control over what RB Barnes decided to do. His infidelity was not about me at all. I think it took a divorce, counseling, and several psychology courses for me to wake up to myself. Yes, Susan's maturity at her age was light years ahead of mine.

"So, what are you going to do?" I asked.

"Well, Sam will keep on being Sam. I realize she's dedicated to being a good minister right now, and her job might be even more difficult if she came out in a relationship with me. As for me, I'll wait. I can be a very patient person if the stakes are high enough. I'm determined to accept her love as friendship for now, and not have any other expectations. No selfish expectations; that's the hard part."

Oh, my Lord, wasn't that the truth? Giving up expectations *is* the hard part. I wasn't sure about Susan, but I knew I wasn't evolved enough to give up expecting what I needed from those I loved.

"You've set yourself a high bar."

"I know. That's one reason I'm telling you this. I'm counting on you to help me stay the course. Give me the Allen eye roll if I get out of line."

I wondered how long Susan would tolerate me as her conscience. I figured about the third time I gave my opinion, she'd tell me to butt out. I smiled and could almost hear her telling me to mind my own business, and that was okay. Susan was certainly old enough to make her own decisions.

I said something encouraging like, "Okay. I'll do whatever I can to help. I'm proud of you for being patient with Sam." Then I remembered she'd said three things. She'd only mentioned two. 'What's the third thing?"

She fidgeted in her chair and put both hands, palms down, on the table. I'd seen Daniel do that. It usually meant I was about to hear something I wouldn't like.

"I can't mind what Daddy told us to do. I can't hang around down here at the beach when I know Daddy is looking for whoever killed Cousin Mac. I have to be there to stand beside him, no matter what. I came over to tell you that Sam and I are leaving tomorrow morning."

"Even though your dad told us to stay put until he feels we aren't in danger?"

Susan looked down at the white tablecloth and released a long sigh. "Yes, ma'am. Even though." She met my eyes again. "But look, I'm not telling you what to do. You do what you feel is right. I won't blame you either way. I just wanted to tell you my plans this morning so we could find you a rental car. Since Daddy's got your Subaru and I'll take my Jeep, I don't want to leave you stranded."

Stranded? The word had a particular finality to it, as though once you were there, returning would be nearly impossible. Was I stranded without Daniel?

My eyes drifted to the bay window and then to the morning sky beyond, an azure blue riding so low on the horizon that it appeared to be a seamless quilt spread atop the ocean. What was it my mother said about the ocean? "It's the constancy of it, Promise, that reminds us of who we are meant to be."

Or did I read that somewhere?

Susan touched my arm. "Did you hear me?"

"Yes. What time are you leaving?"

"About eight."

"I'll be ready."

"You'll be ready?"

"That's what I said, yes."

By the smirk on Susan's face, I'd swear she knew I wouldn't be left behind. "Okay. Cool. So tell me what you did yesterday after Sam and I took off for the village?"

I didn't know where to start. About halfway into my recounting, Susan said she couldn't absorb so much information on an empty stomach and left me to pile a plate high with pancakes and sausage from the buffet table.

My cell phone rang. The number was local, unknown to me. When I answered, a cheerful, male voice said, "Good morning. Sid Balfour here. Dr. McNeal?"

"Yes."

"I have information on the person you asked about. Are you on St. Simons this morning?"

"Yes, I'm at The King and Prince. Would you like to come over?"

There was a pause and then Mr. Balfour suggested, "I live on St. Simons, not far from The King and Prince, but how about we meet at Massengale Park? Do you know the park?"

"Yes, I do."

"Good. In about thirty minutes? Can you do that?"

Sure, I could do that. I'd had my salad supper at Massengale Park the night before. I confirmed we'd meet him there and hung up.

Susan was seriously into her stack of pancakes. "What's up?" she asked.

"That was the man from the Jekyll Museum---the retired newspaper reporter I told you about. He says he has information about Garr Lemley."

"Lemley is the fisherman who was killed back in the early 1950s?"

"Right. You really were listening."

She drew a long sip of coffee. "I always listen, Ms. P. You'd be surprised at how much I retain."

No, I probably wouldn't be surprised. Susan's mind catalogs information like the public library. You want to know who was our fourth president? Ask Susan. You want to know what year Harry Houdini died and what was the cause of death? Ask Susan.

We agreed to meet Sid Balfour together, and I headed for the cashier to pay our bill.

CHAPTER TWENTY-THREE

When Susan and I arrived at the park, Sid Balfour was sitting on one of the concrete picnic tables. His long legs dangled over the edge and his arms were folded over his chest like a bearded potentate. He smiled as we approached and hopped down to shake my hand. As I was introducing Susan to him, I felt, rather than heard, someone walk up behind us. When I turned, Olean Hopper, out of uniform in khaki shorts and a tucked in, green Polo shirt, stood with her hands on her chunky hips. She was not smiling. This could not be a coincidence.

"I thought I'd join y'all. You don't mind, do you Dr. McNeal?"

Sid looked a little sheepish. "Olean is my sister Frederica's littlest one."

Susan's raised eyebrow told me she was wondering just how big the other Hopper children were, if Olean was the little one.

"I called Olean with a couple of questions about this Garr Lemley business, and well…she'll have her say, I'm sure, about why she wanted to come with me."

Susan reminded Olean they had met at Sparrow and Sid suggested we sit at the picnic table so he could show us what he'd found. Susan and I sat together on one of the benches. He and Hopper sat opposite us.

The first piece of paper Sid slid across the table was a copy of a November 1951 Brunswick News article about Lemley being shot. Before I had time to finish reading the piece, Olean Hopper said, "Look Sid, I know you've got a pile information in that file and some copies to give Dr. McNeal, but why don't you cut to the chase and give us the highlights. Then I'll clean up what I need to ask Dr. McNeal and be on my way."

Sid smiled. "Cause it's your day off and you want to make your eleven o'clock tennis match."

Olean ruffled. "Well, hell yeah. What's wrong with that?"

Sid threw back his head and laughed. I had the feeling that teasing his niece was one of his favorite sports. "Stand down, trooper. No harm meant."

"Sure, Sid. Just get on with it. Okay?"

Sid straightened his back and began. "The News reports Garr Lemley died of gunshot wounds at Jekyll the day before the article ran. His body was found by a woman walking on the beach---only referred to in the article as a colored female resident of the island. According to the reporter, Glynn County Sheriff's Department responded. They suspected foul play and the Georgia State Patrol was called in to investigate."

Susan asked, "What made them think it wasn't an accident? Maybe some hunter mistook Lemley for a deer."

"Good question. I wondered the same thing. That's why I called Olean and asked her to look in the State Patrol files to see if there was a report."

"He means he called me at seven this morning, on my day off, and begged me to go to the office and look up the case. "

"Which she was kind enough to do. There was, indeed, an old file on the case. Olean, tell them what it said."

"Not a whole lot really. Lemley was shot twice in the back. Not likely a hunter would hit the mark twice by mistake. No suspects. One lead, it seems by the reporting officer's notes. At the time, there was a convict camp of twelve men working on the island digging drainage ditches, repairing roads, and doing other site work. The officer investigated all twelve and cleared each man. No weapon was found. I guess one of the bulls could have shot him..."

"Bulls?" I asked.

Sid answered my question. "A bull is a deputy, a guard who oversees the convicts while they work."

"Doesn't sound like a camp counselor kind of person?" I replied.

Olean frowned. "No, bulls don't say please and thank you, and one or two psychos were known to work as bulls in the prison system in the old days. It could be Lemley pissed off one of them. But if so, there is nothing in the report about the officer believing the killer worked for the prison system. As near as I can tell, the Lemley case simply reached a dead end and went unsolved."

Susan held up the copy of the newspaper article. "Who was this Garr Lemley guy anyway? This says he was a local fisherman and boat captain. Did he live on the island?"

Sid shuffled through his file folder for answers. "Well, here is what we know. He lived in a tenant house down the road from the old hotel. There used to be three employee houses down there back in the day, mostly used for maids and cooks at the hotel. They are all gone now. Razed in the 1960s rather than be repaired. We know this because I have the Jekyll Island employee records from that time. Got them when I was working on my Jekyll history book. Looks like Lemley moved into one of the houses during the war---around 1943. He's listed as an employee of the Jekyll Island Club as a captain for the island steamer, general handyman, and caretaker for several cottages."

"Anything else? Like family or where he came from?" I asked.

Sid shook his head. "Not many personal details. Except, I cross-referenced him through the Brunswick News back files and the guy was pretty much plagued by trouble and bad luck."

"How's that?" Susan asked.

"In '47, I think it was, Lemley was arrested for assaulting a young woman in Brunswick--- a euphemism in those days for rape. The charges were dropped because both had been drinking at a local bar earlier in the evening. After that, another woman came forward and said Lemley had assaulted her on another occasion. Again, charges were dropped. He was arrested later that year for poaching turtle eggs on the island and paid a healthy fine. I didn't see any other arrests.

"There was one really sad mention of Lemley though. In August 1948 a short piece ran in the News about a nine-year-old boy drowning on the seaward side of Jekyll. Apparently, he fell overboard while fishing with his stepfather, one Garr Lemley. The article said the boy 'suffered from mongolism' and that his mother had died recently from yellow fever."

Susan nearly screeched out the word, "Mongolism? Is that what you said?"

"I'm afraid so," Sid replied. "That was the accepted term for Downs Syndrome back in the 1940s"

"That's terrible," Susan replied. No one disagreed with her.

"Did you say the boy was Lemley's stepson? What was the child's name?" I asked.

Sid looked down at his notes and thumbed through the papers in his file. "You know it's odd, but I don't have the name. I'm thinking the paper probably didn't print the boy's name because he was a minor. There was one other thing though. The article said a brother survived the boy who drowned. No name given for the brother either. Probably because the brother was also a minor."

I nodded my understanding. "And Betty Wu was on the island in 1947, and 1948. Garland mentioned the other day that she didn't leave until Mena Simpson died around 1952. That puts her also on the island when Lemley was killed. At the very least, she had to know about the boy falling overboard and about Lemley being shot. Sid, were there a lot of people living on Jekyll during that time?"

Sid shook his head no. "Hardly anyone. The rich, winter folks stopped coming to Jekyll Island before the war, and when the State of Georgia bought the island in 1947, there probably weren't a dozen permanent residents. The owner of Sparrow Cottage, Mena Simpson, and her staff, being some of those residents."

"So those who had the opportunity to kill Lemley were few."

Sid shook his head again. "Don't know that. Boats could run back and forth from Brunswick anytime. And you heard what Olean said about the prison camp."

Susan added, "Then set aside opportunity. Who had a motive for killing Lemley?"

"Hmmm. Good question," I said. "From what Sid found out, Garr Lemley wasn't exactly a stellar citizen."

"No," Susan added, "sounds like the kind of guy Fletcher Enloe would say *needed killing*."

Olean Hopper stood up and replaced her hands on her hips. "All right. Enough. So what does all this mean, Dr. McNeal? Why are you and the TV woman interested in Garr Lemley? And does this have anything to do with who shot Mrs. Wang? Because you know that's my interest in the matter. I'd really like to solve this issue locally. You know what I mean?"

Yes, I knew what Hopper meant. She'd already told me finding the shooter before RB Barnes did would make her day. And maybe net her a promotion?

"But that aside, I want you to think about your answers to my questions before you speak. Because I'm telling you in advance, I saw your Jeep parked across the street from Sparrow last night when I found Mrs. Wang's mother over there. Also, the vehicle was gone by the time I finished with the old broad and drove back to check. That was you, wasn't it?"

Now how would Hopper know that? She was bluffing. The Jeep was registered to Susan and not me. Still, I thought it best to own up to being there. "Yes. I followed Betty Wu over there from the hotel."

"You followed her?" Hopper sat back down. She must have realized she was in for a long story.

"Yes. I know it doesn't make any sense. But after what happened at the hospital yesterday and the way Betty acted when I mentioned Garr Lemley's name…by the way, did someone from Glynn County Sheriff's Department tell you about the man in Aileen's hospital room yesterday?"

Olean Hopper grimaced. "Of course they did. This is a small community. We talk to each other, and we keep up with each other's business. But I don't know what you mean about the way Mrs. Wu acted when you mentioned Lemley."

I replayed the short conversation I'd had with Aileen and Mrs. Wu about Garr Lemley. Hopper then said, "Okay, so I see why you're interested in Lemley. But don't you think it's a far stretch to think a killing from sixty years ago is connected to Mrs. Wang being shot?"

Now I was going to have to come clean about the tall man I'd seen with Betty last night. Otherwise, how could I clue Hopper in on the fact that Betty seemed to know the man who'd shot Aileen?

"Oh, before I answer that, there's something interesting I learned this morning. Aileen has put out the word that she's writing a book about the history of Sparrow Cottage and the life and times of Jekyll Island. Even though Aileen now says she doesn't remember why she was interested in Lemley, I think the book is the reason. She announced the book at the cocktail party, so I'm thinking someone doesn't want her to find out something that happened around Sparrow."

Olean Hopper groaned. "Another long stretch. Still doesn't link Lemley to Mrs. Wang being shot."

Susan held up her hand like a school crossing guard. "Wait, hang on, let her finish. There's more."

Sid Balfour, who'd been quiet until now, interjected, "Wow, I wish I had my tape recorder. This is starting to get interesting."

"Hush, Uncle Sid. This is serious police business."

"Well, of course it is, honey. I know that, but…"

Hopper cut him off. "Okay. Get to the point Dr. McNeal; my tennis match is in fifteen minutes."

How to get to the point--- compress everything I'd heard between Betty and the tall man? Should I leave out Betty pointing a gun at him? No, I'd have to include that. Besides I'd heard something important in his exchange with Betty and her threat to shoot him. But what was it? He'd said something to Betty about knowing her---the rest of the sentence was hiding from me. I couldn't quite re-call it. Something about how he knew she wouldn't shoot him….

Hopper reached across the table and snapped her fingers in front of my face. "Hey, you still with us, Doc? I'm waiting on your answers here."

"I know. I was just thinking. Making a mental note of the high points so you won't miss your game."

What followed was a truncated version of what I saw and heard while hiding behind a dark corner of Sparrow Cottage. I did have the presence of mind to repeat what the man said about Aileen's actions impacting his business in some way. Though, honestly, as I repeated the conversa-tion, I had to admit that the man did not specifically say it was the Sparrow Project that could hurt his business.

"Just a second," I said, "let me make sure I'm getting this right. He didn't say the Sparrow Project would hurt him, not exactly, but he did say Aileen could hurt his business. And he told Betty Wu that he wouldn't think she would want old memories of Sparrow dug up any more than he would...or something to that effect."

"I ought to arrest you for obstruction of justice---you know that?"

"Well, I guess I do. But I really thought if I stepped out last night and told you, Betty would deny everything. And then she'd know I'd seen the guy, and maybe we would have a harder time finding him. She might even tell him I'd seen him."

Hopper dropped her head and groaned. "Lady, you watch way too much television. How about this version? You could have shown yourself last night, and then faced with your story, Mrs. Wu would have given us the guy's name."

"She wouldn't have done that. I know she's protecting him for some reason."

"You know that? Terrific. We have an old lady with a gun starting fires that could turn the whole island to cinders, and a sniper on the loose. Why does what you think you know not give me a warm and fuzzy feeling? What I know is that now I'll have to go find Mrs. Wu and question her about this mysterious tall man?"

"And you'll miss your tennis match," I said. "Sorry."

Still thinking like a newspaper reporter, Sid took a pad from his file folder and retrieved a pen from his shirt pocket. "Okay. Last night is water under the Sidney Lanier Bridge. Let's stop arguing and be productive. Dr. McNeal, recap what you saw last night for us. First, describe the man. What did he look like? I'll take notes."

CHAPTER TWENTY-FOUR

Satisfied that I'd given all the information I could re-member, Sid closed his pad with a promise to tran-scribe his notes and fax them over to Olean. Then, after a few short pleasantries, he declined a ride home from his niece, said goodbye, and struck out walking in the oppo-site direction from the village. For a big man, he looked light-footed as he strolled down the sidewalk skirting the salt marshes. I believe I heard him whistling *Oklahoma* as he walked.

Olean---still angry with me for being the cause of her cancelled tennis match ---did not say goodbye before she swaggered to her black, Ford Ranger truck and drove away. I took a deep breath as she disappeared down Ocean

Boulevard. Susan made a little whistling sound in my direction but made no comment about Trooper Hopper.

"Hey. Mr. Balfour seems like a nice guy," she observed.

"Yes, he does," I agreed.

"Do you think Olean Hopper's gone hunting for Mrs. Wu?"

"I guess. I'm not sure which dog I'd back in that fight. Betty Wu's a tough one."

Susan nodded her agreement and then stood up and stretched her arms up over her head, bending from side to side a couple of times. "Well, it's just that Trooper Hopper drove toward the village and Betty Wu is staying at the King and Prince. That's in the other direction."

I thought about that logistical issue for a moment. "True. I'm thinking Olean wants to change out of her tennis clothes and into her uniform. She probably wants to look official when she talks to Mrs. Wu."

"You're probably right. Good point. So, what do we do now?"

I stood up and walked around the table a couple of times. The concrete bench was making my butt go numb, and I needed to work the poor-night's-sleep kinks out of my back. "I don't know. Sid wrote down everything I could remember about the guy. Olean will talk to Betty. There isn't much else I know to do."

"Yeah, but from your description, the mysterious man looks like about a thousand other old guys on the Island. Not much for Olean to go on."

"True. Let's hope Olean gets a name from Betty Wu."

"Yes, a name would be helpful. Speaking of Betty Wu, I keep thinking about her purse sitting on the floor over at the Peterkin house. What was she doing over there? Do you suppose she killed the old ladies?"

"Hmmm. I can't imagine why Betty would do that. What possible reason could she have? Besides, I doubt she could have carried the unconscious sister out to the garage and rigged up a carbon monoxide fake suicide."

"You have a point. The sister had to be unconscious. The killer couldn't just tell her to sit still in the car and wait for the sound of a heavenly choir. I'm guessing whoever killed the sisters poisoned them first. But when one of the sisters didn't croak, the killer did a little fast thinking and came up with the fake suicide idea."

A white, First Methodist Church van pulled into the parking lot and unloaded a dozen or so preschoolers and chaperones. When the little people descended on the playground equipment, pushing, shoving, and whooping with joy, Susan and I walked away from the picnic table and meandered down the path to the beach.

I agreed with Susan about the Peterkin sisters. "I think you're right. Toxicology tests will probably show some sort of heavy-duty narcotic present in their bodies. But you know, another reason I don't think Betty Wu killed them is that the carbon monoxide idea feels like a man thing to me. It's something a *Popular Mechanics* kind of guy would think of, not an elderly Atlanta widow in a Chanel suit."

"That leaves us with the tall, older guy. Maybe the Peterkin sisters knew what he was afraid Aileen would discover, if she kept poking around Sparrow's history."

Now that we'd left the shady oaks of the park behind, a blinding glare of late morning sun burned almost directly overhead. So unlike our mountains where sun is more often filtered through a lush canopy of leaves. I paused for a few seconds, searching for my sunglasses in my purse. "Maybe. That takes us back to the original question. Why was Betty Wu at the Peterkin house?"

We stepped from the pathway onto a boardwalk spanning low shrubs hunkered down on the sand dune separating the park from the beach. I stopped to think about my question and leaned against the wood railing. Here and there, a vine bloomed red amid the shrubs, using the foliage as green ladders to reach the light. Susan walked on, then doubled back to stand beside me.

"What? What are you thinking?" she asked.

"Well, here's the thing: I don't believe Betty was over there to find out what secrets the Peterkin sisters knew about Sparrow because she already knows the secrets. Why would she make a trip to Brunswick to ask about something she already knows? No. She must have been looking for new information---maybe about the guy she *suspected* had shot her daughter. Maybe she wasn't sure about him when she drove over to see the sisters.

"I say that because remember, Betty was at the Peterkin house before the guy showed himself at the hospital and before he followed Betty to Sparrow last night. *Now* Betty knows the name of the man who shot Aileen, but maybe when she called on the Peterkin sisters she wasn't sure of his identity."

Susan tilted her head back and closed her eyes. "Ms. P, that is so totally confusing. What exactly are you saying?"

Since I was thinking out loud, I had to hesitate a couple of beats for my brain to catch up with my mouth. "Okay. Here is what I think: Betty went over there because she suspected the Peterkin sisters had seen this tall, older guy and recognized him from a long time ago. Remember, I said that Betty told the guy she'd thought he had died a long time ago. And he said that Aileen could harm his business if she kept digging up Sparrow's past. And he also said something to Betty about being ten years younger than her. Did I mention that to Sid Balfour?"

Susan shook her head. "I don't think so, but why does that matter?"

"I'm not sure, but I think it does matter. Their whole conversation last night sounded like two people who haven't seen one another for many, many years. And if they go back to the Sparrow years, the guy would have been a teenager when Betty was about twenty-six or twenty-seven. She couldn't have been any older than that because she left Jekyll Island in the early 1950s."

"Okay. I think I understand your timeline. We know her approximate age now so we do the math and subtract the years. But why would the Peterkin sisters have seen the older guy? They don't live on Jekyll Island."

"The question is: *when* could the sisters have seen him?"

Susan stepped back, raised her arms in the air, and nearly shouted, "Aileen's cocktail party."

"Exactly. The Peterkin sisters crashed Aileen's cocktail party. Sid Balfour told me that the sisters quizzed his friend from the Chamber of Commerce about a man at the party that neither he or his friend knew personally. The sisters must have thought they recognized the man at the party but weren't sure. So, they started asking around about him."

"Yeah, but Betty Wu didn't know all that. She didn't talk to Sid Balfour."

That fact almost set my brain falling back to square one until something else dawned on me. "Hang on a second." I rummaged in my purse for my cell phone and said a silent prayer that I had service. "I'm calling Garland." The phone rang several times before he answered. "Garland?"

"Yes, who else. I hope you are on my clock today looking for the bastard that shot my wife because Barnes isn't coming back until tomorrow late and, not withstanding the Glynn County Sheriff's deputy still stationed outside her room, Aileen is driving me crazy to leave. She wants to check out of the hospital. I keep asking her what part of *some nut is trying to kill you* don't you understand?"

I had to be rude and interrupt Garland. "I'm sorry, Garland. I know you've had a bad night and morning, but I need to ask you something."

"What?"

"When you got the guest list for the cocktail party from Barkley, did Betty Wu look at the list of names? Did you show it to her maybe?"

"If you call Betty jerking the list out of my hand and telling me to be quiet while she found her reading glasses showing her the list, then the answer is yes."

"Did she mention she recognized any of the names? Knew any of the people?"

The phone was silent for a few seconds. Then Garland said, "No. At least I don't think she did. She did look at it for a long time. But I don't recall her saying anything about the names. Hell, I don't know. Why do you ask?"

How to explain such a long and convoluted reason for my asking? I opted to leave it alone until I could sort it all out. "Just one more thing: you told the story about the Peterkin sisters showing up at the party in front of Betty, right?"

"Yes, I probably did. Well yes, I know I did." Garland's voice reminded me of the tense whine you hear when a tuning fork is struck. "She was there when Barkley and I talked about them crashing the party. Did I do something wrong?"

"No. No. I'm not suggesting that. Is Mrs. Wu at the hospital this morning?"

"No. God has granted me at least one prayer. I guess after last night, Betty is sleeping in. We haven't heard from her this morning. Why are you asking me these questions, Promise?"

Though I wasn't sure Garland really wanted to know the answers, I felt the need to give him something for his questions. "Garland, do you trust me?"

After a long, rather protracted sigh he replied, "Promise, you are about the only person I do trust in this bizarre situation."

"Good. Then know that Susan and I are trying to figure out what happened. So are Olean Hopper and Barnes. Just hang on a little while longer. And promise Aileen anything to keep her in that hospital room with the guard posted at the door. Okay?"

"Okay." Now Garland sounded pitiful.

I felt like a heel hanging up on Garland when he sounded so distraught, but I wanted to look at the party list in my purse. "I'll call you later. Bye now."

"Betty Wu saw the party list?" Susan asked.

"She sure did." I found the list, and we turned our backs to the ever-present wind stirring up sand along the Georgia shore while I flattened the sheet of paper against the railing of the boardwalk. Somewhere on that list had to be a name Betty Wu thought she recognized---a name she wanted to confirm with the Peterkin sisters.

Susan leaned over my shoulder. "Any idea who we're looking for Ms. P?"

"No, but it has to be a name from Betty Wu's time on Jekyll Island---some name that Sid Balfour wasn't familiar with, but that his friend gave the Peterkin sisters when they asked about the man in the summer tuxedo. I'm guessing the person that the sisters saw at the party was someone they'd known long ago but weren't sure was the same person. I'm also thinking the man has to be a newcomer to the island, or Sid would know him." I dialed Sid Balfour's cell number.

He answered on the second ring. "Balfour here."

"Hello again. It's Promise McNeal. Sorry to bother you but I'm looking at the guest list from Aileen Wang's cocktail party. Do you suppose you could call your friend with the Chamber of Commerce and have him take a look at the list, see if one of the names belongs to the man the Peterkin sisters asked about?"

Sid explained that his friend was on a cruise to the Virgin Islands so he couldn't pop over and have him look at the list.

"Well, could I read you the list of names, and you tell me whether you know any of the names or not? We could at least eliminate the names of the people you know."

"Sure. Go ahead."

Susan took my purse, found a ballpoint pen somewhere in the mess, and handed it to me. I read down the list and put an X beside any name Sid knew from either Jekyll or St. Simons Island. We could rule out these names as being our man because he'd already told us he didn't know the man at the party. Five names had no x.

I read the five names to Sid again---just in case I'd missed one he knew. After I thanked him and was about to hang up, he reminded me to call Olen if I found out anything about the remaining names on the list.

"This is serious business, Dr. McNeal. Don't wade so deep into the manure pit that you can't lift your feet back up on solid ground," he warned.

Good advice. I would try to remember it.

CHAPTER TWENTY-FIVE

S usan and I walked up the beach to The King and Prince. The plan was to pick up Sam, have a light lunch, and think about our next move. We had five names on the party list as possibilities. Maybe Betty Wu had recognized one of those names and gone over to the Peterkin sisters' house to confirm they'd seen the man matching that name. Maybe. If so, then one of the names could be our man. It was possible. Then there was always the possibility that Olean Hopper would have a come-to-Jesus meeting with Betty, and then Betty would give Olean the shooter's name. Mystery solved. Then our next move could be unfolding deck chairs on the beach so we could catch some Georgia sun.

The moment we reached the hotel parking lot, my cell phone played Bette Midler singing *I Want To Drive*. I had a voice mail. "Oh, good Lord, Susan. I don't know why you loaded that ring tone in my phone. I love Bette Midler, but come on. Those lyrics are so...so...well, I don't know, sexual for one thing and aggressive for another. It's just not me."

Susan smiled and said, "Uh huh."

We stopped beside Susan's Jeep for me to listen to the message. "This is RB. Got your message. I'm getting a chili dog at the Varsity and will have to call you later."

"Barnes can't talk to you and eat a hot dog at the same time? The man is even more limited than I first thought."

From Susan's tone of voice, RB Barnes had made a lasting, negative impression on her when he called her dad a cowboy. I could have told her that Daniel could care less what RB Barnes calls him, and that I knew from personal experience that staying angry with RB was a total waste of energy. Yes, the man is limited in his ability to empathize, to realize the world does not revolve around him and his desires, and, of course, in his ability to follow a monogamous path. The good news is that I am no longer married to him. Daniel is hands down the better choice of a husband. But to give the snake in paradise his due, RB Barnes is a good cop.

"No, no, that's code from back when we were married and he worked for the Atlanta PD. It means he's on a case, usually a stakeout or undercover, and can't talk. He'll call me when he gets off duty."

"Why'd you call him?"

"I called him early this morning to tell him about seeing Betty with the guy last night. Officially, the Aileen Wang thing is his case."

"Man oh man, you must feel really guilty for not stepping out last night and telling Trooper Hopper about the guy if you called your ex-husband."

I could not disagree.

When we knocked on Sam's door at the Village Inn, she was out of bed, dressed, and insisted she felt better. Susan pressed her open hand to Sam's forehead and declared she was no longer feverish. Sam looked a little peaked to me, and if she'd been my daughter, I'd have insisted she stay in bed. I noticed Sam's suitcase was open on the bed---her clothes neatly folded---ready for the trip home. I needed to pack, too, plus tell the hotel that I'd be checking out the next day.

What a strange trip this had been. A wedding where tragedy overshadowed the joy, the groom left two hours after the ceremony, and we'd hardly set foot on the beach. The thought of leaving the Georgia coast without my fill of the ocean really did make me sad, though with Daniel four hundred miles away and him dealing with the tragedy of Mac's death by himself, I didn't want to stay. Except, I did want to know who shot Aileen. It would be good to have a name for Aileen's attacker before we left.

Fifteen minutes later, Susan, Sam and I sat at a table on the porch at Gnat's Landing Restaurant. Susan and

I ordered fish and slaw sandwiches. Sam decided on the chowder, and while she munched on crackers from a basket on our table, Susan gave her the blow-by-blow account of our morning, as well as an abbreviated version of my encounter at Sparrow Cottage the night before.

At one point, Sam called time out from Susan's story and asked me a good question. "So this older guy---the one you saw at Sparrow who may be on the party list---does he have anything to do with the Garr Lemley person? I remember that yesterday you were all fired up to find out about him and who killed him."

"Yes, I was and still am, though we're kind of out of leads to follow up on what happened to him. Sid Balfour's information is interesting, but it doesn't tie him to the man I saw last night---at least not yet. The party list seems to be our best clue right now to lead us to Aileen's attacker. Maybe when we find him, we'll find out more about Lemley."

My mind replayed what Sid had told us about Garr Lemley. And it was true, I couldn't see any clue that would link Garr Lemley to anyone who would want to kill Aileen Wang, even though my gut told me there was a connection. One thing we did know: there were only a few residents on Jekyll Island when Lemley was killed. Surely Betty Wu knew the man. And what about his stepson---the boy who drowned? Did Betty know him? It would be so much easier if Betty Wu would talk to me, be honest about what she knew.

Then I remembered that Betty Wu had talked to Sam, had told Sam something she considered confidential. Sam wouldn't, or couldn't, tell us what Betty had told her. But was she asking about Garr Lemley for some reason other than curiosity?

Sam raised her forefinger in the air to make a point. "And another thing: what about the carved chair Betty Wu says is cursed? Garland Wang says the chair washed ashore during WWII. And now it's back because Aileen Wang wants to make it part of the Sparrow project. Does the chair have anything to do with Lemley or Aileen Wang being shot?"

I heard what Sam was saying and she brought up good points, though I was pretty sure she didn't hear Garland's conversation at the hospital about Betty and the cursed chair. Wasn't Sam outside with Betty Wu when Garland was telling that story? Had Sam gotten her information from Betty? I was about to ask Sam when my cell phone rang. I punched the little speaker icon so Susan and Sam could hear.

"Hello. This is Dr. McNeal."

"This is Hopper. I caught Mrs. Wu leaving the hotel for the hospital. Thought you'd like to know the old lady denied a man was with her at Sparrow last night. She tells me she knows nothing about who shot her daughter, except it was probably the man she beat with her cane at the hospital. Big Surprise. I finally told her you were there last night and saw her talking with a man---not a good idea in retrospect---but it's done now."

"And what did she say then?"

"She says you lie; you are 'a crazy lady.' She also allows that her son-in-law told her you read tarot cards like a gypsy, and sometimes dead people talk to you."

I'm a crazy lady? This from a person who believes an ancient curse on an ugly chair somehow caused her daughter's gunshot wound?

I grimaced and stole a quick glance at Sam Quinn, wondering what she thought about Hopper's comment. It was a relief to see Sam studying the overhead paddle fan, pretending she hadn't heard what Hopper said about me. Susan only shrugged and smiled. I resisted the urge to defend myself to Hopper, to say that Betty Wu was taking something Garland may have said out of context.

I mean, it isn't as though I hang out a shingle offering tarot readings for five dollars. It's a game I play sometimes to test the accuracy of the cards against life. It's surprising how often the cards mirror what's happening, but I certainly wouldn't say I read the cards as a substitute for critical thinking. I'm an educated person for God's sake. As for the spirits who sometimes people my dreams and walk Fire Mountain near my house, I don't try to explain what I don't understand.

"Did you hear what I said, Dr. McNeal?"

"Yes, I heard you. I just don't know how to respond. I saw what I saw. Betty Wu must have a compelling reason to protect this man, though I can't imagine why, since this person obviously shot her daughter. It doesn't make sense---not yet anyway."

"No. It doesn't. Regardless, the old broad isn't talking. Any ideas?"

I looked at Susan and Sam. Susan shrugged again and shook her head. Sam said nothing and now seemed to be intent on eating her clam chowder. "Not at the moment, but we're working on it."

"How comforting," Hopper replied. "Maybe you could whip out your tarot cards for some answers. Look, I called to tell you this because I screwed up and tipped Mrs. Wu off that you saw her last night. She's probably not going to be happy with you, so you might want to steer clear of her. I can't do anything else about the Wang shooting this afternoon. My boss called in all personnel to assist a DNR search on Jekyll for a cougar seen near the du Bignon Cemetery."

My heart skipped a beat. If a cougar were on Jekyll Island, I may have been in his sights yesterday when I stopped at the cemetery. "Has there been another report since the one you were investigating? I think you said two college kids might have seen the animal?"

"Yeah, there was a second one. Apparently, a man was in the area about daybreak today. He believes he heard the cat scream as he jogged past the cemetery. Then a couple of seconds later, he saw it cut out through the scrub palms and disappear behind the Horton House ruins. DNR has verified a footprint, so now we all go hunting."

"And then what?"

"Don't worry. Little kitty cat won't get hurt. It'll get zapped with a tranquilizer and relocated. I have to go. Keep the cat thing to yourself. Wouldn't be good for the tourist trade, you know?"

"Sure. Thanks for calling. Be careful."

"I'm always careful."

"Wait. Before you hang up---I talked to Sid Balfour again and he helped us narrow down the names on the party list to five possibilities for the shooter."

"That's if the shooter is even on the list. We don't know if he was even at the cocktail party."

"Well yes, that's true. But the list seems like a good lead. And it's our only lead right now. I think we should keep trying to match a name to the shooter."

"Fine. I'll talk to Sid when I get a break from kitty hunting. In the meantime, forge ahead. Get some answers. I really do want to solve this thing locally without that hotshot Barnes. And you owe me for last night, you hear?"

Olean Hopper hung up before I could answer. "Did y'all hear what Hopper said?"

Sam nodded and Susan said, "I heard. It's a good thing we're the only ones dumb enough to be eating outside in the heat, or half of St. Simons would have also heard."

Oh crap, I'd forgotten about the phone being on speaker.

CHAPTER TWENTY-SIX

Dainty, gray birds scoop up bread bits as fast as Betty Wu tosses them from her Ziploc baggie onto the ground. With each mouthful, a bird lifts off the ground with a winged flutter, crying out, "cheep-cheep."

"You foolish birds; nothing cheap in this world," Betty tells them from her seat on the Lutyen bench in the far corner of the Eugenia Price Memorial Garden of St. Simons Island's hospital.

Betty doesn't read historical novels; thus, she isn't aware of St. Simons Island's beloved author. And she could not have said that the comfortable, armed bench was made from a eucalyptus tree and named for an English architect. She does know that the scent of childhood in Taiwan rises from the wood of the bench, wafting up to her as she feeds the birds. This whisper of another time stills her bouncing thoughts. If only for a few moments, she is part of the chirping birds, part of the billowed white and red azaleas blooming throughout the garden like a cotillion of wide, starched skirts.

A calming scent of eucalyptus is something Betty Wu needs on this Saturday afternoon. Though Aileen is improving and suffered no permanent damage from the bullet, Betty worries that her daughter isn't safe---won't be safe until this akuryou, this evil spirit living in that chair is satisfied. What will it take this time to satisfy it? It will want a price for leaving---a price to go back to hell where it lives. But what price? Betty knows the price is hers to pay if she wants to stop the curse. She also knows that she must stop the man she saw last night at Sparrow.

"Ha," she says aloud to the birds. "That boy. He is my problem."

Shoes crushing tabby shell against stone cause her to look away from the birds before she sees him on the path. She turns back to the birds, ignoring him. He moves with no hurry to sit down beside her, silent, waiting. "Ha. There you are. I thought you smart enough to find me here," she says to him.

He crosses his legs and adjusts his sunglasses on the bridge of his nose. She half-smiles to think that maybe his nose is sore because she'd struck him there with her cane. "Well, you aren't doing a very good job of hiding," he replies.

His remark angers her and she huffs up, sitting straighter on the bench. "I don't hide from you. You think I'm afraid of you? Ha."

"You know Betty, you are wound way too tight. You always were. Relax. You and I are really on the same side here. We need to help each other, not fight."

"I sit here long time thinking about Pris and Paula Peterkin. Why you kill them? What they ever do to hurt you? You think you going to help me like you did those old sisters?"

He soothes down the crease in a pant leg before he replies, "Ah, Pris and Paula, two avaricious, old biddies. The chicken women you used to call them. Peck, peck, peck. Remember? No love lost there, eh? Their demise was an unfortunate necessity, but not one you and I need to discuss. You and I can work out our own goals in a far less violent way."

"Why you come back? What you want down here on Jekyll Island anyway?"

"What do I want?" He takes a cigar from the inside pocket of his blazer, lights it, and sucks in a deep draw before he answers. "I want Georgia's crude oil. That's what I want." The smoke rises up in front of Betty like little bee hives, floating skyward.

"Oil? Ha. Now you foolish like those birds. You think all these rich people on the islands will let you build big tall, ugly oil rigs on their green-grass golf courses?"

He uncrosses his legs and slaps his open hands on his knees. "You see? It's that kind of ignorance that I'm up against down here. These people don't understand the first thing about bringing up oil. No rigs on the island my dear lady---everything's so far out to sea the lazy golfers will never know we're there. Out of sight, out of mind. It should be an easy deal. But no, it can't be easy if the government is involved. And the government is involved. They decide who gets the oil leases. I've been working my ass off for two years to close the deal, and now I'm this close to being the first to capture oil off the Georgia coast." He holds up a forefinger against his thumb to show the smallest of margins.

Betty scatters the remainder of the bread scraps to the birds and stuffs the empty bag into her purse. "So, go drill for oil. Who stops you? What's that oil business got to do with my daughter?"

He blows out a long ribbon of cigar smoke and leans closer Betty. "Any question about my integrity will give the bastards an excuse to deny me the leases. What do you think are my chances if your daughter puts the puzzle together? Dredges up old stories about Sparrow Cottage and Jekyll Island for her book?"

Turning and cutting her eyes up at him, Betty measures the rage in his voice. Who is this angry man grown from a silent, sad boy? Mena would say he doesn't know Jesus, "hasn't been washed in the blood of the lamb." Betty considers the phrase she'd heard Mena say so many times so long ago. The image still unsettles her, paints a savage picture in her mind of slaughtered lambs, innocent children, and a bloodthirsty God. She wonders how Mena could love such a Jesus?

Betty lets her memory drift back--- before Mena Simpson, before Jekyll, before earthquakes and paper husbands---to her tiny mother with the bent back and smiling eyes. What would she say about this angry man sitting beside her? Her mother would explain that a long time ago the boy's soul was attached to his beating heart by only a single, frail thread. When the storms came, his soul broke away--- lost to the winds, doomed to wander blind and hungry---until it found his grieving heart again. Her mother would say it was very sad, but sometimes that was the way of the world. Storms come to everyone. And some souls wander many, many lifetimes.

Betty shakes her memories away and tries to dismiss his worries about Aileen hurting his oil business. "That was long, long time ago. Nobody remembers. You worry about wrong things. This day, nobody cares."

He lowers his voice to a harsh whisper. "Yes, they would care. We are talking about a United States government bureaucracy populated by myopic assholes whose fulltime, lifetime mission is to fuck with anybody who is smarter and richer than they are. Believe me, they will care, and I will not get my oil leases."

He pauses for a moment, nursing his cigar. When he speaks again, his voice is composed, almost cordial. "That is why you will cooperate with me in my simple plan to derail your daughter's project. And if you choose not to cooperate, then I will treat your daughter as another unfortunate necessity, like the sisters, and finish the job I so lucklessly botched. Either way, I intend to have those oil leases."

Betty considers what he says. Maybe it is better if Aileen finds another project, one not related to Sparrow and the past. Maybe she should listen to what he has planned. After all, what are her choices? Tell that bossy Olean Hopper woman? Ask Aileen's useless husband for help? Or maybe, Betty considers, it would be better to kill this angry man, squeeze the trigger of the gun tucked away in her purse.

Betty gives that thought space to fill her mind, tries on the possibility. The small pistol had felt good in her hand when she'd threatened him with it last night. He respected her while she was holding her husband's pistol. After all, she was an old woman. Who would blame an old woman? But what if he was right? What if someone did care about what had happened? Where would she be then? Maybe then it would be goodbye to her nice condo in Atlanta. Goodbye to her easy life.

"Tell me. What is this simple plan you have?"

He stands and leans over her, his acrid cigar breath stinging her nostrils. "Meet me at Sparrow at nine o'clock," he says. "And, of course, it goes without saying that you will come alone and not share our conversation with anyone." Without a reply from Betty, he turns on his heels and walks away.

CHAPTER TWENTY-SEVEN

Betty remains on the bench, tapping her cane to a private rhythm on the ground, thinking, questioning if she even remembers exactly what happened so long ago. How her soul became bound to this angry man. Memories lie, she tells herself.

For so long, if those memories slipped into her mind like a snake coiling in the dark, she could will the snake away, make it a shape made of smoke, not flesh and fangs. And if her will was weak, *I'm not that girl anymore* was the charm that could put a heavy box on top of the snake, trapping it inside.

But today, in this garden, still smelling this angry man's cigar and owning the responsibility of keeping her daughter safe, Betty feels the need to remember that girl from so long ago, remember what happened.

Betty concentrates, pealing away the years. Was it morning or afternoon? Why that day of all days? What made that day different? She reaches into her dusty closet of memories and brings out the one thing she remembers that separated that day from all the days before.

It had been bitter cold on Jekyll Island, colder than any other November day since Mena brought her from Taiwan. A freezing ocean wind had ripped inland, cut across the dunes, and blown sand, ferrying tiny ice crystals against Sparrow's windows. The frost on the glass French doors in the living room clung to the panes like crumpled lace. The kitchen sink sputtered ice when Betty turned on the faucet. Mena complained she couldn't draw a bath in her big white tub. There was no heat in the house, except for the living room fireplace. Betty remembers she wore two wool sweaters over one of Jon's flannel shirts.

When she'd gone upstairs to make the bed and gather Mena's dirty laundry, she looked down from the bedroom window at Jon's garden. It was midmorning by then. The oleander leaves still drooped from cold. Betty watched as Mena shuffled around in the garden, stripping off bed sheets they'd draped over her rose bushes the night before. She wore only a light jacket, no hat.

Betty had noticed the wind thrashing Mena's long gray hair in all directions, leaving it in tangles, but Mena didn't care enough to rake the matted hair from her eyes. Mena only cared about the garden. Since Jon died, she'd spent most of her time in the garden. She worked on her knees in the dirt just like Jon used to do, and talked to a Jon who wasn't there. Sometimes, she carried one of his books out to the garden and read to him. Betty gave up reminding Mena that Jon was dead. There was no use trying to tell her what she didn't want to hear.

I'll have to brush the knots out of her hair, Betty decided. *She won't notice them, unless I tell her. Does she even feel the cold?*

Betty had seen something else from the upstairs window: the old black man's wagon lumbering down the river road, passing in front of the cottage. His gray-haired daughter, bundled in a green, threadbare army jacket and faded red scarf, sat tall on the bowed wood driver's seat. Betty watched as the woman gently snapped the reins across the mule's back, urging the animal to keep moving against the cold wind. A sizeable lump of brown canvas occupied the bed of the wagon. Off in the distance, a boat from the mainland eased down the channel toward Jekyll's landing and sounded its deep-throated horn three times.

She's meeting that boat, Betty realized. *What's she hauling in her wagon to send mainland? Must be something big under all that canvas.* When Betty looked down at the garden again, Mena was chasing a sheet across the ground in the wind and was about to lose another as it lifted off a rose bush and parachuted over the garden wall. Betty dropped her laundry basket and ran for the stairs.

Later, after Betty had collected the damp bed sheets from the ground and hung them over chairs in the dining room to dry, she was back in the garden cutting the last of the rosemary. The black man's daughter drove up in her wagon and stopped. "You see what I done?" she called out to Betty.

Betty dropped her pruning sheers into her coat pocket and walked over to the wagon, looking up at the woman. "I see you have empty wagon now."

The woman threw back her head and laughed. Her two, gold front teeth caught the slanted sunlight and threw it back into the clear afternoon with a quick flash.

"I knowed you was watching me from Miss Mena's window. I wants to tell you something fine. Daddy took a crazy notion to sell a pile of our old furniture. He say we getting new furniture from Sears and Roebuck. And you know what? That trader man from Brunswick come on his boat and bought the old stuff off me for cash money. That prissy, white man thinks he be smart. I thinks I got me a hundred dollars for a pile of junk." She laughed again.

Betty smiled. Yes, that was something fine. "Ha. That trader man gets what he deserves. I'm happy for you. Cash money always a lucky thing."

"Yes, ma'am, that's the truth. Well I got to go see about daddy, but I wants to tell you one more thing. That ugly haint-looking chair---the one with the puckered up faces on it---it was one thing I sold that trader man. I suspect since you hate that chair so bad, you be happy to know the ugly old thing be off island now, gone to be somebody else's trouble."

Betty nodded and backed away from the wagon as the woman clicked the reins for her mule to move along. She stood by the side of the road for a time, listening, watching the wagon work its way along the rutted, sandy path, feeling the timbre of the dry oak trees complaining in the cold, island wind and wondering if the curse in the chair rode on the trader man's boat, or if it had stayed behind.

After lunch, Mena went upstairs for her nap. Betty put on her coat, hat, and gloves again. She'd forgotten to collect the morning eggs. When she followed the narrow path behind Sparrow to the chicken coop, she'd seen Caretaker cut through the pines at the back of the property. Even sixty years later, she remembers that his head was down, his body pushing against the wind, and she felt a flood of relief when he didn't see her. Still, she had squatted down on the path, out of sight, until she was certain he was well on his way.

Betty noticed Caretaker carried a wire basket and a metal-headed mallet. She knew what he was up to, had seen him with the basket and mallet before. She made a disapproving, clicking sound with her tongue, assuring herself that Caretaker was turtle hunting again.

He'll walk down the beach some, and then cut over to the creek. He'll find where the young turtles hide. Then he'll bash in their heads, put them in his wire basket. When he gets home, he'll have himself some turtle soup for supper.

While Betty was feeding the chickens and collecting the eggs, she thought about Caretaker and the turtles, about the young ones who couldn't outrun him. And she thought about the day before when he'd let himself into the kitchen---delivering the mail he'd collected from the mainland post office, he said.

He was stinking of whiskey, his dirty hands grabbing at her, pinching her breast. She shoved him away, threatened to cut him with the vegetable knife she held in her hand, but since her sharp words were spoken in Chinese, Caretaker ignored her. *Lucky for me*, Betty thought, as she reached under a sitting hen for an egg.

Over the squawking complaint from the hen she'd robbed, Betty heard Caretaker's drunken insult in her head again. As he'd stumbled out the kitchen door, he called her a whore and slurred, "Just as well, you're a lousy fuck anyway."

Three eggs went into her bowl. *These stingy hens,* Betty thought. *Soon we chop off their heads and make chicken and dumplings with them.* She had wished she could chop off Caretaker's head, boil him down to grease and bones, throw the grease out in the yard for the vultures, and grind the bones for feeding Mena's roses.

It was when she walked the path back to Sparrow that she saw the boy carrying the rifle. He trudged slowly, at the edge of the tall, wind-whipped sea oats on the inland side of the sand dunes. He was taking the same direction as Caretaker. She watched the boy stop, wipe his nose with the back of his gloved hand, and then push on, his feet sinking into the soft sand with each step.

At first she thought to call out to the boy, to warn him to stay back, that Caretaker was on the beach. Then she realized calling out was a bad idea. What if Caretaker was close enough to hear her? What if he saw her? She clinched her jaw and anger flushed into her face before it rained down acid into her stomach. Her bowels churned and rolled. Fearing she would lose control on the path, Betty set her back straight and breathed slowly through her mouth, in and out, in and out, her breaths hanging in the icy November air like evaporating dreams.

When the pain passed, Betty left her eggs in a thatch of grass beside the path and followed the boy.

CHAPTER TWENTY-EIGHT

It was after two o'clock. I'd eaten too much lunch and really needed a nap, but Susan and Sam wanted to explore Redfern Shopping Village, so we cruised through a few of the shops. Sam found a boutique that carried small size shoes and loaded up on three pairs of sandals and a pair of stylish pumps.

As we left the shop, with Susan carrying two of Sam's packages, my new stepdaughter groused, "I can't believe you bought three, identical pairs of shoes. Who does that?"

"They aren't identical. They are different colors, same style. I like them. They are comfortable. Besides, do you have any idea how difficult it is to find a size five sandal?"

"No, I do not. I was born with a size nine foot."

"You were not. Don't exaggerate. How do you like the Sunday pumps I got?"

"They are black and they are pumps. What's to like?"

"Hey guys," I interjected, "there is an art gallery over there. Let's go over. I'd like to browse, maybe pick up something for the guest room."

The merits of Sam's shoe purchases apparently decided, and hearing no objections from the girls, we cut across the asphalt parking lot to the opposite row of shops and entered the gallery. Luckily, the inside temperature felt twenty degrees cooler than outside. Low voltage overhead lighting and deep green, Tuscan gold, and dark blue walls provided a restful backdrop for hundreds of paintings and prints---most by local artists. I could have meandered from one exhibit to another for the rest of the afternoon, enjoying watercolors of local birds, oils of joyful children playing in the surf, or drawings of St. Simons Island historical sites.

In ten minutes, Susan and Sam were bored and motioned they would be waiting for me on the bench outside the gallery entrance. I looked around for a few more minutes and liked everything I saw, but didn't love anything enough to buy it. Then, as I traced my steps back to the shop entrance, I passed a small watercolor grouped with several larger works. It was about the size of an open book and I would have missed it entirely except for the ornate, gilded wood frame that matched another piece I already owned and treasure.

My gilded frame surrounds an equally small oil of dusk closing over the salt marshes, a sky of coral, blue, and pale yellow giving up the day to night. It came from my mother's apartment in Atlanta and I have no idea who painted it or when. I stopped and studied the watercolor. When I realized it was of Faith Chapel on Jekyll Island, I knew I had to have it for my mother's memory and for her love of the little island church. I paid the price for the chapel watercolor, had the salesperson leave it loosely wrapped in the bag, and floated out of the shop to show my purchase to Sam and Susan.

"You're smiling. You must have bought something wonderful." Susan stood up, took my shopping bag, and extracted the painting. Her face deflated. "Oh, it's a church. How... wonderful."

"Don't be sarcastic. It's not just a church. It's Faith Chapel."

Sam stood for a better look. "Is it really?"

I pointed to two crouching forms at the eves of the chapel roof. "Yes, there are the gargoyles we saw. Besides, the artist noted on the back that it's Faith Chapel."

"May I look at it?" Sam asked.

"Help yourself," Susan said and handed over the painting.

Sam took the watercolor and sat down to study it. Susan moved behind her, looked over her shoulder, and said, "Well, I suppose it's a good rendering of the church, but I'm sorry, I can't get excited about a picture of an old church."

Susan's remark didn't dampen my spirit. "That's okay. I bought it for my own reasons and I like it."

Sam handed over my prize and then looked up at me with the smallest hint of a satisfied smile. "I like it, Promise. It's lovely. Well done. Faith must hold so many stories and so many secrets."

There it was. In Sam's smile was a twinkle, a tiny light falling on the seed of a possibility. I asked her, "What were you telling us about the library at Faith Chapel?"

Susan came around to stand beside me, facing Sam. "Which part?" asked Sam. "I remember I rattled on and on about the family records they've kept over the years."

Susan's eyes lit up like a happy dog on the hunt. "Oh boy, Ms. P, I can hear the cogs in your brain clicking over. Go ahead, tell us what you're thinking?"

Before I could answer, my cell phone rang. The caller ID was Daniel's number and I sat down on the bench to answer my husband's call. As Susan and Sam ambled down the sidewalk to give me privacy, I signaled that I would catch up with them as soon as I hung up.

"Well, if it isn't my favorite husband."

"Tell me I'm your only husband. Neither of us needs any more complications in our lives."

"You are, and I love you. What have you been doing today?"

"I had an early meeting with the state investigator this morning. That's why I didn't call you before. I hope you had a chance to sleep in and enjoy your day at the beach."

With the night I'd had and then our meeting with Sid Balfour and the irritable Trooper Olean Hopper, I didn't know where to go with that one. Better to leave it alone. "Hmm. What happened with the investigator?"

"I thought some more about that money in Mac's account and decided I had to trust somebody with what I'd found out. Turns out Mac already reported the deposits to the state boys and they opened an investigation---all on the hush-hush, of course. Nobody in the department here knows anything about it. I'll fill you in on the details when I see you but I'm sure the money has something to do with Mac being killed."

I was thinking that if Mac's office staff and all of his officers were kept in the dark about the deposits, the state must suspect someone inside the department is connected. I asked, "Did someone local make the deposits?"

Daniel didn't answer immediately. When he did, he sounded hesitant. "Well, someone had to have Mac's checking account number to make the deposits. They know where the deposits were made and an agent is going through the bank videos hoping to identify the person. Then we'll see."

"You know, making deposits at the bank doesn't sound very smart. You'd think whoever did it would know banks record every transaction on video."

"Uh huh, you would think. But the investigator did tell me there are ways to fool the camera. Like I said, we wait and see what they come up with. But here is the other thing I wanted to tell you. You are not going to believe this. This is one of your crazy coincidences."

"Daniel, you know I believe most coincidences aren't coincidences…"

"I know, I know. I just can't remember that ten-dollar word you use for when things happen."

"Synchronicity. That the word you're looking for?"

"Yeah, that's it. Are you ready for it?"

"I'm ready."

"Okay. Remember you told me you saw a man running down the beach, twice, with a thunderbolt on his tee shirt? And you asked me what the thunderbolt meant?"

Actually the man was running down the sidewalk on one of those occasions, but whatever… "Yes, I remember."

"Well, I couldn't get the picture of the thunderbolt out of my mind---where I'd seen it---and then about three o'clock this morning I woke up and knew."

I waited while he took another breath. "I saw the thunderbolt a bunch of times over in Vietnam. American boats going up and down the river flying a black flag with the thunderbolt on it. Meant to frighten the enemy. You know, like here we come and we're going to get you. Anyway, I try not to think about the war, so the symbol is one of those things I don't dwell on. But when it came to me in the middle of the night, I realized something else. So I got dressed and went out to my house."

I was having trouble connecting what Daniel was saying. "Why did you go over to your house at three in the morning? I don't understand."

"I'm trying to tell you. I realized the thunderbolt re-minded me of a photograph hanging on my office wall."

Susan had framed about twenty of Daniel's old photo-graphs last year and hung them on one wall of his study/office. I hadn't given much thought to the various fishing and hunting scenes, most with Mac and Daniel or with Daniel and Susan. "Which photograph are you talking about?"

"It's one with me and an old buddy from my Marine days. We weren't that close, but we served in Vietnam to-gether, so you know how that goes. I hadn't heard from him in years, and then he called out of the blue about four years ago. Mac and I met him at his lake house down in Georgia. The photo is of us in his bass boat holding up a string of fish. Good catch, as I remember."

"I'm not sure I remember it. You'll have to show it to me when I get home."

"That's just it, Babe. I can't show it to you. It wasn't hanging on the wall with the other photographs. It's gone. I'm thinking Mac was looking for that photograph when he let himself into the house. He took it. Probably had it with him when the bomb went off."

"But why would Mac be looking for a fishing photograph?"

"I don't know. Here's the other thing: my Marine bud-dy in the photograph was killed in a plane crash the year after the photograph was taken."

Well now, that was interesting. A Vietnam buddy calls out of the blue; they go fishing; Mac takes his picture; the guy is killed; Mac looks for the photograph and Mac is killed. Coincidences?

Daniel broke into my train of thought. "Fletcher's at the back door. I need to talk to him. Let me call you back later, okay?"

"Sure. Say hello to Fletcher and MaMa Allen for me. Love you."

I disconnected the call and sat for a moment digesting what Daniel had said. The missing photograph from Daniel's house was troubling. What if Mac wasn't the one who removed the photograph? What if someone else had been in the house? We needed to go home. Tomorrow.

CHAPTER TWENTY-NINE

When I caught up with Sam and Susan on the other side of the parking lot, the first words out of Susan's mouth were, "Did you tell Daddy we're coming home tomorrow?"

I must have looked addled because then she said, "Hello. Earth to Promise."

"I'm here, and I didn't tell him. I was so engrossed in his side of the conversation that I forgot."

I hadn't answered her immediately because something Daniel said just struck home with me. He'd realized only this morning the photograph was missing. Yet, Fletcher told us when he'd called Thursday about Mac's death that Pate Hoag was asking MaMa Allen to go over to Daniel's to see if anything was missing. Did Pate already know Mac was looking for a photograph at Daniel's house? If so, how would he know that unless Mac told him? Would Mac trust Pate Hoag with that kind of information?

"That's okay. I'm glad you didn't tell Daddy. It'll be better to surprise him."

Yeah, I thought. That's because we both know he would tell us to stay put if he knew we were leaving St. Simons. Although, just now on the phone, Daniel didn't sound as though he was afraid we were in any danger. He sounded more like a man on a mission. Maybe he wouldn't be angry with us for leaving.

Almost as quick as the sweep of a broom, afternoon thunderclouds gathered in the west and the temperature dropped. A brisk wind rustled oak branches hanging over our heads. You could smell the rain coming. We ducked into a coffee shop and ordered three iced coffees. My mind was back on Aileen Wang's would-be killer. I was excited about the idea inspired by my Faith Chapel watercolor and anxious to share it.

"Here's what I'm thinking: we believe the shooter is somehow connected to Betty Wu and her years at Jekyll."

Susan looked doubtful.

"Well, okay. I believe that. We can at least agree that there are five possible names on the party list for the man in the tuxedo. What if we could match one of those names with information recorded in the Faith Chapel records? Link that name back to Jekyll Island when Betty lived there?

"Maybe our shooter was born on Jekyll and there is a birth record at Faith, or maybe he was confirmed or married there. I say we make one more run over to Jekyll Island and have a look. Then, we go home tomorrow knowing we followed every possible lead. With only five names to check, it shouldn't take us long."

Lightning crackled overhead, a three-beat clap of thunder responded, and the heavens opened up with a vengeance. Susan leaned over the tiny, marble bistro table to be heard above the rain pelting down on the coffee shop roof. "I say we find old Betty Wu, gang up on her, and explain the wisdom of telling the truth. She knows the guy's name. She needs to give it up."

A tanned, white-tennis-dress clad woman waiting in line for her order turned around and shot us a suspicious eye. I smiled at her while I said to Susan, "You don't really mean gang up on her."

"Yes, I do. She's making this way more difficult than it needs to be. I'm not saying do the old lady bodily harm or anything, but maybe if all three of us corner her, she'll see reason."

Sam stirred her drink with a straw and studied the table-top. "No way," she said. "Count me out of that plan. I can't be an adversary to Mrs. Wu. She trusted me with her...well, with something in confidence. But look. I think it's a great idea to go over to Faith Chapel and check out the records. Make sure you look at the Prayers Of The People book."

"Why?" Susan asked.

Sam looked up at Susan and hesitated for a couple of beats before she answered, "Why? Well, just because."

"Brilliant," quipped Susan, "just because. Best reason I know. Hey, you sound like you aren't going with us."

Sam took a long sip of her drink. "I'm not. Tell you the truth, I feel rotten and a little feverish. I'd appreciate it if you would drop me off at the Inn so I can lie down."

I knew when we picked her up before lunch that Sam didn't look well enough to be running around town. "Do you have aspirin for your fever?" I asked.

"I do, and I'll take a couple when I get back to my room. Right now I just want to curl up under the covers for awhile."

The rain shower was fierce but short. We were parking in front of The Village Inn on Mallery Street within a half hour. Susan walked upstairs with Sam to get her settled in while I waited in the car. I rested my head back against the seat and closed my eyes. A nap would be wonderful.

Just about the time I felt my body beginning to unwind, I heard a rap-rap on the hood of the Jeep. Then a voice called out, "Hello, hello."

Through half-opened eyes, I saw the smiling, gray-bearded face of Sid Balfour approaching my open window. "Hey. I knocked to get your attention. Didn't want to startle you--- in case you were asleep. Busy day, huh?"

I fully opened my eyes and sat up straighter. "Yep. You certainly look a lot happier than when we left you a few hours ago."

Sid leaned down into the open window and braced himself with both hands against my door. "I am happy. And you will be, too, when I tell you what I found out."

This sounded important. I motioned for him to move back so I could get out of the car, and he opened the door and offered his hand to me. "What did you find out?"

Grinning ear to ear, he explained. "Remember I told you our mystery man was wearing a summer tuxedo at Ms. Wang's cocktail party?"

I nodded. "I remember. You said all the other men were in casual slacks and blazers, and he was wearing a fancy tuxedo."

"Right. So I got to thinking after we talked this morning. If I were concerned about making a fashion statement in a tuxedo, I'd probably want to have the suit cleaned, or at least pressed, before I wore it to a party. Now here is the deal: there are no dry cleaners on Jekyll Island. So I figured the guy would bring his tuxedo to one of the four on St. Simons rather than drive to Brunswick, because rich folks like to shop where other rich folks do. I also figured there couldn't be too many guys getting summer tuxedos done up on the island, so I decided to visit the St. Simons cleaning establishments and ask a few questions."

"And people at the dry cleaners actually talked to you?"

"Yes, ma'am. Sure they did. Thirty years as a newspaper reporter taught me being shy doesn't get the story. Besides, most people actually want to tell you what they know---makes them feel more important."

"And?"

"The fourth dry cleaners is located down the street from here. I got lucky with that one. Our guy's last name is Coleman. No first name or phone number, but Coleman is the name."

"What makes you so sure?"

"Well, for one thing, like I said, a tuxedo isn't the usual island attire. The others haven't cleaned a tux since the after Christmas party rush back in January. And the young woman at the cleaners said Coleman's was the only tux they've seen in over a year. Plus Clip Coleman is one of the five names we decided are possibilities from the party list, right?"

"True. But Coleman is sort of a common name. There could be several on St. Simons. Did she remember what Coleman looked like?"

"No. She didn't remember. But think about it. Yeah, maybe there are several men named Coleman on the island, but only one got his tuxedo cleaned and only one guy was wearing a tux at the party. It's got to be him."

"So you just now got the name from the dry cleaners?"

"Correct. About two minutes ago. I saw you sitting in the Jeep as I was walking back to my car. I'm about to call Olean on her cell and tell her---in case she strikes out with Betty Wu."

Susan walked up beside us. "Tell Olean what?"

I recapped Sid's story and Susan raised her fist in the air. "Yes!" she cheered.

Her enthusiasm made me smile. Then I remembered Olean might not answer her phone. "Sid, Olean called me a couple of hours ago. She found Betty. But Betty insisted there wasn't a man at Sparrow last night. She also said she can't do anything else today about the guy because she's been called over to Jekyll. They're looking for a cougar."

Sid looked surprised. "Cougar? You sure?"

"Yes, that's what she said. But look, try to call her anyway. She may be able to pick up if she knows it's you. Susan and I are headed for Jekyll now to follow another lead. If we see Olean, we'll make sure she knows about Coleman."

Sid fished his phone from his pants pocket, gave us a happy wave, and fast walked down the sidewalk.

"Wait," Susan said, "why do we need to go to Jekyll now? Sid will give Olean Coleman's name."

"Because we have nothing to link Coleman to Aileen, or Betty Wu, or anything that happened at Sparrow Cottage way back when---nothing to tell us why Coleman would want to shoot Aileen. If Betty sticks to her story about not seeing a man last night, what do we have?"

Susan's shoulders slumped. No more cheers. "Nothing except that Coleman was at the cocktail party with about a hundred other people."

"Right. We need to know why Coleman feels threatened by Aileen's Sparrow project. What does he think she will find out that would hurt his business? And for that matter, what is the man's business? And why is Betty Wu hiding what she knows? Since Betty isn't sharing, we need something to put us on the right trail. Speaking of which, as Sid mentioned, Coleman's first name is listed as Clip on the party list. I can't imagine a mother naming a son Clip. I'm thinking it's a nickname---one of those guy things that men hang on a buddy. What do you think?"

"Yeah, sounds like it."

"But why Clip? Short for Clipper, maybe?"

Susan shook her head no. "You are so sheltered Ms. P. How about gun clip? You know, the thing that holds the bullets."

"Oh, of course. I didn't think of that."

Susan smiled at me. "That's what I mean---sheltered. If you are going to be a true mountain woman, you have to get familiar with our redneck ways, at least learn the parts of a firearm, even if you won't learn to shoot one."

A true mountain woman? Could I ever really be that? Would I always have *sheltered flatlander* stamped across my forehead? Would I ever be able to call the mountains home?

Susan was saying something else.

"I don't see how the Faith Chapel records will answer any questions, but your instincts must be kicking into over-drive so I'm trusting you. Besides, I don't want to get back home and you tell me for the next ten years that we could have figured it all out if only we'd looked at the chapel's records. So let's go. It's getting late. Like your good neigh-bor, Fletcher Enloe, is fond of saying, *daylight's wasting.*"

CHAPTER THIRTY

As much as I like Jekyll Island, I have to admit I was getting tired of the eighteen- mile drive from St. Simons Island over there. I hoped this trip to Faith Chapel would be the last until Daniel and I returned to Georgia's coast for a real honeymoon. I looked over at Susan and wondered what she was thinking. This vacation turned fact-finding mission certainly wasn't what she'd expected. My guess was that she'd hoped the wedding celebration for Daniel and me would ignite a similar romantic fire with Sam. Instead, she'd spent her time ferrying me around and bumping up against boundaries in her relationship with a sick Sam Quinn. That must smart.

As Susan made the left turn off St. Simons via the Torras Causeway onto Highway 17 heading south to Jekyll, I decided to approach the subject---gingerly. "I'm sorry our beach trip hasn't worked out the way you'd hoped. You and Sam must be disappointed, especially with Sam being sick and all."

"Don't worry about it. Sam will be fine. It's just a bug. Nothing serious. You and Daddy are the ones whose wedding and honeymoon were trashed."

"Well, I wouldn't exactly say trashed. Our ceremony at Crane Cottage was beautiful. I'll always remember the sound of the ocean from the garden and the fragrance of the flowers. But certainly, with the Aileen Wang drama, and worse yet, with Mac being killed, it has been…" I stopped because I didn't have the words to explain. Susan nodded, kept her eyes on the highway, and avoided any further mention of Sam and their relationship.

I changed the subject. "We haven't talked much about Mac and what happened. How are you coping?"

Susan's mouth tightened and then twisted to one side. After a few seconds, she answered, "Coping? I don't know if I'm coping or not. I know I'm pissed that some asshole would do such a thing. *Could* do such a thing---in broad daylight---right in front of our house. Makes me madder than hell. I know that Daddy is devastated because he and Mac were so close, but Daddy is also a fighter. He won't rest until he hunts down Mac's killer and walks the son-of-a-bitch down the hall to death row."

"I'm sure you're correct about your dad, but what about you? Are you devastated?"

"Me? Tell you the truth, I'm very sorry that Mac died, very sorry, but I wasn't that close to him. I always felt I was the little kid who got in the way of his and Daddy's fishing trips and other guy stuff. After Mama died, Daddy pretty much took me everywhere with him and I think that was too much for Mac."

There seemed to be more that she wanted to say, so I waited. About a mile down the road, she picked up her thoughts and said, "The other thing is I've always felt Mac spent a lot of energy trying to be like Daddy---to copy him. That irked me. Like the way he kept his hair permed so he'd have Daddy's curly hair, and how he'd show up with some ole thing about a week after Daddy had gotten the same thing. And I thought Mac was kind of pompous, sometimes---too full of himself. I know I'm sounding critical of Mac. I think I'm feeling guilty because I didn't really love him that much in life. I know that sounds terrible, but it's the truth. Bottom line is: I'm worried about Daddy. I can't help Mac now, but I can get my tail back to Perry County and try and help Daddy."

Susan certainly gave me an ear full, though none of what she said surprised me. I'd noticed the strain between her and Mac. Susan has a way of cutting her feelings into a conversation with sarcasm that's hard to miss. I'd heard her wield her sharp tongue at Mac on several occasions.

Usually Mac managed a sharp comeback, but he wasn't as proficient with the verbal barbs as Susan.

"I'm concerned about your dad, too. But on the phone he sounds focused on finding out what he can, but he also sounds cautious. Your dad is a fighter, that's true. But he's a smart warrior. I trust him. He won't go off half-cocked."

"I hope you're right. Still, I need to be there with him."

"We both do. This time tomorrow we'll be most of the way back to North Carolina. Then we'll all sleep better."

After another mile or so, I felt I needed to say one last thing about Mac. "I understand what you said about feeling Mac couldn't handle sharing Daniel with you. I felt Mac's jealousy, too, especially after he realized your dad and I had a serious relationship. Mostly I wrote him off as being a slightly self-centered person who needed to be the center of attention. You know, kind of like Garland Wang--harmless, and a good person underneath, but somewhat irritating. Now I wish I'd tried a bit harder to get to know Mac. Made more of an effort."

"Yeah, me too. Below the pompous exterior, Mac was an honest person. He tried to be a good sheriff, and he cared about the people of Perry County. And he was family. I mean, my gosh, he and Daddy saw each other about every day their whole lives, except when Daddy was in the Marines and Mac was in the Army. And even then, karma landed them in practically the same rice paddy in Vietnam, and they ended up hanging around together over there."

The mention of Vietnam made me think of the missing photograph. I almost asked Susan about it, but decided Daniel would want to tell Susan about the photograph himself. Instead, I changed the subject and asked whether she thought Sam would be up to the long ride home the next morning. Susan replied that she hoped so, and we drove the rest of the way in silence.

When we pulled into the gravel parking lot beside Faith Chapel, it was four thirty, an hour from closing. Not much time to go through about a hundred years of church records. I noticed the only other car in the lot was a yellow VW Bug. Before I could mention that the vehicle looked like the one we'd seen on Thursday, the rear door to the chapel opened and a young, blond woman in a black skirt and white blouse stepped out.

"Isn't that the woman Sam met over here on Thursday?" Susan asked.

"I believe it is. Is she the same pastor Sam had the appointment with yesterday?"

"You know, I'm not sure. I can't remember her name."

"Well, she's waving at us, so I think we are about to be introduced."

I waved back and we parked. She was waiting for us by the rear chapel door when we approached.

"Hello," she said, extending her hand to me, "You must be Dr. McNeal and Susan Allen. I'm Bebe Sloan--- spelled B-e-b-e, but pronounced *Bay Bay*, by the way. Don't ask why. It's too long of a story. Let's just say it's a Southern thing. I'm the vicar of Holy Nativity over on St. Simons and a volunteer here at Faith Chapel."

She quickly shook my hand and then took Susan's. "Sam Quinn called me and explained you are in somewhat of a crisis and need to search our chapel records. We don't have a lot of time before I'm to lock up, but since I'm familiar with what's covered in the records, perhaps if I help you, we can find what you are looking for."

Susan and I followed her through the rear door of the chapel building and down a short hallway into a room not much bigger than a broom closet---the library Sam had mentioned. An old-fashioned, schoolhouse-globe light fixture hung in the center of the space, adding light to the one, small, horizontal window at the end of the narrow room. Along the longer sidewalls, dark mahogany-stained bookcases held rows of red, journal-width books on one side and thicker, black-bound books on the other.

"Here we are." Rev. Sloan said and waved a hand in the air like a magician just about to pull a rabbit from her hat. "The Jekyll Island Club memories. Sam says you have five names. You want to know if they appear in any of the records?"

I stepped forward. "Actually, we've narrowed our search to two names. We have a last name for one, Coleman, and we think he was born around---I did a quick calculation based on Betty Wu's age and him being ten years younger---1935, give or take a couple of years. We're looking for birth records, confirmation, anything. The other person we are interested in was an immigrant from Taiwan. We only know her first name, Betty. She lived at Sparrow Cottage and was employed there by Mena Simpson."

"Ah, I see. Well, I know Sparrow Cottage, of course, and the Simpson family name. They became members of the Jekyll Island Club about 1915. Mena's maiden name was Peterkin. Her family was old Brunswick. After she married one of the Simpson sons, she became a Methodist missionary. Later, she lived year round at Sparrow for many years. For some reason her husband stopped coming to Jekyll Island even for the winters and remained in Grand Rapids, Michigan where he managed the family's furniture manufacturing business. Certainly, Mena Simpson probably had household staff, though employees aren't generally mentioned in the Club records."

Rev. Sloan paused, took a stick of clear, lip-gloss from her skirt pocket and coated her lips before she continued. "The name Coleman doesn't sound familiar. I can tell you they were not one of the wealthy northern families who were Club members. Maybe Coleman was also an employee. We'll have a look."

She waved her hand over the bookcases. "Let me explain what we have. The black books begin in 1888. They contain entries by various Club members who reported Island news, like who came for the season, who gave parties, who brought whom as guests, who got engaged or married. An entry in 1915 mentions the first coast-to-coast telephone call, made from right here on Jekyll Island.

There is even a list of the wild game hunted by Club members---the number of deer or pheasant taken during the season, that sort of thing. So you see, the records are varied.

"In case you didn't know, *the season* was when the island was open to guests--- usually early January until April. You'll find famous names like Rockefeller, Morgan, Pulitzer, and Vanderbilt all through the black volumes. But, as I said, the records don't usually say anything about employees. And, oh yes, the black books stop at the end of the 1935 season. During that time, the Club was faltering because of the terrible economic depression. Membership was shrinking. Hardly anyone returned the next season. The Club's financial troubles continued, and then when America entered WWII, the island was closed to visitors.

"Once the war was over, the State of Georgia bought the island for $300,000 with the intent to run it as a state park. Now, of course, we have the Jekyll Island Authority as the governing body. So, all of that being said, it would seem we have only one year in the black books to check for Coleman and Betty."

My head was spinning from all the information Rev. Sloan had managed to reel off in just a few seconds. Her final remark did stick with me, though---only one of the black books would have any information about Betty and Coleman because the records stopped at the end of 1935.

I plucked one of the black books from the shelf. It began in 1900 with a list of the first guests arriving on Jekyll for the season. An early entry stated that Club President Charles Lanier had announced the Clubhouse season rate for a room with a private bath would be $13.50 per day. As interesting as that was, it wasn't the information we needed. I began to despair that our trip to Faith Chapel was a waste.

CHAPTER THIRTY-ONE

"And the red books?" asked Susan.

"My favorites. Anyone who visited Faith could leave a prayer request in the red book. They go forward from about the time Faith Chapel was completed in 1904 until the early 1950s when the practice of leaving prayers was stopped for a time. We call the red books: The Prayers Of The People. In the late 1980s, we resumed the practice of leaving the red book in the chapel beside the votive candles. Now we have people from all over the world visiting and leaving prayer requests, or simply their own prayers, in the book."

"Okay, Ms. P," Susan said, "this is your party. Where do you want to start?"

Given what Rev. Sloan had told us, it would seem we had a narrow window of opportunity. "Let's start with the years we think might be relevant. We think Coleman was born about 1935, so we begin our search then. That gives us one, maybe two, black books to look through, if we look at 1934 also---just in case Coleman was born earlier than we think. I'll take the black books. Rev. Sloan, why don't you and Susan take alternate years in the red books beginning at 1934."

"Please call me Bebe. That sounds like a good plan. Just one thing though: you will notice that the red books are not identified as to years on the spines. You have to look inside the front cover for that information. So as Susan and I look through a book, why don't we stack it on top of the bookcase? That way we won't get confused as to whether we've checked that book or not."

"Great idea," Susan said and took two red books from the shelf. One she handed to Bebe, and one she opened. "Let's do it."

The Reverend Bebe Sloan smiled and looked as though our hunt was the most fun she'd had in weeks. I found 1934 and 1935 in the black books and pulled them out. The first thing that struck me about the entries was that each person who'd taken on the task of recording Club events had impeccable penmanship. How different the flowing handwriting was from my in-a-hurry scrawl. That was the good news. The bad news was that for a person like me, used to typed words produced in Times Roman, 12 point on my computer, the longhand was slow going to even scan an entry for the name Coleman or Betty. By the time I'd checked my two books and found nothing, I noticed Susan and Bebe had stacked five red books on top of the shelf.

"You guys are moving fast."

Bebe Sloan sighed. "Are we? I was afraid I was reading too slowly, lingering on the sorrows these folks brought with them to Jekyll. Some of it will break your heart---death, sickness, despair, even among the rich."

Susan added another book to the top of the stack. "But no mention of anyone named Coleman and no prayers for Betty?"

Bebe shook her head. "No. I'm afraid not."

I removed the next red book from the shelf. "What year did you just finish?"

"1940," answered Susan. "I did find a prayer for all the people in harms way in Europe. Maybe the person is refer-ring to Hitler on the march? I notice many of the prayer requests are signed with initials and no names. That one about Europe is signed M.S. Could be Mena Simpson."

"1941 for me," added Bebe. "I see what you mean by the initials. Let's try to remember the handwriting and see if we can at least decide if M.S. is the same person."

"Gotcha."

I began to look through 1942. Interesting. Many of the prayers were signed with M.S. The first prayer that meant anything to me was in April of that year. M.S asked for

God's mercy for the men aboard the tanker torpedoed by Germans off the coast. This must be the event that resulted in debris from the wreckage washing ashore on Jekyll. With that debris, the carved chair Betty Wu believed to be cursed had arrived. I read the prayer aloud and continued searching. More and more, the prayers were made by M.S.

A few minutes later Bebe hit pay dirt. "Hey, listen to this from August 1948. It's signed by M.S and says, 'We pray that Our Lord and Savior will gather little Bobby Coleman into His loving arms on this day. We also pray for Bobby's brother Freddie, another child in need of Our Savior's grace.' Could this be the Coleman you are looking for?"

Susan looked up from her reading. Bebe handed me the book and I read the prayer aloud again. "This prayer has to be around the time the boy drowned while fishing with his stepfather, our infamous Garr Lemley."

Bebe frowned. "Oh dear, are we also looking for the name Lemley? If so, I missed that direction and haven't searched for that name."

Susan and I exchanged we-are-so-dumb looks. "It's okay," I assured Bebe, "we didn't think to include Lemley because we weren't sure how he fit into the puzzle with Coleman. Now I think we know."

"We do?" Susan sounded unsure.

"Yes, we do. Sid Balfour found the newspaper article about the boy who drowned in August 1948. Garr Lemley was mentioned as the stepfather who was with the boy on the fishing boat. But remember the Brunswick News didn't give the child's name---just that he was survived by his brother. This prayer was offered in August 1948. Bobby Coleman had to be the child referred to in the newspaper article. Freddie must be the brother who now goes by the nickname Clip Coleman. And M.S. must stand for Mena Simpson. We know she was on Jekyll at the time. Otherwise, we'd be plagued by way too many coincidences."

"And you don't believe in coincidences," said Susan.

"Not usually."

"Okay, let's say you are correct. Why is Freddie Coleman, our Clip Coleman, running around at Aileen's party in the summer tuxedo?"

"I don't understand," Bebe Sloan interjected. "Please don't tell me we are looking for Coleman because he wears a tuxedo?"

I tried to explain. "No, no. Not just the tuxedo. We think Clip Coleman shot Aileen Wang because he believes Aileen knows something terrible about him---or she will know something if she keeps digging around into the history of Sparrow Cottage."

Bebe looked puzzled. "Okay. And how does this tie in with Betty Wu?"

Interesting. I was sure we'd only given the Reverend Sloan Betty's first name. Sam must have mentioned Betty Wu when she called her. The Betty Wu connection explained why Sam urged us to look through the records, and why she called her fellow priest and asked her to guide us. Sam couldn't tell us what Betty Wu had confided, but she could point us to the truth. But what was the truth? What could Betty Wu have told Sam?

I let the mention of Betty's last name pass and answered Bebe as best as I could. "We don't know yet how it ties with Betty Wu, but we know that Freddie Coleman could have blamed Garr Lemley for his brother Bobby's death. After all, Lemley was with the child when he mysteriously fell overboard and drowned. And we know that Betty was living on Jekyll Island when the child drowned and when Garr Lemley was shot. She had to know Freddie Coleman and Garr Lemley.

"In any event, let's say Freddie blamed Lemley for his brother's death. And also, Freddie's mother died only months before his brother went fishing with Lemley and ended up missing. We don't know if the boy's body was ever found. Two traumatic events in such a short time period would have been devastating for any fourteen- year-old. With his mother and brother gone, Freddie was left alone with Lemley. And from what Sid said about Lemley, the man was likely violent. Who knows how badly Lemley treated Freddie. Add possible abuse to a belief that his stepfather was responsible for his brother's death and you have a festering wound that could erupt in murder."

Susan looked skeptical. "You're saying Coleman was fifteen or sixteen when he shot his stepfather in the back?"

Bebe answered for me. "Unfortunately, it happens. Just listen to the national news. There's no shortage of troubled teens out there who pick up a gun."

"Yeah, that's true," agreed Susan. "So, Ms. P, do you think Betty Wu is protecting Coleman because he was so young at the time?"

That was possible, though a niggling feeling in the back of my mind told me there was more to it than that. Betty might shield Coleman under some circumstances, but I didn't think she'd endanger her daughter to protect him.

Bebe looked at her watch. "We only have ten minutes before I have to close Faith for the night. What do you want to do now?"

I made a quick decision. "I'll finish the 1948 book. You guys jump ahead to the next year for any reference to Coleman, Lemley, or Betty. And remember Wu is Betty's second husband's name. We don't know her last name when she lived on Jekyll."

They nodded and reached for the next year's red book. I read forward a few pages after M.S.'s prayer for Bobby and found another interesting entry. This one would give us Betty's previous name.

"Hey, here is something. We are still in August 1948. Listen to this: 'we pray for the soul of our beloved Jon Chou who passed into glory this day from the summer fever. The empty space left by his passing can never be filled. Oh Lord, be with me and with Betty as we travel our lonely road of grief.' Another coincidence, or do we assume Jon Chou was Betty's paper husband?"

"Assume," said Susan.

I read the prayer again to myself. "Hmm. I think we can also assume that Jon was more than an employee to Mena Simpson. Her grief sounds very personal, to me."

We scanned as many pages as we could in the remaining minutes, though found nothing except further evidence of Mena Simpson's growing habit of leaving prayers in Faith Chapel's red book. Yet, I did notice Betty was not mentioned again. I hated to leave with so many pages unsearched, but understood that Rev. Sloan had no choice but to usher us out and lock the doors of Faith Chapel.

"I'm here tomorrow if you want to continue looking," she offered when we stood in the parking lot.

"Can't," said Susan, "we have to leave for home in the morning---that is if Sam is well enough to travel. This bug she's gotten has her feeling pretty rotten."

Bebe extended her hand to Susan and then to me. "Yes, I understand. I'll pray for Sam and for you. Exposing the truth can sometimes be a perilous path."

We thanked Rev. Sloan for her help and then watched her drive off in her little yellow VW Bug. Susan turned to me. "You don't suppose yellow VW Bugs are the standard issue for Episcopal priests?"

I smiled. "No, I don't think so. More than likely the fact that Sam and Bebe Sloan both own yellow Bugs is simply one of life's few coincidences."

"Hmm. If you say so. What do we do now?"

I extracted my cell phone from my purse. "We call Olean Hopper and tell her Freddie Coleman is our man.

Our job is finished. She can use whatever sources she has to find him."

"With just his name, sounds like a needle-in-a-haystack kind of mission to me."

I punched in Hopper's number and waited. "Maybe not. Hopper seems pretty determined to solve Aileen's case on her own---before RB can hog all the credit." When Hopper's voice mail answered, her stern voice ordered me to leave a message.

"Now what?"

My idea was a long shot, but worth a try. "Let's drive around the island a bit. If Hooper is still out looking for the cougar, we might spot her vehicle on the road."

"Okay, but not for long. I want to get back to St. Simons and check on Sam. Plus, we need to pack if we're going to leave here early in the morning."

By six thirty we'd encountered two teams on the cougar hunt. Neither included Olean Hopper. Neither could tell us where to find her. Our only recourse was to hope that Sid Balfour had been able to reach his niece, and that she would pick up my voice mail detailing Clip Coleman's name when he lived on Jekyll and his connection to Garr Lemley.

CHAPTER THIRTY-TWO

When Susan and I returned to St. Simons Island from Jekyll, she dropped me at The King and Prince and headed back into the village to check on Sam. We agreed she would call me about nine to let me know how Sam was feeling and if we were still set to go home the next morning. I was exhausted from rushing around all day on minimum sleep from the night before and decided to have a light supper at the hotel and get to bed early. But first, I went upstairs to my room to wash my face, drag a comb through my salty, tangled hair, and call Daniel. I was anxious to share the news that we'd discovered the name of the man who'd shot Aileen. He answered on the second ring with a loud hello rising above considerable background noise.

"You sound like you're in a disco."

Daniel laughed and I felt better already. "No, no disco. It's Saturday night; some fool is playing *Staying Alive* on the retro jukebox Susan put in, and the dinner crowd is rowdy."

"Oh, you're at the restaurant?"

"Yeah, we're short staffed. Ben called me in to man the register, which is okay. I like watching the cash pile up in the drawer of our little barbecue investment. Tonight is super packed. I just talked to Susan to report we are still in business and all is well. She says Sam has some ugly virus. Fever, the whole bit. I'm sorry to hear that. What a bummer to be sick at the beach. You all right?"

"Oh yes, I'm fine. No fever. No virus. Just tired."

"What are you doing tonight? Going barhopping in the village?"

"No. I'm over the bar scene, thank goodness. Just about to have a little supper and hopefully turn in early. I miss you. Wish you were here to warm my bed."

"I wish I were there to warm more than your bed."

"Oh my goodness, Mr. Allen, whatever do you mean?"

A second sexy laugh from Daniel was music to my tired heart.

"Hang on, Babe. I need to ring up this ticket."

I waited while Daniel chatted up customers and took their money. Shortly, he was back on the phone. "It's so crazy busy I might have to hang up, but I'm glad you called---for several reasons. First off, I love you. Secondly, two interesting things have happened since we talked earlier."

I sat down on the bed and kicked off my sandals. "I'm listening."

"When I got to the restaurant tonight, yesterday's paper--- which I hadn't seen--- was on the counter. The front page was all about Mac of course. Just about broke my heart. They ran that photograph of him from last year's election. You know the one. He's grinning like a fool and holding that cute, curly-headed baby girl."

"What did the paper say about the explosion?"

"The whitewashed version from the state boys is that the explosion is under investigation. They hinted a fuel line leak could have been the cause. The newspaper was all over that and even ran some stats about recent automobile manufacturer recalls---deaths due to faulty parts and that kind of thing."

"A fuel line leak? You mean they didn't mention the bomb?"

"Correct. Personally, I don't think anybody with any sense will believe the story about a fuel line failure. I mean, even twenty years ago when I went through law enforcement training, we could tell pretty quick if an explosion was a bomb or not."

"Wait. You did the law enforcement training course twenty years ago?"

"Yeah. Haven't we talked about that?"

I couldn't believe what I was hearing. How could I have known Daniel for over four years, married him, and not known he'd gone to school to be a cop? "Well, as a matter

of fact, no we haven't. Was this something you conveniently left out of your life history? How could that piece of information slip your mind?"

In a flash, I had a good idea why Daniel could
have let the information slide into the background.
He knew my ex-husband was a cop, and knowing
Daniel, he didn't want any bad taste I had for cops
in general, and RB Barnes in particular, to cloud our
relationship.

"Babe, why are you getting upset about this? It isn't
as though I did ten-to-twenty for bank robbery. I went
through the training, passed the course, and was offered
a job by Perry County. About that time, I found myself a
widower with a little girl to raise, so I took the job with the
post office instead. Do I need to explain why I thought
being a mailman was a better idea for a single dad than
being a deputy sheriff?"

"Was this before or after Mac went with the sheriff's
department?"

"Just before, as I remember. Why do you ask?"

"Oh, just something Susan said about you and Mac always doing and having the same things. Nothing really. It
doesn't matter. So, was the front page story in the paper
the interesting thing you wanted to tell me about?"

"No. I have to talk fast. Two parties are headed up
front to pay. On page five of the Friday paper there was a
small article saying Alton Hazlett will retire from the sheriff's department at the end of the month---two weeks from

now. Can you believe that? I talked to Alton yesterday. He didn't say a word about retiring."

"That's kind of bad timing for Hazlett, isn't it? I mean he was Mac's second in command, and you thought he'd be interim sheriff until an election."

"That's right, I did. And it is really bad timing. But you know Alton must have given Mac his notice several days ago for the news to get in the paper yesterday. Maybe he'll change his mind and stay until we get a new sheriff. You'd think he would want to stay until they catch the SOB who killed Mac. Here's the other thing. Pate Hoag came in the restaurant tonight, ate a barbecue plate, and when he came up to check out, he said he and I needed to talk. His words were, 'soon and in private.' Wanted to know if he could come by the house tomorrow."

"What'd you tell him?"

"Two o'clock tomorrow. I have to hang up now. I'll call you later, about ten."

"Okay. I love you."

"I love you, too."

After I hung up, I sat on the bed, thinking. Why wouldn't the state investigator say Mac was the victim of a bomb? As tired as I was, it still took me only two seconds to answer my own question. They wouldn't want to send out a message to the citizens of Perry County that the sheriff's department was so weak it couldn't even protect one of its own. That would be bad public relations, and it might cause some folks to panic, think Perry County was having some kind of major crime wave. We weren't, were we?

And what could Pate Hoag possibly want to talk to Daniel about? He said *in private.* What was that all about? As I followed rabbit tracks in my mind, searching for anything I could recall about Pate Hoag, anything Mac had said about him, I realized I hadn't told Daniel about Freddie Coleman. My news would have to wait until later. That is, if I could stay awake long enough to talk to Daniel later.

I checked my cell phone for missed calls, hoping Olean Hopper had tried to reach me while I was talking to Daniel. Nothing. Then I noticed the room phone's message light was blinking from its stand on the bedside table. It took me three tries to get the hotel's sequence of commands correct and retrieve my phone message. The message was Barnes returning my call from earlier that morning. He was still occupied with a case, but said he would be back at St. Simons late Sunday afternoon. We would talk then. He also said he'd talked to Olen Hopper and she'd filled him in on my "adventure" at Sparrow.

His final snarky comment was: "Once again, you are busy obstructing justice and making my work more difficult."

What a prick was my first reaction. The second was that I probably deserved his comment. Well, the good news was that Susan, Sam and I would be more than half way to

North Carolina by the time **RB Barnes** returned to the island.

The bed felt so good I stretched out for a five-minute rest, but then fell sound asleep on top of the covers. When the cell phone woke me, it was dark outside and the bedside clock said nine thirty-five. My mouth felt like a band of gypsies had camped out in there and left all their garbage behind. My eyes were grainy with sleep, and I was wicked hungry.

I fumbled for the phone and tried to clear my throat enough to answer like a person who hadn't been rousted from the dead, which is what I felt like.

"Ms. P?"

"Yes, here."

"You don't sound like yourself. You okay? You aren't getting sick are you?"

"No, no, I'd fallen asleep. How's Sam."

"Well, that's why I'm calling. I got her to eat a bowl of soup and drink a ginger ale. She's gone back to sleep, but honestly, I'm not sure she's well enough to make the drive tomorrow. Did you already tell the hotel you were checking out?"

"No, not yet. Are you thinking we should stay another day?"

There was a long silence on the other end of the line followed by a breathy sigh. "Yeah, I'm afraid so. What do you think?"

"Well, I talked to your dad earlier, just after you did, and he seems okay. I miss him and I'd already gotten into the mindset of traveling tomorrow, but really it would probably be better to give Sam another day to kick the virus. I say we plan on leaving Monday morning."

"Okay. Let's do that. I'll call you in the morning."

I said goodbye to Susan and hung up. I was sorry to hear Sam was still sick and even sorrier that we would be at St. Simons when RB got there on Sunday. No doubt he would enjoy giving me hell about not stepping out of the shadows last night and telling Trooper Hopper about seeing Coleman with Betty Wu.

Then I realized there was a bright side to it all. Susan and I had learned Coleman's name and established a connection to Garr Lemley. We had answered the question of who shot Aileen. Now all RB and Hopper had to do was find Freddie Coleman. Surely, the gift of the shooter's name would buy me a pass on RB's anger. And if it didn't, oh well, I'd weathered worse storms than my ex-husband's temper.

CHAPTER THIRTY-THREE

It was too late to order supper in the hotel dining room, but my growling stomach was telling me I needed to feed it something. While I washed my face and brushed my teeth, I considered my options and realized that without my Subaru or Susan's Jeep they were few. The late night room service menu didn't list anything that really appealed to me, so I investigated the mini-fridge in the room. There was a demi-bottle of white wine---it looked good, but I knew better than to drink wine on an empty stomach---three wedges of Laughing Cow cheese, an orange soda, and an apple. After wolfing down the cheese with the apple and drinking part of the soda, I went into the bathroom to take a shower and wash my hair.

My mind usually wanders from topic to topic in the shower. I can cover a lot of territory between soaping up and rinsing off. Maybe it's something about the hot water massaging my brain cells through my wet hair. During this particular shower, I was thinking about Betty Wu and why she was protecting Freddie Coleman.

Though we hadn't confirmed my suspicion that Freddie Coleman killed his stepfather, we knew he had opportunity and motive. And the prickling on the back of my neck told me Freddie had, indeed, killed Lemley as well as the Peterkin sisters. Betty must know Freddie killed Garr Lemley. She certainly knew that if Freddie had been a better shot, he would have killed Aileen. Then why would she shield him from Olean Hopper? Did Betty think that somehow she could convince Coleman to back off? Leave Aileen alone? Why would she think that? If I were Betty Wu, and didn't want to expose Coleman to Hopper, how would I stop him from hurting my daughter? Well, there *was* the pistol Betty was lugging around in her raincoat pocket...

As I dried my hair, my thoughts flipped over to Alton Hazlett and why he had decided to take early retirement. Leaving the job early would probably cost him in retirement benefits. What would make early retirement worth it? Maybe he or his wife had health issues? The room phone rang and I cut off the hairdryer to answer it.

"Hello."

A pleasant young man asked, "Am I speaking with Mrs. Allen?"

Mrs. Allen? Would I ever get used to being called Mrs. Allen and not Dr. McNeal?

"Yes."

"Ah, sorry to bother you. This is the reception desk. A woman who says her name is Hopper is here asking for your room number. May I have your permission to send her up?"

"What does she look like?" I'd learned to be cautious, even though I sometimes ignored caution.

The young man cleared his throat and hesitated before he spoke. "Well, she's medium height, has sort of short, light hair. Caucasian."

He wasn't telling me much. "Is she in uniform?"

"Would camo pants, snake boots, and a black tee shirt be a uniform?"

"Probably not. Is she skinny, or fat? How would you describe her build?"

This time he didn't hesitate before he answered, "Linebacker."

I don't know much about football, but I was pretty sure we were talking about Trooper Olean Hopper. "Thank you. You may send her up."

I grabbed underwear, navy blue cropped pants, and a tee shirt from my suitcase. Thirty seconds later, Olean Hopper paced the floor of my room and grilled me about the message I'd left on her phone. I repeated what we'd found out at Faith Chapel and she wanted me to repeat the prayer about Bobby Coleman, word for word. When I told her I wasn't sure if what I said was exactly what was written in the book, she fussed at me because I hadn't thought to copy it down. Well, maybe I should have written it down, but what mattered was that little Bobby Coleman was probably the child who drowned while he was with Garr Lemley, and Freddie Coleman was his brother. Freddie had to be our Clip Coleman from the cocktail party list.

"Look, I know we don't have the guy's driver's license to prove Clip Coleman is Freddie Coleman, but don't you think the possibilities are likely enough to go looking for Mr. Coleman?"

She stopped pacing, faced me, and planted her hands on her hips. I was thinking someone should really have a talk with this woman and tell her that particular body language, of which she seemed to be so fond, is too aggressive to engender cooperation from anyone. But then I realized Hopper didn't care if she got cooperation. What she was after was obedience.

"Don't talk down to me, Dr. McNeal. I *am* looking for Coleman. It's my day off and so far I've run my ass all over Jekyll Island hunting a cougar that probably exists only in someone's imagination, and now I'm over here on St. Simons chasing a crazy Chinese lady who probably won't tell me jack shit---for the second time today."

"Someone's imagination? What about the footprints y'all found?"

"Maybe DNR is wrong. Maybe the print belongs to a bobcat. Who knows? Don't change the subject."

"I'm not changing the subject. Are you saying you came over here tonight to talk to Betty Wu again?"

Hopper slicked her short bangs back off her forehead and groaned. "Yes. Yes. Yes. I came up empty-handed running Coleman through my local resident sources, and since we don't know his car tag number, or even what he drives, I can't locate him by his vehicle. He's probably leasing a house or condo in the area, but it'll take time to check that out."

I had an idea and reached for my phone. "I can't believe I didn't think of this sooner. Hang on." I dialed Barkley's cell number and waited. No answer. When it rolled over to voice mail, I left a message. "Barkley, this is Promise. Since you sent out the invitations to Aileen's cocktail party for the Sparrow project, I'm thinking you have addresses in your computer for everyone on the list. I need you to look up Clip Coleman's home address and call me back. I'm sorry to bother you, but this is an emergency. I need it ASAP. Tonight. Like right now. Thanks."

Hopper sank into one of the chairs flanking the French doors to the balcony. I could hear the draw of the ocean above her as she spoke. "Oh well, good try but no cigar."

"Don't be so sure. Barkley is the best-organized production assistant in the business, and he never goes off line when it comes to Aileen's needs. He'll call back."

"Maybe. In the meantime, as I was saying, my plan was to confront Mrs. Wu with Coleman's name. Maybe if she knows I have a name for the shooter, she'll tell us how to find him. However, Mrs. Wu is not in her room and her Cadillac is not in the parking lot. The front desk kid remembers her coming into the hotel around suppertime. He does not remember seeing her leave. I called that idiot attorney son-in-law of hers and he says she left the hospital about six o'clock to have supper in the village and then go to bed early. He has no idea where she might be and frankly didn't seem too upset that I couldn't locate her. Mr. Wang tells me his mother-in-law has a mind of her own---one that functions un-like reasonable people's---and there is no telling where she might go. I'm hoping you've seen her here in the hotel. Without Betty Wu, I'm out of ideas."

"Your plan sounds like a good one, but I haven't seen Betty." I ran down a mental list of possible places Betty might go at ten o'clock at night. "Maybe she went over to the grocery store."

"No. I checked. Where else would she go?"

Where would she go? What would Betty do? Just what I'd been thinking about in the shower---how could she as-sure Clip Coleman that Aileen's Sparrow project wasn't a threat to him? I didn't believe Betty could reason with a killer like Clip Coleman unless she had something big to offer him---something that would keep his secret a secret. I grabbed my sandals from under the edge of the bed, threw my cell phone in my purse, and snatched my room key from the dresser. "Come on. I know where Betty would go."

Following me out of the room, Hopper complained as we walked. "You don't know. Not really. You're just guessing---another one of your suppositions, like Coleman killing Garr Lemley. Where are we going?"

I managed to pull on my sandals as we reached the stairs to the lobby. "Sparrow Cottage. Betty would burn down Sparrow to stop Aileen, just like she tried to burn the cursed chair last night. She would reason that with Sparrow gone, Aileen won't find out about Coleman and then his secret will be safe. If his secret is safe, Aileen is safe."

Hopper stopped and reached for my arm, pulling me up with a start. "Holy Mary, Mother of God, is that old woman capable of burning down Sparrow?"

I gave her a what-do-you-think look and rushed down the staircase. "Where is your truck?"

She led the way to the parking lot. I'd barely climbed into the cab of her Ranger before she threw the truck into reverse and backed out.

"Are you going to call for a fire truck and maybe another deputy in case Coleman is there with her?"

Hopper didn't take her eyes off the road. "Are you kidding? You think I want to look like a fool if you're wrong? I'm officially off duty. We'll ride over there and take a look around. If we see anything that looks like trouble, I'll call for backup. And when we get there, you stay out of my way. You got that?"

Before I could answer, Hopper pulled into an empty parking space at the edge of the village shopping area, put the truck in park and slid out of the driver's seat. I watched as she reached under her seat, took out a metal box, unlocked it, and removed a pistol. Once the handgun---smaller than the one I'd seen her with when she was in uniform---was holstered at the small of her back and under her tee shirt, she replaced the metal box under her seat and got back in the truck. She didn't say a word to me about the gun but that was okay. I really didn't need a tutorial on why Olen Hopper thought she needed to be armed.

Hopper's dashboard clock read a few minutes after ten o'clock. Daniel had said he would call me back about ten. What if he called while we were looking for Betty Wu over on Jekyll? I thought I should call him before he called me, so I dialed his cell phone. While it rang, one or two pangs of guilt stabbed at me because I knew there was no way I was going to tell Daniel where Hopper and I were going. I was prepared to excuse my prevarication by telling myself I didn't want to worry Daniel until I remembered how angry I'd been with him because he'd conveniently left out taking law enforcement training from his bio. Okay, no excuses, I'd tell a lie and suffer the consequences later. I was relieved when Daniel's cell rolled over to voice mail. I left a message saying I'd called to say goodnight and that I loved him. Neither statement was a lie.

As we drove across the causeway onto Jekyll Island, Barkley called back. He'd searched his database for Clip Coleman and found that his invitation to the party was mailed to an address in Arkansas. The other address Barkley had for Coleman was in care of Spector Oil, LLC in Oklahoma City.

"What exactly does Spector Oil do?" I asked Barkley. After he gave me a quick rundown on the corporation, I thanked him, promised to call him the next day, and hung up.

It was disappointing to learn Barkley didn't have a Jekyll Island address for Coleman. He must be getting his mail forwarded to Jekyll from Arkansas. However, I did learn about the business Coleman was afraid would be jeopardized by Aileen's Sparrow Project. According to Barkley, Spector Oil was well known for locating crude oil. I could have kicked myself. Barkley had told me before that Aileen wanted him to set up a phone call with T. Boone Pickens---think T. Boone Pickens, think oil. Aileen must have suspected what Clip Coleman was up to.

But now we had it. The key was crude oil. Clip Coleman was making plans to drill for oil off the Golden Isles of Georgia. To garner support from local residents and politicians, Coleman would need to be perceived as a white knight, a super good guy. Ugly skeletons falling out of the closet tend to diminish a knight's holy aura, and good guys seldom shoot someone in the back---even if that person is a murderous stepfather.

I could only speculate about the amount of money Coleman thought he'd make off Georgia's coast, but no matter the amount, my guess was that he was willing to kill for it.

CHAPTER THIRTY-FOUR

Tracking Betty Wu down on Jekyll Island felt like a movie played alternately in fast forward then paused to still frame. I know I gave my statement to the officers who responded to the scene, and I believe what I told them was factual. It's just that what happened seemed so surreal.

Olean Hopper drove into the historical district past Sparrow Cottage to the end of the road. Then she turned around and drove past Sparrow again. That's when we spotted Betty's Cadillac. She'd parked beside the cottage between the crumbling tabby wall of the abandoned garden and a pair of French doors leading into the house.

Hopper slowed. "I'm going to pull off on the other side of the road where you parked last night. Then I'll go see

328

what Mrs. Wu is up to. You stay in the truck. If I'm not back in fifteen minutes, call 911."

I watched Hopper get out of the truck, reach for a flashlight under her seat, lift up her shirt to pat her pistol, and then stand under the cover of oleander bushes for a moment before she sprinted across the road to the right side of Sparrow. She was following the same route I'd taken last night to spy on Betty. That was good. I remembered the kitchen door was on that side and should offer easy access into the house. In seconds Hopper was out of sight.

I would have followed Hopper's directions and remained in the truck---maybe---if I hadn't noticed a dark object leaning against a tree on the same side of the house she was approaching. The longer I stared at the shape, the clearer it became. I was sure it was a bicycle, and equally sure someone other than Betty Wu owned it. I tried to be still and wait, but I kept worrying that Hopper hadn't seen the bike and wouldn't be prepared if she found Coleman in the house with Betty. Finally, I put my cell phone in my pocket and eased out of the passenger side of the truck into the darkness.

Somehow, I managed to cross the street and find my way to the cottage without tripping and falling on my butt. I remember pushing against the kitchen door, feeling my heart pounding in my ears, and the sensation of the old door giving way and swinging open. Even without a flashlight, when I stepped inside I could make out the layout of the room. Some of the upper cabinets were missing doors;

there were no appliances; a wood, farm table---minus chairs---sat in the middle of the room. Off to my right, a large, white sink stood on metal legs, moonlit under twin kitchen windows.

The floor was swept clean of debris and, except for the one mouse scurrying to find safety from my footsteps, the room didn't appear to be too badly kept, considering that the place hadn't been lived in since before I was born. I wondered if Aileen's Sparrow Foundation had tidied up the cottage prior to her cocktail party. My next thought was distress about my open-toed sandals---just in case the mouse was a member of a large family.

I listened before I moved deeper into the house. Nothing but dry palm leaves scratching against each other outside. Where was Hopper? Why didn't I hear her? And where was Betty Wu? My mind flashed a picture of the Peterkin sister lying on the red rug of her foyer, pink fingernails on curled dead hands. Oh Lord, I prayed, please don't let...

I took a couple of tentative steps across the kitchen floor, then circled the table, and moved through an opening leading---I assumed---to the dining room. The almost square space was empty. Overhead, centered in the coffered, dark wood ceiling, wires protruded as a reminder that a chandelier had once hung there.

Moving along the perimeter of the dining room, I eased around an archway leading to a foyer tiled with large, terracotta squares. Once I stood in the darkened foyer, I could see the living room beyond, illuminated by moonlight seeping from the yard through the curtain bare French doors. The large room looked to have wainscoted, wood paneling much like the dining room ceiling. The floors were tiled to match the foyer. If the rest of Sparrow Cottage was as grand as what I saw, I could understand why Aileen Wang wanted to restore it.

I was thinking that I would tiptoe into the living room and have a look around for Olean Hopper when someone grabbed my arm and jerked me downward. I lost my balance and sat down hard on the tile floor.

Olean, squatting beside me, held my arm in a vice grip. I could feel her warm breath on my cheek. "Stay down," she whispered, "out of sight of the French doors in the living room."

"Okay. Why?" I whispered back.

"Because out those doors is a huge, live oak tree. Under that oak sits that stupid chair old Betty tried to burn last night."

"So?"

"Shut up and let me finish. There is a guy sitting in the chair, facing into the moonlight like he's sunning himself."

"Must be Freddie Coleman. I think he rode a bicycle over here. I saw it outside leaning against a tree. Probably rode a bike so his vehicle wouldn't be spotted near Sparrow. Is Betty Wu out there with him?"

"No. And I've looked around the first floor. No Betty."

"How about upstairs?"

"Can't get up there. The staircase looks like it caved in."

"Really?" After seeing how neat the old kitchen looked, I was surprised Aileen would leave the staircase in rubble for her cocktail party guests to see. Then I thought: maybe she wanted to dramatize how badly the house needed repair. Aileen loves drama. "Well, if you can't get upstairs, then Betty couldn't either. She must be here on the first floor. Unless she's wandering around out there in the moonlight with Coleman."

"Coleman isn't wandering around. I told you. He's sitting in the chair facing the house, smoking a cigar."

I was sure I'd misunderstood. "What did you say?"

"I said, smoking a cigar."

"Why would he sit out there, smoking a cigar?"

A mew, more like a cat in distress than a human cry came from behind us. "Shit," said Hopper. "Stay down. I'll have a look."

She made a dash for the rear of the foyer where it opened to another room. I crawled along the wall until I found the bottom newel post for the stairs. When I pulled myself up by the post, I saw what Hopper meant about the staircase caving in. A large dark hole yawned from midway up. Then I heard the cry again. This time more faint but nearer. Then Hopper was back beside me.

She whispered, "Did you hear it? It's over here. Close."

"Yes. Can you shine your flashlight into the hole where the stairs fell in?"

"Sure. But what if Coleman sees the light?"

I thought for a second or two. "That's not an unhappy cat we're hearing. Give me the flashlight. I'll check. You go back to the living room doorway so you can see what Coleman's doing. If he starts this way, you'll have to stop him."

Olean handed me her flashlight and drew the pistol from her holster. I waited until she was at the doorway and then climbed the five remaining steps of the staircase. Leaning over into the hole, I switched on the light. Betty Wu was lying crumpled on her side in a pile of splintered wood. She didn't call out or say anything at all, though she turned her head toward the light, pawing at the brightness with one hand, and then quickly looked away.

I remember thinking it was a good thing she could turn her head. That meant she wasn't paralyzed. Maybe she could walk if we helped her up and out of the hole. Then we could get her and ourselves out of the house and away from Coleman. That is if Betty was willing to give up whatever plan she had that brought her to Sparrow at ten o'clock at night.

As I was thinking about how to reach Betty and extricate her from the fallen staircase, the beam of the flashlight bounced off a small, bright object lying beside her. I stared for a moment before I killed the light. What was I seeing? A necklace?

"Betty," I whispered into the black hole, "it's Promise and Olean Hopper. Try to be quiet. Coleman's just outside the house. We'll get you out."

Olean tugged at my arm. "I think I know why Coleman's smoking that cigar."

Before I could ask her why and tell her I thought I smelled gasoline, a noise like dragon wings beating the air swooshed behind us and a column of yellowish light jabbed into the foyer from the living room doorway. Fire. Freddie Coleman had set fire to the house.

Then, when the dragon's wings gave way to the sizzling sound of fire crawling up the living room wall, I heard a two note scream from outside---growling, guttural, and hissing at the same time. It was animal; it was big and it was angry.

Olean tugged at my arm again. "We have to get out of here."

"I know, but I found Betty Wu. She must have fallen into the hole where the stairs used to be…"

Olean took the flashlight from me and moved to the collapsed stairs. Past caring if Coleman saw the light, she shone the beam into the darkness.

"Get that outta my face," Betty spit at her from atop rotted wood.

Olean cut the light and turned back to me. "Well, we know the old broad is alive."

I was about to ask her if she had a plan to raise Betty out of the hole when glass popped and shattered to the floor of the living room. I flinched and pressed myself tighter against the wall. The fire was in the house. "We need a plan," I said. "Any ideas?"

Hopper backed down the stairs. "Come on," she directed. I followed. She turned into the hallway beside the staircase and twisted the glass knob of what looked to be a closet door tucked underneath. The door opened and we stepped in. "Kick," she said and raised a healthy leg to pound the closet wall with her booted foot.

Because I'd been dumb enough to wear sandals, I couldn't imagine my efforts amounting to much, but I remembered Susan summoning the strength to kick in the garage door at the Peterkin house and gave it my best try. Old, brittle plaster crumbled and fell from the closet wall. Behind the plaster we found thin wood strips nailed horizontally onto studs. The old wood splintered as we kicked, but with Hopper's physical power and my realization that we either get Betty out through the closet or not at all, we managed to make a sizeable opening.

Olean shone her light into the cavity behind the closet. We could see Betty, still lying on splintered wood and not making any effort to get up. My hopes dropped to the bottom of my stomach when I realized that Betty couldn't get up and wouldn't be able to walk out with us.

We pushed through the hole in the wall and knelt beside her. Hopper grazed the area around Betty with the flashlight. I noticed the small, shiny thing again and reached down to pick it up. In the dark space abandoned by the flashlight, I grasped the object by a chain. My hand traced the cross shape and the human form cast onto it as I slipped the crucifix into my pants pocket.

Hopper breathed heavily beside me. I smelled smoke, and when I looked up through the stairway hole to the foyer, flames licked the doorway to the living room. The fire was one room away from us. As soon as it found the dry staircase, it would go like a tinderbox.

"She's passed out," Hopper said. "She can't walk. We're going to have to risk moving her. Look, we can do this. She probably doesn't weigh ninety pounds. Help me get her raincoat off. We'll make a sling out of it and carry her that way."

When I moved Betty over to slide her arms out of the raincoat, she woke enough to moan before she went out again. I hoped she would stay unconscious until we could get out of the house. As Hopper tucked Betty's coat underneath her, a heavy object fell from the pocket, making a solid thud on the floor. "Well, great God-a-mighty, the old broad really is packing a gun. Can you believe that?"

Of course I believed it. I'd seen the gun the night before and heard Betty threaten to use it. "Forget the gun. Have you got a good hold on your side of the coat? If we don't lift together we're liable to dump her off."

"All right," Hopper replied. "I've got my side. We'll lift on three. When we get out into the hall, keep your head down; looks like the smoke is blowing our way."

Hopper carried one side of Betty's raincoat and I took the other, trying my best not to flail Betty about as we walked. Once we squeezed back through the closet and out into the foyer, I kept my eyes straight ahead---didn't look to my right. I didn't want to know how much fire was already consuming the living room.

As we maneuvered Betty through the moonlit kitch-en, the dark smoke following us burned my throat and I coughed. Then my hip bumped the table sitting in the center of the room and I stumbled. We almost dropped Betty. Hopper cursed, then coughed, cursed again, and then tightened up on her side of the raincoat. We were level again and inching to the door.

Just as Hopper freed one hand and opened the kitchen door, glass shattered above our heads and I knew the fire had reached the upper floor. I kicked the door wide for us, and the first one out of the house was the mouse I'd seen coming in---at least I assumed it was the same one. Once we were outside, we carried Betty well away from the house and eased her down on the ground. Almost immediately, sirens wailed in the near distance and I felt we would be okay---until I thought of Coleman. His bicycle was still leaning against the oak tree. Where was he?

I turned to Olean. "What about Coleman? Do you think he walked away?"

"I'm on it," Hopper replied and flipped her cell phone to working mode. "You stay here. I'm going out to the road to meet the fire truck."

This was one time I would follow orders. I was too tired to argue and sat down beside Betty. Hopper sprinted out into the street, waved at the fire truck, and then signaled Betty's location to the ambulance and state patrol car that followed. In less than five minutes, Betty was loaded on a gurney and the ambulance was pulling out on the road in front of Sparrow Cottage headed to St. Simons Island Hospital.

By now a small crowd had gathered to watch the fire. I was just as curious as the other folks about the damage, so I crossed the street and walked down the verge of the road closer to Sparrow's other side to get a better view. From there, I watched two fire trucks spraying water on Sparrow's tabby walls and tile roof. Smoke plumed from broken windows. It looked as though Freddie Coleman had started the fire on the left side of the house---where the French doors opened into the living room. Betty Wu's Cadillac was a charred metal whale beached near the French doors, though the live oak tree Coleman had sat under and the cursed chair looked undamaged.

Olean Hopper stood near the oak tree talking to a fireman and waving her arms in the air. Presently, the fireman left, came back with a tarp, and used it to cover something the ground. A couple of minutes later a second ambulance arrived driving at normal speed and pulled in beside Hopper. I knew from the murder scene at Paul Tournay's house in Atlanta that an ambulance in no hurry is not the one you want to be riding in. When the tarp and its contents were loaded into the ambulance, and it pulled out onto the main road, Hopper looked my way and then crossed over to me.

She scrubbed soot from her lips with the back of her hand. "I guess you saw. We found Freddie Coleman."

"Under the tarp?"

"Yeah. Looks like the cougar got him. His neck's broken. He's as dead as he'll ever be."

CHAPTER THIRTY-FIVE

I knocked twice, opened the door of the hospital room, and stepped inside. "Hey Mrs. Wu. We're going home tomorrow morning. I wanted to stop by and..."

"And what? You come here for me to say thank you for saving my life last night? Makes no difference. Waste of your time. I'm going to die anyway."

I took a couple of steps closer to her bed. "Well, I suspect we'll all die sometimes, but I didn't come by for a thank you."

"I know everybody die. But I go soon, very soon. I know because they put me in room number fourteen. Number fourteen is bad fortune for Chinese lady like me. When you say fourteen in Chinese sounds like 'must die'. And besides, I heard that evil spirit, that akuryou, scream out for me at Sparrow house. She calls my name."

I hesitated telling her about Coleman in her condition, yet she needed to know. "That wasn't an evil spirit screaming, Mrs. Wu. Trooper Hopper is pretty sure it was a cougar. There were fresh footprints outside near the house."

"Ha. Cougar. Big cat. Don't you know evil spirits can be any shape they want?"

"Olean Hopper believes this particular cougar attacked Freddie Coleman last night outside Sparrow Cottage, after Coleman set fire to the house. I suppose he knew you were trapped inside?"

"Sure, Freddie knew. He saw me fall. Left me to die, burn me up with the house."

I nodded. That's about what we thought. "Olean Hopper believes the cougar was resting up on one of the limbs of the live oak beside the cottage and probably jumped Freddie from behind; broke his neck. Mr. Coleman's dead."

"Dead you say? Well, maybe this akuryou is good luck for me after all. So why you come to see me then?"

I took the crucifix from my pocket and offered it to her. "To return this to you. The chain must have broken when you fell."

"Mena's Jesus. That's good. I'm glad you found it, but I don't need it anymore."

"Should I give it to Aileen for you?"

"No, Aileen is practical girl. No need for Mena's Jesus. Give it to that Sam Quinn girl. Maybe she needs it for good luck."

"Is that why Mena Simpson gave you the cross? For good luck?"

Betty squeezed her eyes closed and frowned as though pain had ripped her flesh. Once she'd gotten her breath, she told me about the cross. "No. I tell you what happened. I don't care now. Mena didn't give it to me. Mena was sometimes kind, always stingy. I trusted her when she told me she was saving money for me every month in a glass jar in her closet. This was instead of paying me salary. When Mena's heart stopped beating, just like a rundown watch, I called her doctor, but I knew she was dead. We were alone at Sparrow. No Jon, no Caretaker, no black man's daughter.

"While I waited for the boat from the mainland, I searched for the glass jar---my savings for my new life. It was in the closet just like Mena said. But you know that jar---it had a lousy three hundred dollars in it. Twelve years I worked for that spoiled woman and that's all she left me. In 1952, three hundred dollars good money, but not enough for those years I cooked and cleaned for Mena. I was angry. So angry I could have....don't know what...but very angry.

"I go to her dresser and I take two pieces of jewelry---gold butterfly pin with ruby eyes and fancy, diamond bracelet. Even hiding that pin and bracelet in my purse, I was still angry with Mena. That's why I took the Jesus from around her dead neck. That same day, when the doctor came in the boat for Mena, I put Jekyll Island behind me. All these years I didn't come back to that sad place---not until now."

Betty raised her face to me. I didn't comment. She narrowed her eyes and continued, disapproval and defiance in her voice. "You ask what I do, a Chinese girl alone who'd never been anywhere in America except Jekyll and Brunswick? I made a new life. That's what I did. I bought a bus ticket to Atlanta. Then I rode all the way to that city in an air-conditioned bus with a big dog's picture on the side.

"Turns out that bus was good luck for me. In Atlanta, Mena's jewelry found my husband George. He brought his nice suits to the laundry where I worked. We talked. One day he told me he bought and sold jewelry. I want to sell Mena's jewelry, so George buys. But I don't sell the Jesus. For some crazy reason, I can't sell Mena's Jesus. Soon George and I marry. We are happy for a long, long time. George was Aileen's father and he loved her very much. Now I say you give Mena's Jesus to that freckled-faced, lady priest. You do that for me?"

I nodded and put the crucifix back in my pocket.

"You going to tell Aileen her mother is a thief?"

"No, ma'am. It's your story to tell, not mine. What about Garr Lemley, Mrs. Wu? What happened to him?"

Another wince of pain passed across Betty Wu's face as she pulled herself up in the bed. I reached to fluff her pillows closer to her back for support, but she waved me away.

"Ha, Caretaker. Worse than thief. I try to forget him but his smell follows me. Sometimes I stand in my own house and there he is, bringing that stink he had on him, rotten like his soul. "

Betty gathered a fold of bedcovers in each hand, squeezing until the fabric disappeared in her fists.

After a few seconds she spoke again, her voice matter-of-fact. She may as well have been reading a grocery list. "First the evil chair washed up on the beach. Then, very soon, the curse brought him to Jekyll Island. That was during the war when honorable men were away fighting the Japanese. But he wasn't honorable. He knocked on Mena's door one day looking for work, made himself useful because he could ferry the boat and fix many things. During the war everything broke, no parts to make new---everything goes for soldiers. Because the island needed him, he took what he wanted, even if it was a poor Chinese girl with no say.

"Then he did worse than that. After his wife died, Caretaker drowned her not-right son---the one who was Freddie's little brother. He kicked the boy and that cursed chair he was sitting in overboard like a rusted out bait bucket. Then he lied. Said the boy fell overboard. There was nobody to make him pay for what he did."

"Except Freddie?"

"Yes, except Freddie. At first I didn't tell; didn't say I was on the beach road and saw them out in his boat; knew he shoved the boy overboard. Who could prove what I say? Not me. Caretaker could swear I lied and nothing would change, except he would punish me. Then…" Betty hesitated before she finished her sentence. "Later I told Freddie. He hated Caretaker already because all the time Caretaker beat him like a mule for no good reason. Just like me, nobody to help poor Freddie. Soon, I tell him: you have to stop that Caretaker; you have to punish him for drowning your brother. Everyday I tell him. Over and over."

"Until Freddie finally took a rifle and shot his stepfather?"

Betty nodded. "I saw Freddie walking to the beach carrying his rifle. I knew Caretaker was also walking that way to hunt turtles. I told Freddie many times to punish Caretaker. So that thing Freddie did was my fault. He was only a boy, sixteen, too young to carry a man's sorrows. Too young."

Betty stopped her story and stared out the window. I turned to see what she was looking at---ribbons of white clouds trailing across a flat blue sky---but knew she was seeing sixty years ago.

That was when I remembered Garr Lemley had been shot twice in the back. And, I recalled something Freddie Coleman had said to Betty the night I overheard their conversation at Sparrow. He'd said to her that he didn't think she could shoot him, not unless his back was turned. At that moment, I understood why Betty had protected Coleman.

Into Betty's silence I asked, "Who shot first, you or Freddie?"

Her dark eyes darted to mine. She did not flinch or look away. "Me. I shot first. I took the rifle from the boy, aimed, and squeezed the trigger. It was November, very windy; my fingers were cold. I was not a good person with a gun. Freddie said my bullet only wounded him in the shoulder, so he took the rifle and shot again."

One of the nurses came into the room and went through a checklist of Betty's vital signs. "Now Mrs. Wu, your temperature is fine, but you need to relax. Your blood pressure is way too high. We need you strong for your surgery tomorrow. How you doing with the pain? Is that hip hurting you real bad? You need me to get you another one of those little pills?"

Betty growled no, and pulled the covers up around her chin. "No pills. Pills bring bad dreams."

There really wasn't anything else to say. I knew the rest of the story, sad as it was. I touched Betty Wu lightly on the arm, told her I would say a prayer for her surgery going well, and turned to leave. The nurse was still hovering over her patient as I closed the door behind me.

Olean Hopper was waiting for me in the hallway outside Betty's room. She looked about as exhausted as I felt. "So, how's the old broad doing?"

"Me or Betty Wu?" I asked.

The hint of a smile settled on Olean's face. "Well, if the shoe fits…."

"It doesn't. I'm not ready to be an old broad just yet. Betty is in pain from her broken hip, of course, but she seems to be faring okay, under the circumstances."

"Did she ask about Freddie Coleman?"

"Not exactly. But I told her what happened to him. She didn't seem to be sad about it. If fact, I think what she said was him being dead was good luck."

Hopper frowned and slowly shook her head. "I'm telling you, that Mrs. Wu is some tough old woman. I'm glad she isn't my mother."

"Yeah, I know what you mean, but I think she and Aileen have an understanding. And it may not look like it to an outsider, but I believe they love each other."

"Yeah, I hear you. Strange family. I saw Garland Wang downstairs. He's even concerned about Betty. He told me they're going to bring Aileen up in a wheelchair to see her mom before she goes into surgery."

"That's good." I waited for Olean to ask me if I'd found out anything else about Freddie Coleman, or Garr Lemley, from Betty, but she didn't.

Instead, she said, "I came over to St. Simons to pass along some news to you."

Hopper was smiling like a cat after snaring a juicy goldfish, so I figured her news must be good. "I'm listening."

"Earlier this morning, one of the officers hunting the cougar was in du Bignon Cemetery and noticed one of the grave slabs looked like it had been moved. He didn't think he'd find a cat in the crypt, but he was curious enough to slide the slab back to see if a grave robber had been poking around. In the crypt, he found a nylon, zippered bag containing an expensive assault-type rifle. My guess is RB Barnes will trace the rifle to the bullet he found and then to Freddie Coleman."

I heard RB's voice behind me. "Someone taking my good name in vain?"

Olean bristled up at the comment. I ignored it and turned around to say hello. RB, being RB, had to get in the first word. "I hear you two ladies cleaned up the Aileen Wang case for me."

I groaned, knowing he would have to follow his back-handed compliment with something derogatory. He did not disappoint.

"I also hear you both acted like amateurs and nearly got yourselves French fried."

I rose to the bait. "Well, you heard wrong. Trooper Hopper was well in control of the situation. Lucky for you she did your dirty work for you. Not to mention she saved Betty Wu's life."

He thought about that for a moment, chewed his infernal, Juicy Fruit chewing gum, and then smiled. "You need a ride back to the hotel, Dr. McNeal?"

"As a matter of fact I do."

One of The King and Prince clerks had dropped me off at the hospital on his way home from the night shift. Not that I wanted to ride with RB Barnes, but there was no way I'd let him think he'd irritated me to the point that

I'd avoid being in the same car with him---that would give him too much pleasure.

I shook hands with Olean Hopper and returned her all-knowing, wise-woman look confirming the victory for solving the Aileen Wang case was hers alone.

RB had the last word. "Hopper, we'll get Mrs. Wu's statement after her surgery, when she's a little more coherent."

Olean nodded, and RB and I headed for the elevator.

CHAPTER THIRTY-SIX

S am was on the mend by Monday morning, so about the same time Betty Wu went into surgery, we loaded our suitcases in the Jeep and said goodbye to the beach. I'm sure Susan was more than ready to see St. Simons in her rear view mirror. But leaving was bittersweet for me. Part of my heart always stays with the sea. I rolled the window down as we drove off the island, savored one last breath of the salt marshes, and vowed Daniel and I would return.

We made the trip from St. Simons Island to North Carolina in record time. With each mile, I missed Daniel more and more. We had a marriage to build and a deep sorrow left by Mac's death to heal. With Aileen Wang's drama put away, I found I was anxious to begin both.

Familiar road signs told us how far we had to go and how far we'd come. With each marker, the green mountains of North Carolina took on a sharper focus in my mind, pushing St. Simons Island to the background--making the beach a hazy dream of someone else's past. What would it take to heal Daniel from the pain of Mac's death? I was certain, knowing Daniel as I did, that time alone would not be enough. Daniel is a man who believes in honoring responsibilities. He also believes that what's right is right, and what's wrong needs to be stopped.

From the back seat, I could hear Susan and Sam up front chatting about friends they shared and Susan's restaurant venture. Susan was telling Sam that she intended to add smoked trout to the menu. My mind would not rest on the everyday. It went back to Daniel and what might happen. MaMa Allen is fond of saying that when we worry, we borrow trouble from tomorrow. That may be true, but knowing that doesn't stop my mind from visualizing the trouble I can feel marching my way.

Daniel was not likely to sit on the sidelines and wait for his cousin's murder to be solved. Someone had killed Mac because he was sheriff of Perry County, because he knew something. And that same person was either looking for the photograph missing from Daniel's house, or already had it.

And what about the money deposited into Mac's checking account? Was the money linked to Mac's murder? The only thing we knew about the money was that Mac had reported the deposits to the North Carolina State Bureau of Investigation. Did the person who made the deposits believe Mac would keep the money and wait for more? *Surely not.* Then why deposit the money in his account?

At early evening light, Susan turned off the state highway onto the winding, back road to my house on Fells Creek. There, in the magic of dappled shadows, I was witness to a miracle. Sometime during the past week, spring had finally arrived in Perry County. All along the roadside slopes, hundreds of mountain laurels were in full bloom. Clusters of thumb-sized, umbrella-shaped white blossoms hung from waxy green bushes as tall as my barn. I smiled and hoped Daniel had remembered to water my tomato plants.

Speaking of Daniel, he was happy to see us, and the kiss he gave me was a promise all its own. Though I have to say, he didn't seem surprised that we were home. In fact, he had the grill going and steaks seasoning on a platter in the refrigerator. My guess is that he called The King and Prince and learned that I'd checked out, but I didn't ask. I would prefer to believe that the man just knows where I am at all times.

MaMa Allen was still staying with my neighbor Fletcher Enloe, though I wondered if she truly felt unsafe in her own house, or if she had gotten used to Fletcher's company. If the latter was true, then I was convinced Mrs. Allen was a saint. They brought ice cream and joined us for supper served on the picnic table in the back yard. My hound Alfie also joined us. I was so glad to see him that his drooling on my white pants went unmentioned. We didn't discuss Mac's death. I think we were all avoiding the subject for the moment, perhaps trying to gain strength to weather the sorrow.

Later, after Fletcher and MaMa Allen walked back through the pine thicket separating his house from mine, and after Susan and Sam said goodnight and closed the door to the guest room upstairs, Daniel and I were alone in the great room. We snuggled on the sofa, Daniel gently stroking my arm and humming a tune I didn't recognize. I thought to ask him what it was, but didn't want to break the moment with conversation. Alfie yawned and circled around on the rug in front of the fireplace, nesting down for the night. I had closed my eyes, thinking it was bedtime for us, too, when Daniel spoke.

"Babe? You asleep?"

"No. Just resting."

"I reckon you'll tell me about the Wang business tomorrow."

"Uh huh."

"Okay. I'm glad y'all came on home. You're safe and we're together. That's all that matters. Don't you think?"

I thought I heard a *but* in his voice and opened my eyes. "Yes. That's what matters." I sat up, waiting for him to share what was on his mind. When he hesitated, I asked, "What is it, Daniel?"

"We're going down to the courthouse tomorrow to finish up the getting married thing, right?"

What a puzzling question. "Well, sure, if you want to go down tomorrow, we can do that. Did you think I'd changed my mind?"

He kissed me on the forehead. "I was hoping not. I just needed to hear being my wife was still what you wanted, that's all."

Why did I know that he was skirting around something? "What is it, Daniel? You might as well go ahead and tell me. If whatever it is makes me angry, then so be it. We'll work it out."

He cleared his throat, kept his arm securely around me. "All right. I wanted to go ahead and tell you tonight because I don't want you thinking I'm hiding anything from you---and because someone might say something down at the courthouse."

"Say what?"

"You remember I told you Alton Hazlett went ahead and retired early?"

"Yes, I remember."

"Well, the county commissioners asked me to take the job of interim sheriff until they can call a special election---it'll only be for a few months."

I shot up off the sofa and almost tripped over Alfie. "What? Daniel, how can you consider doing that? How can *they* consider you doing that? You don't even work for the sheriff's department."

He stood and held me by the shoulders. "Babe, don't panic. Listen to me. I think they want me because I'm not in the department. The SBI suspects someone inside the department had a hand in Mac's death. They don't know who they can trust, except me."

My ears were ringing and I felt the steak I'd eaten for supper thinking about coming up. "Oh Daniel, please don't do this. You'll be the killer's first target. They're using you as bait; that's what they're doing."

He drew me into a tight hug. "I know that. But don't you see? This is the best way for me to find Mac's killer. I haven't agreed, not yet. I told them I'd need to talk to you first. If you say no, then I won't take the job."

Pushing out of his hug, I looked up at him. Was he telling the truth? Would he refuse the job if I said no? He held my gaze, did not flinch, and I swam in the darkness of his brown eyes, floating on the truth he'd once whispered--- *I'll never leave you.* At that moment, I knew he would say no for me. I also knew that, with or without a sheriff's badge, he would hunt down Mac's killer.

After considering the devil or the deep blue sea, I said, "Just for the record, I'm not calling you Sheriff Allen in bed."

CHAPTER THIRTY-SEVEN

Betty Wu died during her routine hip surgery. She shouldn't have, according to the doctor; there were no complications, aside from the fact that her heart stopped and they were unable to revive her. Old age would be the cause of death on everyone's lips, but I wondered. From time to time, in the years to come, I would think of Betty Wu and of how an angry river becomes a killing flood because of one single drop of water. I suppose an angry river can rage inside every quiet heart, feeding on the hurt it endures and waiting for that one drop of water.

Aileen went back to Atlanta, back to being a shining star of the late afternoon talk shows. Her Sparrow restoration project was permanently shelved---off limits for discussion, according to Barkley. I have no idea what happened to the hideous carved chair. Susan thinks we would find it sitting in Paul Tournay's Atlanta house, holding court in his living room while Paul and Barkley regale dinner guests with their version of a Jekyll Island tale of murder and curses. I hope not. Some things are better not taken home.

Sid Balfour published a popular novel based on the Jekyll Island incidents. Fortunately, he kept the names and actions of those of us who were there murky enough so that only Aileen is recognizable in print. Here is what he wrote about the Monday after Sparrow Cottage burned and the cougar killed Freddie Coleman:

Before daylight, A.J. Voight, a somewhat dyspeptic little man with failing eyesight and ears designed for a much bigger head, strode down the short pier and dropped the three steps into his state-owned boat. He was five days from retirement with the Georgia Department of Natural Resources, Wildlife Resources Division. Today was his last Monday on the water.

With more shadows than light to guide him, A.J. did not notice the boat sitting a little lower in the water than usual. And because his sense of smell had begun to betray him as miserably as other parts of his worn-out body, he didn't detect a musky smell of big cat.

Voight turned the key. The Evinrude rolled over like a trusty old dog, and he eased the small craft out into Jekyll Creek, steering slowly toward the marshes south of the island. This was his patrol route, his territory, his home, and he'd be damned if he would miss one single day of being alone on the water. No, he wouldn't give up his boat until the five days were up, and the boss asked for his keys.

"Damned pricks," he mumbled. "Young farts warming a desk. Don't know crap."

He was glad they hadn't bothered him yesterday to hot-dog around hunting for a rogue cougar some fool swore had killed a man over near Sparrow Cottage. Frigging waste of time, A. J. muttered to himself. With all the easy game available on the island, he doubted any self-respecting cougar would go after a human---not unless she was cornered. And who'd be dumb enough to do that?

Besides, he grumbled, how would a cougar get onto Jekyll Island anyway? It wasn't like a cougar would hitch a ride across the causeway in some damn city-dude's fancy SUV. No, like as not, the whole story would turn out to be a hoax. The coroner would decide the poor bastard got drunk, fell in the yard, and broke his neck against a big old oak tree. Even a city-dude's head ain't hard enough to go against an island oak.

In the stern of A.J's boat, the cougar was lying still, uncertain if peeking out from under the tarp covering A.J.'s fishing gear was a safe thing to do. And then, too, she was sleepy, full-bellied from last night's hunt when she'd been lucky enough to bring down a small deer behind the village stables. She closed her eyes and drifted toward dreams. Deer was good eating; rabbits were even better. The human she'd downed wasn't fit to eat. That's why she'd left him on the ground, sorry she'd bothered.

As day opened up the doors of heaven, and sun slanted across the water from the east, A.J. cut his engine down to idle, waking the cougar. She peeped out from under the tarp to see A. J.'s back to her, his scrawny backside lifted up into the air. She watched as he leaned way out across the bow into a float of marsh grass and netted a squawking bird. Silently, she crawled from under her cover on her belly, and while A.J. was hoisting the bird up onto the bow and untwisting it from his net, she eased over the side into the shallow waters of the channel.

"Sons' of devils, lazy fishermen, throw their shit everywhere; don't care what gets hurt."

Once the bird was free from the net, A.J. tucked it securely under his arm and used his pocketknife to cut away the plastic soda bottle ring choking it. "There you go, old girl. Try to stay away from those plastic deathtraps. I won't be out here next week to watch after y'all."

After he released the bird back into the water, he cut each remaining circle of the plastic used to bind the eight-pack of cola and stuffed the pieces into his pants pocket.

Then with a salute to the liberated bird now pecking at a small crustacean in the grass, A. J. Voight powered up the boat.

With strong, even strokes, the cougar paddled to the muddy bank, shook herself off, and moved into the cover of a bramble thicket at water's edge. She turned, following the boat with her suspicious yellow eyes, and then when it puttered out of sight, she skulked into the open, sniffed the salty air, and surveyed her new territory. The slash pine forest and inland swamps around her were a delicatessen of appealing smells. She licked her lips and loped into the green cover of trees, salivating from the prospect of fresh game. But first she would find a mound of dried deadfall to burrow beneath, mark it with her scent, and make ready for the cubs she would soon birth.

All in all, I think what Sid wrote was pretty good and certainly put a sharp perspective on the place we humans occupy in the great scheme of the universe. I wonder if he shaved off his great, bushy, gray beard so as not to be compared to the late Monte Woolley at book signings.

Sid Balfour---a great name for a novelist. Don't you think? I should call Sid one of these days and tell him all about what happened when Sheriff Daniel Allen was tracking down Mac's killer. Who knows? He might want to use the story for another book. Yes. I'll do that as soon as I can talk about it without shivering.

A NOTE TO THE READER...

Thank you for being here and choosing another Promise McNeal mystery. Without you, the stories would be forever locked in my mind.

St. Simons Island and Jekyll Island are magical places for me. Each visit there is a blessing. I hope this story does justice to the Golden Isles, her history, and her people. Please remember though, history is sprinkled in for flavor, events are fictional, and my characters do not live in the flesh. If there are differences in locations found on the map, please be kind. As a writer, I have the privilege of creating a world within the pages of the book.

Jekyll and St. Simons brim with interesting history. A German submarine did sink two tankers off the coast of Georgia in 1942. And in 1900, The Jekyll Island Club members who came south to winter on the island did comprise one-sixth of the world's wealth. While revisiting the fascinating history of Jekyll Island, I found publications from the Jekyll Island Museum, and books by Tyler E. Bagwell and William Barton McCash and June Hall McCash helpful.

And Thank You...

I am grateful to family and friends for encouraging me to tell the stories. Thank you to my patient husband Rick for making the writing possible. Thank you Dee, my compass for all things story related, and Karen, the tireless reader who thinks commas are "fun." And thank you Kevin with The Malabar Front. His creative covers get the books *off the front porch and running with the big dogs*.
See You Next Time...
Morgan

ABOUT THE AUTHOR...

Morgan James was born in middle Georgia and called Atlanta home for many years.

She now lives in Western North Carolina. After writing for newspapers, magazines, professional publications, and training manuals as part of the necessary paycheck-world, she has returned to her love of telling the stories of the human heart. James is also the author of the Promise McNeal mysteries, Quiet The Dead and Quiet Killing, and the contemporary Southern novel, Sing Me An Old Song. Her work has been called: "...lyrical...everything a Southern mystery should be." Fans may follow her at www.morganjameswrites.com and at www.Goodreads.com.

Made in the USA
Charleston, SC
10 September 2014